ONE

RAGE VENGEANCE MURDER

K. J. MCGILLICK

ONE

ISBN-13:978-1717304537
ISBN-10:1717304532

DEDICATION

In memory of my grandparents Florence and William

Dedicated to my son Mark-Michael and grandchildren
Rinoa and Jude

ONE

One
One symbolizes the leader
One is the loner who will not follow the crowd.
In science, hydrogen is the atomic number 1.
Ares the god of War is the first astrological sign in the Zodiac.

$$1 \times 9 + 2 = 11$$
$$12 \times 9 + 3 = 111$$
$$123 \times 9 + 4 = 1111$$
$$1234 \times 9 + 5 = 11111$$
$$12345 \times 9 + 6 = 111111$$
$$123456 \times 9 + 7 = 1111111$$
$$1234567 \times 9 + 8 = 11111111$$
$$12345678 \times 9 + 9 = 111111111$$
$$123456789 \times 9 + 10 = 1111111111$$

It all comes back to ONE
Consequences of my making nipped at my heels.
I was ready.
Tick Tock.

ONE

Azar

THE CHEERFUL LIGHTS OF THE RUTHLESS CITY, PARIS, WERE extinguished long ago. I hoped today that a man—no, not a man, a monster—would feel the flame of his life doused and soon snuffed out completely. I wanted the body and mind of Adrien Armond to slowly decay in a prison cell isolated from human contact. Existing in darkness, unable to sleep, reason, or think. I wanted Adrien to be the victim of his screams. More than that, I wanted him trapped in his mind with no means of escape, begging for death every day. And denied the release from that torment.

I was here in Paris for one purpose: a trial. The trial for a man I needed to see condemned by his peers and sentenced to a life without hope. My judgment had already been pronounced on him for his transgression against me, but my sentence was still to be carried out. I needed his blood flowing between my fingers as I watched the light in his eyes disappear in death. For now, it was enough for the citizens to condemn him.

Adrien Armond a physician, businessman, husband, murderer, and thief. A butcher in league with the devil who stole my kidney. A part of a team who operated an organ harvesting ring and I was a victim. Oh, they thought because the recipient was my father that my consent should not be necessary, family and all. They thought wrong and with bad decisions come bad consequences. There was no proof of how many people died or were maimed because of my father's deceptive techniques and Armond's skill as a physician. Lives were robed, and people were sold into trafficking because of him, but he walked free of those charges. That one act changed my life forever.

Vengeance is Mine, and recompense; Deuteronomy 32:35.

Today Adrien Armond would stand trial at the *Cour d'Assises* in Paris. A jury of citizens and three trial judges would judge him for the premeditated attempted murder of his wife, Isabella Armond. The motive stated by the prosecution was financial gain. If they knew the breadth of all his crimes, he would not be sitting in a chair in France. He, along with my father, would be sitting in front of three judges at the International Criminal Court at The Hague for their crimes against humanity. But the ones who knew where the proof of their crimes could be found would never come forward— the refugees who were scattered to parts of Europe unknown or dead.

Would he recognize me from the time he spent with me in the surgical suite when he stole my kidney? Most likely not. I was forced to let the French have their turn with him and then he would be mine. The death penalty was not a tool of punishment in the French world. However, it certainly was in mine.

I took great care to arrive every day in disguise to listen to the arguments of the prosecution and Armond's attorney, a vile little man, who appeared as sinister as his client. I carefully weighed the testimony and demeanor of the witnesses and found the prosecution's case lacking. The gun wasn't loaded, and he had not brought the gun with the express intent to murder his wife. The prosecution could not prove intent and they had been so certain they would convict him on this one crime they did not charge him with any others.

ONE

What the testimony revealed was more a crime of passion and opportunity. His attorney discredited witness after witness as Armond remained expressionless even as his wife told a passionate tale of how he tried to steal her mind and take her life.

By day three, the *judge d'instruction* declared the prosecution had overreached its charge. The prosecution had not proved the elements of the crime necessary to convict him of the charge of attempted murder. The case was dismissed, and Adrien Armond was now a free man. The legal system in France may be finished with him. But I was not. The game I started the night he tried to kill his wife was still mine to play.

TWO

Azar

Three months later—Washington, DC

WASHINGTON, DC, A CITY RIFE WITH GREED AND CORRUPTION. It was home to some of the biggest criminals in the world masquerading as politicians who were elected to represent and protect people. For the next few weeks, if my plan executed correctly, this would be my home base. I would return to London when things concluded. If not, I would be dead along with millions of others.

It took years to gather the resources for my plan. And even more time to lay the ground work to allow me the opportunity to be in the right place at the right time to effectuate it. This job was a mere stepping stone to give me cover to perform the tasks necessary to move the enterprise to completion.

"Ladies and gentlemen, please join me to welcome our guest Ms. Azar Abed to our oversight department. Ms. Abed is a member of our London office where she is an integral part of the Global Risk Management team. She has an undergraduate degree from Oxford University, a graduate degree from the London School of Business and Economics and has more credentials than I can list in this brief introduction. In addition to her duties in the Risk Management Department, she is London's liaison with the IOR, otherwise known as the Vatican Bank. As you are aware if you read the memo, and I am certain you all have, she is here to do a comprehensive risk management assessment. Anything she requires or requests, you have my approval to provide to her. Consider her my ancillary arm," Mr. Dexter said as he stepped away from the back of his chair he had used as support.

"Azar, let me introduce our team to you. We'll go from the front of the table coming around to the right and back around. That's Daniel who steers the ship for Investment Banking; Paul is in charge of Securities; Max heads up the Investment and Lending; Josh keeps the Investment Management team moving forward; and Liz corrals the Research team." Mr. Dexter turned to his team. "You'll have the opportunity to get to know each other later as you'll meet with Azar to discuss your various departments. Right now, I hope we're all prepared to present your 2017 Summary Report and a brief 2018 Goal Marker plan." A curt bob of the head let me know introductions were completed and he was ready to move onto other business.

The group nodded at me in greeting, computers were set to their presentations, and pens lifted to take notes. I was grateful that I was spared any chitchat or forced to laugh at lame jokes.

For the next two hours, each department briefed me as I cherry-picked the information I would need to move my personal agenda forward. London, Paris, Barcelona, and Rome were all in place for me to hit the go button, starting the countdown toward financial Armageddon. Now I needed DC and New York linked in to watch one market after another crash and burn. Global economies would fall. That was my plan pure and simple. The people who hurt me would feel my wrath. Collateral damage was expected, and those involved would have to accept their fate.

At the conclusion of the last presentation, we dispersed for the next meeting. This meeting was nothing more than a boring run-down of what 2018 would hold for the US sector. As the speakers droned on I focused on my target, Paul from Securities, who discussed the push and pull between steady economic fundamentals and unsteady undertows of the economy. This was the area that would suit my needs the most and help me flesh out my plan. However, with the emergence of a new player on the market, Bitcoin cryptocurrency, I had to work that into my plan to get the most bang for my buck. If the financial wizards didn't see the 2008 crash with all the red flags waving in their faces, I knew there would be total financial devastation when my stealth plan hit their shores.

Ah, the business world... how I despised it. Everyone wears a mask when they have something to prove. It's when you don't have something to prove that you can remove the mask, and it's only then your true self is revealed. But in this room, no one ever dropped their sparkling Venetian mask. The game was always business.

I swept my gaze to each woman in the room, lips revealing false smiles as they assessed what type of opponent I would make if I threatened their position. On the other hand, the men looked at me differently, from a sexual angle. However, in truth I was neither competition nor a potential sexual liaison. I had an expiration date here. All I needed was information from the supercomputers in this building and a back door to set my plan in motion.

Two men in particular have been brazen enough to openly stare at me Max and Josh. Neither man would be helpful for my agenda, but both men were attractive if a fling was on the menu. So predictable. A coy smile paired with a come-hither raised eyebrow thrown their way would be a sure distraction. Throw in an ankle twist to showcase my heels and they would not care if the bull market turned bear. Who would be the first to approach? Both were good-looking, poised. Neither understood I was so out of their league.

Mr. Dexter proclaimed the meeting over and people scattered much like I would imagine old-time sailors jumping from a rat-infested ship. With a bit of a swagger, Josh held eye contact as he approached me. His style said he was confident, open, a true alpha male, and above all, a true player. I appreciated that he recognized and exceeded the standard that working in an investment firm required a certain uniform. His expensive attire and a haircut undoubtedly cost as much as a mortgage payment. Brilliant white veneers showcased a perfect smile. It was obvious he was prepared for battle in the business world, putting forth his best armor to portray him as a worthy opponent. I assumed he was an extrovert, but likely closed off emotionally, communicating only to gather information not to exchange it. I studied him during the meeting watching for his tell, everyone had one. He twisted his pen nimbly between his fingers over and over when he disagreed with something. An impulse he should curb.

He purposefully stepped into my space, testing my boundaries. This better not be his *A* game. How should I play this? Take a step back and let him think he is the dominant here? Or stand my ground to let him know I'm in control.

"Azar, I want to personally welcome you as a guest here at the Washington branch. Max is preparing to head to Amsterdam on a matter that just popped up. I am next up on the list to escort you to lunch. However, I have a lunch date with family and I would be pleased if you joined us." His mouth morphed into a crooked smile. "And if not, we can reschedule for tomorrow."

My first instinct was to dismiss the invitation. But this opportunity could provide insight into his vulnerabilities as he interacted with a family member. Determining how to exploit someone's soft or weak side was always an advantage I never passed up.

"I'd love to." I turned to leave the room to retrieve my coat and caught his eye. "Let me fetch my coat."

A raised eyebrow that traveled into flirtatious territory told me he found my British accent a cross between charming and humorous. That's so cute that he's underestimating me.

After grabbing my coat, we met in the lobby. We walked shoulder to shoulder to the main revolving doors. I was clearly a foot shorter than him even in five-inch heels, but I had no doubt that anyone spying us could tell I was in charge. I allowed him to play the gentleman and hail a cab. I slid across the seat behind the dark-skinned foreign driver who made it a point to hold eye contact with me a little too long. As if he could see through my mask and was on guard around me.

As we rode in the taxi, Josh explained the restaurant we were going was a favorite of his because it was family run, an oddity in a city overtaken by restaurant chains.

When we arrived at the restaurant, I understood. From the greeting he received, the staff knew him well as they exchanged playful barbs that only people comfortable with each other can do.

A young woman air kissed twice with him and then escorted us to a secluded booth in the back. The green leather horseshoe-shaped booth worn from use reminded me of days gone by and time spent in SoHo when I was happy.

A man who looked exactly like Josh, his twin, sat at the heavy wood table. Whereas Josh appeared to be an alpha metrosexual, his brother was clearly an earthy and rugged alpha. His brother's hair appeared well-kempt in a natural way, without the use of products to tame it. His body clearly benefited from a serious workout regime.

Sitting next to the man was an elderly woman with short, cotton-white hair and owl-like black-rimmed glasses. She was wiping the silverware with a vengeance and arranging it in its proper place setting. She must be their grandmother. A quick bro hug between the brothers led to the man at the table being introduced as Jackson. The woman's name, Mary.

"Josh said he was having lunch with his family, thank you for allowing me to join you." I flashed my most brilliant welcoming smile. The smile I'd practiced for years and that served me well. I extended my hand in greeting to the woman and said, "You must be their grandmother. Thank you for sharing your lunch-time with me."

I met her steely assessing gaze and tilted my head, another practiced move meant to put people at ease. All part of my bag of tricks to mimic normal reactions of warmth and happiness.

"Grandmother?" She laughed heartily. "My dear, whatever would make you jump to that conclusion? We aren't related, but there is no one that has a place in my heart like Jackson—the flame there burns bright for him."

The shock must have immediately registered on my face. I felt my lips part involuntarily and could sense the heat and redness rising from my chest to my neck. It was nearly impossible to catch me off guard and clearly this revelation did.

"Mary, for the love of God and all that is holy—" Jackson started, clearly annoyed as he turned his body to face her.

"It's true, strictly speaking." She huffed and squared her shoulders as if insulted. "I didn't say the flame was the lick of the devil's tail, she jumped to the wrong conclusion."

"Settle down, you two," Josh interjected with a chuckle. He clearly had done this dance with them before. Who are these people?

"Azar, please excuse Mary's attempt at humor," Jackson said, garnering an eye roll from Mary. "Mary is a friend's aunt and I'm babysitting her for a few weeks," he reported with a tone of annoyance. "Mary, no one finds that even remotely funny so open your humor bag and put that one back inside."

"Babysitting. my ass. Don't listen to him. He is my partner for the next three months while I complete my field hours toward my private investigation requirement." She gave him a bit of a sarcastic but satisfied look under her lashes.

I laughed and suddenly realized I was the only one laughing.

"Seriously?" I was more than shocked. "I don't mean to be rude but—"

"You're going to ask if I'm too old to be an investigator?" she asked with a dismissive wave. "Trust me I've been down that road.

Age is a number. The government tried to gently dissuade me from pursuing my new career. They even got downright ugly. This is America and what do you do when someone taunts you? You sue their ass, by God. I sued and won. So not only did they have to let me enroll in the private investigator course but paid me a nice settlement for my age discrimination suit. Winner, winner chicken dinner. You ever need a good lawyer, I've got a kickass one. Her name is Eloise and she is soon to be Jackson's wife."

This time I waited for a cue to see if anyone else laughed. They didn't. On the contrary, everyone appeared uncomfortable.

"What? Why do you two always look like you are sucking lemons when I talk about pursuing PI work?" she asked, a bit indignant, looking between Josh and Jackson.

"Because, Mary"—Jackson emphasized her name with a touch of distain, "you wound up calling on a number of law enforcement officers to testify as to your qualifications and put everyone on the spot. Not to mention Eloise, the attorney you mentioned, seemed to enjoy it way too much."

She shrugged clearly not persuaded by what he thought or said.

"Bite me, Jackson. Might I remind you, El received a huge cut of the money as part of the age discrimination case settlement. Her attorney fees will wind up paying for most of your fancy-schmancy house when it is finished. I didn't ask them to volunteer to help me, we subpoenaed them. All I did was ask everyone to tell the truth. You have to get tough like me. Too much meditating with you people. I hate to see you sushi eaters at ninety," she declared with a sense of authority.

"Please don't feed into her," Jackson plead to Josh with a shake of his head.

"Boys, enough of the twattle. Tell me about this beautiful young lady with us today," Mary said as she looked my way. Her glasses must have weighed a ton because when she moved her head they spilled down her nose.

ONE

Our server took our order, giving me a flirtatious smile and wink. I declined his attention with a turn of my head.

"Mary, this is Azar," Josh offered. "Azar is from our London office and is here for a few weeks undertaking a global oversight and risk management assessment of our office."

Mary gave a low whistle and shook her head.

"That sounds like a very important job." Mary reached for the sugar, catching Jackson's attention.

"It is, Mary. One wrong word from Azar and heads will roll," Josh said with a laugh.

If the man only knew how true a statement that was both personally and professionally.

"Then I'd say you must be a highly intelligent and resourceful young lady. That sounds like a very difficult job. Would it be too impolite to ask your background?" Mary tilted her head, assessing Azar.

"Yes, Mary, it would be very impolite." Jackson shook his head ruefully.

"Certainly, it's not but it's pretty boring. I'd much rather hear about you're work as a private investigator." Mary's work was not at all of interest but would take the focus off of me.

"Nope, Azar, not going there because there will be too much fiction intertwined with the facts and my head will explode stopping and explaining the difference between the two to you." Jackson took a sip of his black coffee that looked steamy enough to burn his tongue. Josh looked on in amusement.

"Okay, I'll go ahead and answer Mary's question to prevent an altercation in public," I laughed and patted her hand. Knowing my canned speech would easily roll off my tongue, I continued, "I have a degree from Oxford and the London School of Business and Economics. My tenure with the firm has been approximately six years and my present assignment is to gather information to ensure we are meeting regulatory standards. In the global department, we each have a specialization and my area is making certain that we are in compliance with Anti-Money Laundering standards."

Mary sat a little straighter and Jackson's face took on a bit of an alarmed look.

"Please continue," Mary encouraged.

"In lay terms, that's about it," I said.

"Don't be shy, Azar. Dazzle Mary with what you do," Josh said, delivering a playful elbow nudge.

"The office of foreign assets control and international sanctions program is under my purview if that's what you are alluding to." I'd stated this, my expertise, probably hundreds of times before in front of thousands of people.

"And—" Josh prompted as if he had a secret to share.

"I also laisse with the IOR or as most people know it as—"

Mary interrupted this time. "The Vatican Bank." She squealed and clapped her hands excitedly, beaming a smile so bright I thought she might blind us.

"Azar, you are in for a treat for lunch. Mary is a bit of an IOR authority, she practically stalks them. We all are a bit surprised they haven't reached out to obtain a restraining order against her. Don't be surprised if she picks your brain for what you know about the IOR's inner workings during lunch, but feel free to shut her down." Josh exchanged what could only be described as a mischievous look with Jackson.

"Sorry, but I have to step in here. There will be no picking of brains. That's a no, a big no, a hell no. A not happening no. This lunch conversation will remain light and you will not badger our lovely guest." Jackson turned to Mary. "Isn't that right, Mary?" He placed his hand gently on her arm and shook it slightly to gain her attention. "Because I won't sit here while you take off on one of your wild rampages."

The table went quiet and time stood still.

Mary looked at Jackson's hand on her arm. "Jackie boy, I have a fork and I know how to use it, so you might want to remove your paw before I impale it." He quickly complied, and Josh chuckled as he watched their interchange.

Turning her attention back to me, Mary offered a somewhat conciliatory smile.

"Azar, I see I may be out-numbered here by the boys. However, maybe if you want to get together some-time to talk shop, we can." Mary leaned a little closer to me.

"Sorry, Mary. There will be no exchanging information with the private sector. No offense, Azar. My brother hears that all the time, and Mary will as well," Jackson said as Mary scowled. "Remember those papers you signed? I think they encompassed shop talk and I recall something about jail time."

Seriously, who are these people? Who goes around threatening a little old lady who wants to play a bit of cops and robbers in her dwindling years.

"So be it. I'm allowed to have lunch with the lovely Azar, I assume?" she asked. "Or is she considered a foreign agent because she is from our cousin country England?"

"Going too far, Mary," Jackson said with an eyebrow raise. "Apologies, Azar. When Mary is too caffeinated or sugared up, things go sideways quickly. And without warning."

"Azar, I would love to extend a lunch invitation to you. These two dullards are not very good stewards of goodwill. I hope you won't be too busy to meet my niece and her husband. I don't know if you like art, but they are both art aficionados. Maybe we can interest you in a day at the National Gallery and some lunch?" Mary winked.

"Mary, I would love that and thank you," I said with another hand pat.

The National Gallery, like so many other museums, probably held its fair share of forged art a subject near and dear to my heart.

It took me a moment to disperse the thought from my mind

about how many forged paintings had passed through my hands working with my father in my earlier life. I tolerated a financial symbiotic relationship with him until he stole my kidney. At the time, he was dying, I was the only match for the rare tissue we shared. Without a thought, he made arrangements for me to be transported to Iran where my kidney was removed without my permission by the viper, Adrien Armond.

I was lost in my thoughts about my plans for his demise when I heard my name.

"Azar, such a beautiful name. Is it Persian?" Mary asked with a somewhat inquisitive look.

"That's rather incredible, Mary. Not many people can delineate the heritage of my name," I said a little mystified.

"Yeah. Mary's a real fount of information," Jackson said sarcastically. "If you value your privacy, Azar, you'll take the fifth and not answer any more questions."

"Did I not solve the Roselov case? My mind is like a steel trap that collects random trivia, Jackson. That and my ability to put random facts together is what keeps our world safe." Mary turned toward him. "And don't say government secrets. It was national news except I wasn't credited. Only the government received acknowledgment."

What was going on? Who was this woman? I had to hold my breath, get control and not start shaking. How could she know Dmitri? Or more important, was it possible she had something to do with his arrest?

"Don't even go there in front of guests, Mary. Your name was withheld for your protection. And enough about Roselov. He is in a coma and will hopefully die a quick but painful death like his partner Khalid," Jackson said pouring another glass of water.

Wait. What? Dmitri was in a coma? Khalid dead? I thought they were in prison awaiting trial. They were naming business associates of my father—men who made my skin crawl that were part of his initial plan to tip the world economies. The handful of times I met Roselov, I had the suspicion he'd always weighed if I was worth more dead than alive.

"Poor man," I interjected. Was it not polite, even expected to use that turn of phrase for a person in a coma? I had to tread lightly here because I had no idea what I'd waded into with this conversation.

"Poor man, my ass. He tried to kill my niece with that other jackwad Khalid. Surely you must have heard it all over the news? We busted up one of the biggest art forgery ring in the United States, maybe even the world." Mary peered at me as if I was from another dimension.

"Mary—" Jackson interceded. "Once again, you've traveled into territory not fit for lunch conversation. We need to end it right now."

I was having none of that, this discussion was something quite useful.

"Mary, I knew about the incident from the press coverage and just didn't connect the name. It was around the time of the Easter attacks that dominated the news. What happened?" I prodded hoping to extract some information about my father's business partners.

But just as Mary was about to take off like a train off its tracks, Josh placed a barrier to any further mention of the topic at hand.

"Hey, guys. Lighten up. We're supposed to be introducing Azar to America and enjoying each other's company for lunch. Let's change the subject." Josh shifted uncomfortably in his seat. "Jax, you think the Pats are going to the Super Bowl again?" And with that, Jackson and Josh went down an American football hole, reeling off statistics. I tumbled into a mental fog, lost in my thoughts.

I wanted to steer our talk back to Roselov. There was no doubt that even from prison Dmitri and Khalid had a hand in the Easter attacks that blew up St. Peter's, Westminster, and Notre-Dame. Dmitri was the money and Khalid the weapons.

I leaned in to engage a more intimate conversation with Mary while the men were still distracted.

"It sounds as if you were involved with some seriously disreputable people," I lead with, hoping to get her to open up.

But as she was about to answer, Jackson interjected shaking his head, "Mary, seriously, not the time and not the place."

As he finished his sentence, lunch was served, and the conversation turned to areas about what I should see first as I settled in town. None at all of interest. Years of my practiced smile bore fruit. People wanted to take me in and connect as friends.

As they droned on with their boring conversations, the mention of Roselov brought me back to how after I recuperated from my surgery I had scoured the earth for my father and lost his trail in Russia. His kidney broker business had collapsed, and his known accounts languished. It was not a leap to determine he was dead—the best-case scenario. Although I would've taken great satisfaction to watch him suffer as I carved his body up the way he had his puppet do mine.

As we finished lunch and Josh paid the tab, I turned and spoke to Mary.

"Mary, could I possibly take you up on that art gallery offer? I love art, too, and I understand that the National Gallery rivals some of our best European museums." Certainly, I could get more information from her without these two around distracting the conversation.

"I would love that, Azar." There was a twinkle in her eye as she studied me.

Was I playing her or she me?

Mary and I exchanged personal information. Josh mentioned that he had the bill covered and we could leave as we wished. I departed for a meeting with an SEC agent a few streets away, but I had a plan in hand.

Bracing in the death trap the Americans called a cab, I huddled in the back seat while the driver weaved in and out of the traffic that crawled through DC.

My phone pinged with a text from Marcello. **Done.**

That's all the text said and that's all I needed. Excellent—our plan to start manipulating grains commodities in the world markets which was the cornerstone of the plan to crash all the markets one at a time was set in motion. Starve the markets with a side benefit of killing off a portion of an overpopulated world. The crops in India, China, and Chile had been dusted with an herbicide that interferes with their growth and killed the crops. Take out the food supply thereby halting trade and export of food, the result was the economy crumbling.

Another text: **It is going to be a bad flu season and bacterial infections are on the rise. However, we need to discuss further.**

Perfect. We were offered Crimean-Congo hemorrhagic fever, Ebola, Lassa fever, MERS, SARS, Nipah, and Rift Valley fever samples and had to make a choice soon. I was still in negotiation for smallpox samples. I felt smallpox would be a good complement for the biological portion to continue panic while the markets crashed.

A well-executed virus at airports and cruise ships and under my guidance a bacterial outbreak would be unleashed worldwide. Pharmaceutical companies, pariahs that they were, would up the price of antibiotics and viral treatments. Supply and demand would prevail. The pharmaceutical stocks we invested in would rise quickly and we could cash in sooner rather than later. Health insurance stocks would drop based on the money required to treat people, hopefully recorded as the worst world pandemic hopefully in history.

If played right, our financial plan would have people dying of disease, famine, and suicide. Overpopulation of the world was unsustainable. We were just helping it along.

THREE

Adrien

PARIS WAS NO LONGER A SAFE PLACE FOR ME. MY STORY AND FACE were too well-known. The removal of my two fingers, courtesy of Ivan Roselov, was priority for treatment immediately after it occurred. However, not such a priority for the French prison system. The months I languished in jail awaiting trial without treatment rendered them useless appendages and complications arose. It wasn't until after my release that I was able to have the issues addressed by competent, but uncaring, judgmental doctors who used to be a part of my circle. They were willing to take my money but unwilling to show me respect. People would pay for their transgressions against me. However, until my money was back in my hands, I had to keep that mantra, day after day as I searched for Azar Abed and the money she stole from me. An eye for an eye.

The life I had relied upon and taken for granted came to an end when Avigad involved me in the theft of his daughter's kidney. He needed to save his own life and he decided she was to be sacrificed. His renal failure had worsened to the point his life would certainly end sooner rather than later, and he was determined to live even if it meant stealing an organ from his daughter. His madness in the end drove me to kill him before he stole my life. Although I returned her kidney to her, her anger knew no bounds and she extracted her revenge on me for my part by stealing all my hidden funds. She left me all but destitute save the funds I had hidden which were not within my reach until the trial had ended and I was free.

One thing Avigad taught me was how to hide money. Sometimes hiding it in plain sight worked the best. Other times, it had to be layered through several channels. A bit complicated in to-day's world driven by regulations.

I was forced to sell the last of the gallery paintings just months before the walls of my life came tumbling down which brought a tidy sum of 300 thousand US dollars. After cleaning it through four banks and two luxury cars, I was able to convert it to cash and tuck it away in a safe deposit box in New York. Now it was time to re-trieve that money. Another insurance policy involved a storage facil-ity in Maine owned by another cell member, Jude White. I was able to arrange for some paintings to be stored that contained informa-tion in the frames I could trade on very soon.

A trip to the US was necessary to start rebuilding my life and I was indeed fortunate that the Paris sweep had not discovered my other two passports—one Italian and one Canadian. Since the US appeared to have a better relationship with Canadians these days, I determined it would serve me better to travel under my Canadian passport. My cover? A Canadian software engineer, a rather innocu-ous cover that I knew just enough about to bore people to death if they tried to engage me in a conversation about it.

Unlike many other people in the world who loved the energy and buzz of New York, I did not. After my incarceration, the nonstop motion and never-ending sea of people surrounding me had an ef-fect that brought me to the point of a panic attack. After my release from prison I became a bit of a recluse, kept my own counsel and preferred it that way. I had the rest of my life planned and once I retrieved my funds from Azar, I would live out my live on an island in the Pacific far away from the despicable people that inhabited the rest of the earth.

Money had become an issue for me, making a trip to New York to retrieve some of my secreted funds necessary. Although traveling under another identity, New York hosted an enormous Russian population. Consequently, a place I shouldn't linger for long. The Roselovs' reach was long. I never knew how Avigad had secured the false documents he always provided but the last two in my possession should do fine for what was needed. However, it troubled me to use them even for a restricted time as I had every reason to believe his Russian contacts were involved in procuring the documents. If my use of the passport hit their radar, it might produce a problem.

I had to remind myself I was here for one purpose. I needed to retrieve my funds to tide me over and also meet with a man who could assist me in moving the cash to offshore accounts. Something I had always done myself but now lacked the necessary credentials to do so without possibly hitting someone's radar. The plan was relatively easy. Warren Goldberg was to meet me at the bank. I'd add his name as someone allowed to access my safe deposit box. In turn, over the course of two months he would make several visits to the bank and remove the cash to off-shore accounts for me. Three hundred thousand dollars being removed in a duffel bag all at once might garner some suspicion. Warren was possibly the only person I trusted, and he had served me well over the years. In return, my investments had benefited him as well and he was more than happy to continue our arrangement. He had recommended an associate, code name Melzar. What kind of name was that? Code or not. These people with their cloak-and- dagger nonsense. I needed them and if it meant achieving my goal I'd play along.

Warren said he had every reason to believe this Melzar character could find Azar Abed and help me retrieve the money she stole from me. Everyone had a price and Melzar had his—it was steep. Once the details were ironed out as to remuneration for their service the hunt for Azar Abed was on.

Within a week of Melzar coming on board, my investment in him had returned a dividend. Azar Abed was in Washington DC representing her firm. My mission in New York finished, I traveled to Dulles airport without any problems using my false identity as a Canadian software engineer. I knew I was watched all the time— fear from my time in prison no doubt. If Azar hadn't stolen my money, I never would have wound up that night in my old home trying to extort money from my estranged wife, Isabella, or getting stabbed by her and arrested for attempted murder. Azar, that bitch would pay.

I had just crossed the threshold of my hotel room when I received a call from the person I had struck a deal with to find out how Azar had hacked into my funds and where they were at present. The man drove a hard bargain. Anything he recovered, he kept fifty percent and if there was an increase in the funds due to market flux that would include interest. If the funds had lost value, it would include the value at the time they were withdrawn, either way a win for him.

"Yes, Melzar. What do you have?" I asked, hoping for good news as I removed my scarf.

"I have recovered one-point-two million euros in six accounts, one is a Vatican bank account. I have to say, Ad, that was pretty sloppy work on her part. I've found that a crack in the back door wasn't there unless someone didn't care if you found it. She must have grossly underestimated your tenacity. I've transferred your portion in the account you specified and by the end of day tomorrow it will be dispersed into eight more, and finally, twelve between the UK, the USA, and every off-shore we can tap into. I am avoiding Switzerland because they're persnickety and looked too closely at unverified transfers after their last go around under the US terrorism laws," Melzar said. It was a modulated voice which I am certain was filtered so I could never identify the voice. But that was fine with me. Compartmentalization always worked well.

"Excellent news," I replied as my day just got a little brighter. "You found her and now the money. I have to say, job well done and worth every penny."

"Ad, I have to ask you once again, are you certain you want me to leave a digital fingerprint that she can find?" He was greatly concerned. "This chick seems pretty clever, and frankly I don't want her knocking at my door. Maybe she or someone wanted you to find the money."

"I'm absolutely certain." I had plans for Ms. Abed. Six months in jail had left me plenty of time to think about my retribution. "I have this well thought out and no one will ever find you. I have one more job and it will be a bit tricky and out of your realm possibly because this is more something old school and low tech," I said hoping to pique his curiosity with a little tease.

"Shoot," His response was immediate and for a moment the modulated voice seemed to have a touch of inflection.

"There are paintings sitting in a London warehouse controlled by the Roselov family, although the building itself is buried in paperwork as a British corporation. The paintings there are under Iranian diplomatic protection. I would like my paintings back. But without my initial contact who helped me store the paintings there, I am a bit hamstringed." I walked that proverbial line of telling the full truth and stopped short of lying.

"I see," the modulated voice returned. "I have to be honest, Ad. I have a symbiotic relationship with the North Koreans, Chinese, and Russian hackers but Iran not so much. Send me the details using the encrypted portal I set up and I will tell you if it is possible. If

I can do it, I will."

"Expect the information you need within the hour. For all I know they've been moved but I highly doubt it." As Avigad was dead and he'd negotiated the deal I doubted any instructions to move the paintings had been authorized. "I also have paintings in a storage facility in Maine under the name of Jude White that I will want transported soon. This is just a low-tech breaking and entering. Can you accommodate me?"

"Of course. Send the information with instructions and the Maine storage facility I will throw in for no service charge," he replied.

This was a good day. I had recovered in essence a quarter of my money she had stolen and located Azar. However, thinking this was a touch too easy niggled at me. Was she setting a trap? No, I'm paranoid. It was a damn shame that the forged paintings we worked so hard to move around the globe after Isabella was declared incompetent were confiscated and sitting locked up in an FBI evidence vault never to see daylight again. I could feel the irony taunting me knowing the authentic artwork confiscated at the New York auction house was donated and transferred to museums by Isabella. Such a selfless act, so Isabella.

At some point, I would turn my attention to Isabella and decide how she should be punished. But I didn't have the inclination to do that right now. That would be a plan that would take serious planning because of Isabella, she deserved my full attention. Of everyone involved, her betrayal hurt the most. If she hadn't stabbed me I never would have spent time in prison. I'd dispose of her and the Europol agent in the pursuit of my justice.

FOUR

Jackson

THIS WOULD HAVE BEEN A PERFECTLY FINE DAY IF I HADN'T RECEIVED my official FBI assignment—a six-month stint with Mary as my quasi partner. Her foray into being a licensed private investigator still gave me chest pain.

The assistance she provided with closing the Roselov-White case earned her gratitude from the bureau despite her stunt of suing the government. Had it not been for her astute observations of Jude White, we never would have closed that case. It still boggles my mind she learned enough Russian to translate what the men involved had discussed, leading to their ultimate capture. She was part of that case, and now I was stuck with her. She had passed all the qualifying criteria, save for age, but that was remedied with a lawsuit. It had been my request she not be assigned to work my latest case for more reasons than I could verbalize. However, she charmed the right people. She was joining the FBI, I was mentoring her in law enforcement tactics and techniques. Thank God her citizen audit had a termination date.

Now, here we sat at the kitchen table speaking about the upcoming day. My stomach clenched at the thought of spending hours with her and now those hours had turned into months. There was theory that the message you send out to the universe is what you get back, good or bad. What had I done to bring Mary into my professional life. Maybe I needed therapy or at the very least a voodoo cleansing.

"Morning, partner." My fiancée, Eloise, greeted Mary with a comical evil laugh as they fist-bumped each other. "Again, Mary, I want to thank you for choosing me to represent you in your age discrimination suit. Your generosity in remuneration was overwhelming. The house is almost finished, and I want you to know there will always be a room there just for you. And I hope you use it often."

"Can't take it with you, El," she sighed. "And knowing your children will benefit from it makes me feel all warm and tingly. Especially when Jax has to explain how my money helped him. And I certainly will take you up on your offer. So much shopping, so little time."

"Eloise, you won't be laughing when Mary tries one of her crazy stunts and we wind up on the evening news, a compilation recorded by twenty cell phone cameras and sent to the network," I warned. This statement, although true, garnered the evil eye from Mary. Receiving it made me shudder.

"Mary, would you care for another cup of coffee?" Eloise taunted, smiling wickedly as she held the coffee pot out.

"No, she would not," I immediately answered. "Coffee with Mary must be earned."

And as if I were speaking gibberish, Mary ignored me. She raised her cup and Eloise filled it. To the brim.

"Just great. Now she will have all the fuel she needs to taunt me in the car, trapped alone in traffic." Eloise already knew this, but her insolence wasn't amusing.

"Jackie boy, here's how I see it—" Mary started as she opened her hard-covered composition book with its black-and-white-marbled cover. She called it going old school, I called it irritating.

"Mary. you don't have enough information to see anything yet." She did but I wasn't hearing it this morning.

"As I was saying," she continued, riding roughshod over me.

"The Easter attacks on Westminster Abbey, Notre-Dame, and St. Peter's and the havoc it caused has become a memory. It occurred eighteen months ago, and the news cycle is now filled with new information closer to home. More isolated terror attacks by lone wolves, and God help us, those horrid school shootings."

Eloise sat at the chair next to mine, put her legs up on the one opposite chair and was settling in to listen to Mary. This all done to encourage her. This was not good. At all.

Mary glanced down to review her notes running her finger down the page. "I have studied the patterns of how this has affected the global markets and see the Easter attacks as phase one—"

"Phase one of what?" Eloise asked as she shifted her weight and brought her coffee cup to her lips.

"Some type of global financial restructuring," Mary replied stirring her coffee with way too much sugar. "The markets have been on an absolute roller coaster and there are several sectors that stand out more than others."

"Oh my God. No, no, and no. You are not going to walk into a conference room today with the best and the brightest and open your mouth about conspiracy theories," I warned, and my stomach twisted and turned with anxiety. "When did you start studying micro and macroeconomics to figure that out? Specifically, deciding what patterns influence the markets?"

Eloise put her hand up to stop what she knew was about ready to turn into a full-on rant from me.

"Jackson, I understand you are a totally black-and-white person and your mind works as though it was a computer running algorithms. Mary has the wonderful ability to think outside the box." She smiled at Mary as if she were her partner in crime. "And I know you hair trigger and shut down when she talks about certain financial institutions, but I want to remind you that last December she called it as the deputy director of a certain financial institution was escorted from the premises along with another banking official. And this whole Russian dossier playing out in the government—can't say she was wrong about that either. Right?" Eloise said. Was she trying to push my buttons? "Hear her out."

I slumped angrily in my chair, crossed my arms defensively and hoped it would signal to them I didn't want to hear any of the information Mary was ready to impart.

"Jackson, would you please pass me one of those warm Krispy Kreme?" Mary winked.

"No." I was circumvented by Eloise scowling at me. She handed Mary two donuts just to spite me.

"The other day I was sitting in a coffee shop where I heard some Chinese business men discussing problems with crops—"

"Okay, stop right there. If you are going to partner with me, you can't be making wild assumptions based on overheard conversations at a coffee shop. Our work is all about deducing. I believe you are acquainted with the word deduct which means to derive as a conclusion from something known or assumed. Gathering facts and then coming to a conclusion. Not making your ideas become a part of a fact pattern. How do you know they were Chinese and not some other Asian culture? If they were speaking another language, how do you know what they were talking about? Did you scribble words in that marble notebook to Google later? Were they using hand signs or drawing pictures? And don't tell me the Rosetta Stone again because I won't believe you."

She raised her spoon and tapped it lightly on the saucer. I don't know if it was to stop my soliloquy or just to annoy me.

"Because they spoke Mandarin Chinese. Keep up, you are putting a drag on the conversation, Jackie," she said ready to dive in again.

"Stop. How do you know it was Mandarin Chinese?" Let her explain that one first.

"Because my real-time translator hearing aids told me so," she replied and tried to continue.

"Hearing aids. I didn't know you had hearing aids. Did you disclose that on your physical?" I hoped she didn't, so we could terminate her learning foray for nondisclosure.

"Jackson, settle down and let her continue. I bought her a pair of the new earbuds that translate something crazy like forty languages in real time," Eloise said as she stood to retrieve flavored creamer from the fridge. "How about letting her continue. Maybe take notes with the questions you want to ask and hold them until she's finished like a good boy."

"Earbuds—" I started. What the hell were earbuds that translate languages in real time?

"Jax," they yelled in unison and I raised my hands in front of me in surrender.

"Let me start again for the slow people here," she said as she looked pointedly at me. "And don't interrupt." I hated when she raised her crooked index finger at me like a frustrated school teacher.

"What are the things that are out of our control as normal people when it comes to an attack?" She looked at me as I opened my mouth and closed it. "Financial market attacks, and biological and chemical attacks. Mostly biochemical attacks because they involve soft targets. Our government can't monitor every building, the warehouses used by the food industry or even the aqueducts. They can't totally monitor recycled air or stop sick people from flying internationally."

She sat forward, forearms on the table, pen tapping a staccato tempo on her notebook. How irritating. She continued her conspiracy theory rant despite my objection. Beautiful.

"I have to admit most of what they were saying I couldn't follow. It was very technical financial information. The gist of the conversation was about the different countries' global exports and market potential. However, I did pick up enough to come back and do some research. Apparently, the Chinese crops had started to fail for no known reason and they were worried. Did you know that in addition to rice, the Chinese are the leading producers of wheat and the number two producer of corn? No? Me neither. I also had no idea that their agricultural exports feed twenty percent of the world population. Putting that idea into play, I thought what if another world player targeted China and their economy. What if someone did something to make them take a step back from being number two as the world's largest economy. They are on our heels to take the number one place and should surpass us in 2035. That is an economic fact. Who would then be in place to vie for the number two position on the world economy stage? Would it be the US? What could you do to the first runner to destabilize a country? My guess: food and exports. If they can't feed their own people how can they keep up their export to other nations? What would be the result?"

"Prices would rise, and other nations would become better import-export partners," I said. It was a pretty reasonable answer.

"Expand your thought process here, Jackson. Let's play what if. What if Chinas' agricultural market crashed? How would that impact the rest of the world? Would it change how they treat our US debt because they can call it in at any time to bolster their economy? Would it lessen their influence over North Korea? Would it impact its ability to continue being a world-class trading partner?" She sat back and pressed on her fingers with her numbered questions. "If their food exports failed would it impact their growing military because they would have to divert their money to survive?"

"Mary, I have no idea and I am certain there are people in think tanks all over the world who watch for these changes and have a plan to deal with them." I was ready to be done with this conversation.

"What if after someone set their sights on China and collapsed their markets they went after India and Brazil's crops? Did you have any idea that US soybeans is a fifty-billion-dollar business. Wipe out soybeans then you are killing a big part of our own economy. What would happen? Stock market wobble? Yes, but maybe even something worse." Yes, she was off and running now and there was no stopping this runaway train. You just had to wait for it to crash or derail.

"Fascinating," I said hoping she would catch my twinge of sarcasm. I was done and ready for this to end.

"Drones, that's how you do it. The watch dogs of the sky, the satellites, will be looking for errant crop dusters. But drones would be a better delivery system," she opined. "Our world is so interconnected with global exchanges that it's easy for a domino effect to cause a chain reaction tipping one loss against the other. There are only so many dominoes before there are no dominoes left to tip."

Not one bit interested in her what-ifs, I checked my watch hoping to close this down.

"We have forty minutes to get to the meeting. Chop chop." I clapped my hands together and stood up, physically letting her know I was truly done and ready to end this conversation. "Let's move out. Save the world on your own time."

It's not that her concern was unfounded, but it would take millions of dollars to put such a play into action. And hopefully manufacturing of the chemicals needed to produce such chaos would hit government radars pretty quickly. Plus, I had an ace in my pocket. Josh would be one of the first to see market shifts. I couldn't believe people all over the world weren't tuned into this being a possibility. We kept a tight watch on Russia; if this threat came from anywhere it would be Russia.

"I'm sitting here in your kitchen drinking your coffee. Whose time is it if not mine? Have I clocked in yet?" she challenged.

"And leave those earbuds home. I don't want anyone accusing you of spying for us," I ordered. Clearly, I was talking to myself. Unless I did a search and seizure I am confident the earbuds would travel with her.

The drive to Langley as always was tense and road rage was a definite possibility. Traffic in the best of circumstances had me on edge but when I drove alone I could at least listen to my audio books. However, today the plus side was Mary remained quiet and focused as she filled her book with notes. I glanced her way every once in a while, as she googled various sites with her government-issued phone and scribbled more notes. At some point we would be called on the carpet for whatever crazy sites she was visiting, akin to undergoing a colonoscopy. Her shenanigans would surely impact me in some way, and when she decided to detonate, all I could see was my career would be in her path of mass destruction.

The morning meetings went smoothly. Mary maintained a quiet presence. She scribbled in her book and it looked like she was studying people who presented their subject matter to determine if what they reported was trustworthy. She asked no questions and offered no opinions. Thank God.

I should have seen it coming, and it's never good to let your guard down even for a moment with Mary.

"Do you think you can get me into the cyber security department for a few days?" Mary asked out of the blue. And there it was, the beginning of the end.

"That's an easy one, Mary. No. They don't need your kind of crazy over there. They have enough on their hands," I stated without even having to think about that possibility as I opened the door to my office for her.

"That big guy Frank was talking about how money laundering is no longer done as frequently through brick-and-mortar stores. He insinuated that digital fronts and cryptocurrency have taken the place of nail salons, gas stations, restaurants, right?" She tilted her head.

I nodded.

"He said brick and mortar was only used now when they added money to their legitimate business bank deposits. They would add a little from their dirty money, so it is mixed. But that takes a long time to integrate, money and people get impatient. Stop me if I misunderstood, Frank said eBay is now exploited as a new revenue path and might inadvertently be a new money laundering front. Someone wants to buy something illegal, so the means to make the purchase is through a legitimate pay source. The person that wants to buy something illegal—let's call them A—opens up an eBay account. The person that wants to sell something illegal—let's call them B—opens up an eBay account. Person B puts something of inconsequential value on eBay for sale that no one would want much less pay the crazy price the seller is asking. Make sure I have the flow right," she said referring to her notes.

I leaned back to take in what she was saying so that in the end I could discount her theory with a valid argument.

"Person A wants to buy drugs, B wants to sell him drugs. But B doesn't want to launder the five thousand dollars of cash over a period of time. The speculation I have read on the internet is that B puts something up on eBay, a few somethings, each for sale at a thousand dollars apiece that no one but a crazy person would buy. The article says person A then uses a PayPal account which connects to his bank accounts to purchase these items at the one thousand a piece on eBay. PayPal and eBay don't know the real value of the items or that they are worthless because who has time to monitor millions of items. Plus, PayPal and eBay each collect a fee for their part and are happy. Neither PayPal nor eBay have any clue they are helping to launder money. If they have an inkling, the profit they make from fees makes it worth their while not to scrutinize every transaction and who wants to get sued for accusing someone of doing something illegal? It would cripple the companies to monitor each and every transaction. The money A paid through PayPal from his bank account gets deposited into B's bank account and the money is considered clean. Later B and A meet up and A gets his drugs and B has clean money. Or maybe B ships it through UPS or

FedEx if it's another state, or hell I don't know by courier or even pizza delivery. Is that right?"

I had to think a moment to make sure she wasn't asking a trick question.

"Right." I concurred so far.

"If someone wants to sell a piece of art or Beanie Baby on eBay and jack the price up they can, as the value is in the eyes of the buyer. But since they will receive a 1099K form for sales more than twenty thousand dollars or two hundred sales they probably need to have a bunch of open businesses to stay under the radar. Which I'll have to look into closer because some of those Beanie Babies were selling for over a hundred grand at one time. Was it real or a money laundering scam? If they sold the Beanie Baby once would it hit someone's radar? Maybe not, maybe it would be classified a collectible," she postulated as she brought up a recent Beanie Baby sale.

Looking at the product, it did seem odd that someone would pay such a price for what had originally sold for five-dollars. But again, supply and demand.

"Your man in there also insinuated that online gaming is popular to launder money. I understand that because you keep intermingling cash. It would be the same as if you were gambling at a casino. You bring cash, turn it into chips, and no one asks where the cash came from. The one that threw me a bit was the people playing online games and using it to money launder, so again, stop me if I'm off base. These people buy some digital game, like World of Warcraft as an example, because it is so popular. And what it comes down to is criminals create a scenario where it is possible to convert real cash for virtual products or services within the game and then convert it back into clean money in other bank accounts. Some kid buys a sword or potion from the game and the person collecting on the other end now has a purchased product. That money that purchased the product was dirty and gets cleaned through buying the potion or whatever. And online gambling like poker or fantasy football is an open field as well. I don't understand the Bitcoin stuff yet, that's for research tonight. I think he called it cryptocurrency."

"Yes, cryptocurrency is a real thorn in our side because it's a great way to launder money. It isn't a real currency and thus cannot be valued on the open market or taxed," I said.

"Next"—she continued as if I hadn't spoken. "I was fascinated how he postulated that some job websites and freelance websites use escrow accounts that allow criminals to open up an account looking for a legitimate service and then open another account with a different IP address claiming to be able to fulfill that service. But it is opened by the same person and they are just moving money from one place to another, yet it looks legitimate. The money would then be released and laundered through the site without any service taking place. That's quite brilliant."

"Your assumption on that is correct too," I replied, rather shocked at her ability to grasp the concepts so quickly.

"Okay, so that's why I want in on cybersecurity. I want to understand how these hackers and jackers work. If it's this easy to launder money digitally why don't the hackers just swarm in and steal all the money in these accounts as they are waiting to be released. If PayPal holds your money for even one hour why not hack in and steal the money sitting in the accounts. I have the FBI's money laundering schemes down. I need a challenge. I need access to cybersecurity."

"Sweet Jesus, Mary, take a course at a community college. You can't go wasting government resources for your whims." I knew saying this was a waste of my breath. Sometime by the end of the day she will have bullied her foot in the door of cybersecurity even without my help.

"I don't plan to ask them to teach me cybersecurity 101. I have a list of things I am particularly interested in," she responded. "Both internet threats and how people can plant a worm. I want to learn about bots and click farms."

ONE

"Why in God's name do you want to bother some unsuspecting person doing their job?" I asked with no intention of helping her.

"Because just like you people didn't see Sopia coming until she was fished out of the St. Charles River, you aren't seeing phase two of global meltdown coming. This isn't a religious holy war knocking at your door. This is the 1929 Great Depression on steroids coming your way, including a global collapse," she announced and closed her book.

FIVE

Azar

SOMETHING WAS BOTHERING ME, ALERTING TO A SENSE OF DISQUIET. Some people called it a sixth sense, I just called it intuition. My nightly routine before sleep included checking my offshore funds to ascertain what, if anything, had changed that day. I watched for fluxes in the market and trends as my plan worked its way around the globe. If anything changed I could readjust quickly. Nothing had changed that I had not expected but something had felt off. Several of my accounts had a pending status and it was impossible to ascertain if that meant they were doing something within the bank itself or if I should be concerned it was directly to do with me. Sleep had evaded me but had finally claimed me for an hour when my phone broke through the silence of the night. I patted my bed to find it. Bringing it to my face I saw it was four in the morning and it was Marcello calling.

Marcello had been my lover, confidant, and business partner since our time at Oxford. We were a match made in heaven others might say made in hell. Our goals in life aligned perfectly, and the endgame we aspired toward was a similar destination. We both wanted money, an abundance over it. We both needed power and control. But I craved one more thing, one more step toward happiness. I demanded revenge. Revenge on people who, since I was a child, underestimated me and treated me as if I was an inconsequential person. He was from a family with old mafia ties. My family was nouveau riche and employed unsavory business tactics. Together we exploited what we'd learned from our families.

I was barely able to grouse a hello when he started speaking in rapid-fire Italian. At the end of the statement two things were apparent. First, someone had removed over 122 million dollars from several of my accounts in one fell swoop, perfectly timed to leave my accounts at precisely the same minute. Thus, the pending status. Second, as a precaution to stop the bleed, Marcello had tried to move money from an account with a small balance. As the money was moved from one account to the other through cyberspace, it was snatched.

Although I wanted to say it was impossible, I knew it was not for I had done it myself.

"Wait, how do you know where my funds are and why are you monitoring them," I asked calmly, but went on frenetically with, "And how did you get access?" Panic started to hit me. I was a lone wolf in the world of finance and never ever shared my information. Marcello was my best friend and business partner, but I would never share that information with him. Ultimately that meant sharing control of my life with another and that wasn't happening.

"It's clear, the hacker was looking for you personally," Marcello shared not answering my question.

"Hold on one minute. Let me get out of bed, wake up my computer, and get a cup of coffee. I'm walking to the kitchen now. It will take me about five minutes so hang in there. To fully understand, I need to follow this step by step." My money, who the hell would even know where to start to look for it? Offshore accounts are numbered and even withdrawals went through numbered credit accounts. Names were never disclosed.

Coffee brewing, computer powered up, and my accounts now in view, my stomach lurched and started to churn. Involuntarily vomiting would not be far behind.

"How?" I asked myself more than I was asking Marcello. But he was as adept as I at cybertheft and I was confident he already had the answer.

"I have been on this for three hours already. It appears spyware was surreptitiously installed on thousands of financial institutions' computers worldwide. This person or more than one person used software that allowed him to remotely watch workflows and transfers of money between banks or money being deposited. Lurking and studying. Probably looking for dates or patterns. Now I know what you are thinking ransomware but no, there was no money stolen or information held hostage. Consequently, that angle is moot." He sighed into the phone. "Giving you the most simplified explanation, it appears that after breaching the back door of thousands of financial institutions, it allowed him to send a worm to study flow patterns. And I emphasize study because until last night no money was removed from anyone at any time. It's still recent and we are continuing to piece it together. What my people are picking up is that the worm sat and collected data and patterns daily. Since money wasn't touched, financial institutions weren't looking for anything in particular. Also, nothing moved, remaining undetected."

Marcello paused to let me catch up. "The hacker or hackers traced patterns back to when you relieved Adrien of his money and zeroed in on those dates and geographic places where you moved the funds. He followed the flow from there to the end destination your present accounts. Apparently, you must have left a back door open when you depleted his accounts," he reported.

His explanation was too simplistic for me. And even as confident as I was that Adrien would be convicted and imprisoned for life, I still would have sealed any and all back doors.

"No, absolutely not. It's not possible. I have a sequence of events that I follow when I leave, and no way would I leave a door open or a scintilla of data to mine. Marcello, I need to know the exact spyware used, when it was planted, and the location of the person who did this. Also, who are your people? Who has had access to my information?" Now I sounded fully hysterical.

"Azar, we are already on that but the feedback we are getting is that once it was taken from your account it bounced around the world and has fingerprints of Russia, Ukraine, China, and Eastern Europe. The worm has infiltrated thousands of institutions in over one hundred fifty countries. But it appears yours were the only accounts where money was taken by this particular operation. We covered all tracks to ensure the banks in question will not notice it and to avoid getting you targeted with an open account investigation status. This is where it gets interesting, so focus. An ATM associated with our legitimate business, yours and mine, was targeted and hacked in New York and spewed out twenty thousand dollars from our legitimate business bank account. Unfortunately, the man at the ATM was unidentifiable because the camera was disabled. However, we obtained footage prior to it being disabled. The person of interest caught on the camera looked like Adrien Armond, only a bit on the shabby side. Whoever hacked this bypassed the daily allowance to retrieve money from an ATM. Additionally, this person targeted a specific ATM. Azar, I question if Adrien has the resources to pull off such a thing. And if he does, is he in NY? Was he the man collecting the money?"

"Absolutely not. After I generously offered to return money to him, he tried to betray that offer I clawed back the money and left him destitute. And offshore banks have always been foolproof." My mind couldn't keep up with this new information. "I'm telling you there's no way possible he could pull this off. Frankly, to be so brazen to steal from an ATM with his prior history would be demented. Careless is one thing. But to commit an obvious crime? No, I am not buying it."

"Azar, this is unprecedented and frankly creates a problem for how we're going to pay for the virus shipment that's on its way and the bacteria that will require a hefty payment next week. The money for the payments was to come out of your accounts. The accounts that are now one hundred twenty million lighter. I will repeat, although I don't need to, this part of the plan is yours. I can facilitate it, but I will not fund it. I have told you the risk is too large for the payout."

He didn't speak for a moment. "My guy in Atlanta is ready to ship what he has been able to replicate as well as our supply contacts in Germany and Algeria. We need to determine if this is going to impact the timeline. Let's face it, that ATM spew was not an accident. It was planned to get our attention. The money came from our account not a random hack and spew. It troubles me that the man knows that we are connected through a business. This was supposed to remain separate, a Chinese wall and no mixing of funds. He targeted our account. It will take two minutes for the bank to connect us with that account. This hack was him thumbing his nose at us. Also, if he accessed that account, is his next step going after my business accounts? This is getting far more complicated than I signed on for and I don't like complicated." Marcello's message was clear.

"I'm on my way from Rome. Text me the address and code to get into your home. By the time I get there, I should have more information. As a precaution, I've frozen all the accounts and will get them moved by late morning your time," he advised.

People may call me obsessive and that trait has served me well. I was not one to be made a fool of and there was no way I had made such a mistake as to leave a backdoor open to be robbed blind. Marcello had my antennae up. His cadence was too quick, and he had too many answers to questions I had not yet posed. I didn't like this one bit. If he even thought to betray me he would be missing his dick and bleeding out in my bed before he could scream for help.

"Marcello, I ask again. How do you know my financial information and have access to my accounts?" I demanded. My money was mine and mine alone to control.

"Seriously? That's you question? You should be thanking me for getting out ahead of this mess. I'll talk to you later." He hung up, clearly irritated.

After we disconnected I was afraid to check my accounts in the event the worm was attached to another account and once I accessed it would give the hacker more information about any of my other accounts. What a nightmare. It had to be Adrien but how had he gathered enough money to pay someone to do this? Marcello had said there were fingerprints of Russians so could the Roselov clan be involved? That would make more sense. But why would the Roselovs help Adrien target me? No, that was just crazy. Adrien was nothing to the Roselovs.

If Adrien knew I was in NY and had found my accounts, then he would know or have some inclination where I was residing for the next few weeks fairly soon. How could this have turned against me so quickly? This wasn't the time to panic and make a mistake born out of fear or anger. What advantage he had over me must be flipped quickly. If he had hackers, then he knew where I worked and my daily schedule. Now everywhere I looked in this city of millions, in my mind I'd imagine him walking three people behind me. At least I knew to arm myself now. He had my money probably well-hidden and if I killed that little bastard I would lose millions. Those millions were my guarantee to the biochemical warfare I was about to unleash on people who had underestimated me and, in their underestimation, treated me as if I was a bad joke. As a child I was helpless to fend against their bullying and torment. Now the tables would be turned on them and anyone who had the potential to hurt me.

Many nights as I tried to find sleep, the only thing that brought me rest was a line from *Romeo and Juliet*. A line spoken by Mercutio before he dies cursing both the Montagues and Capulets, "A plague o' both your houses!" Although Mercutio couldn't make good on his curse I, however, could literally effectuate such a plague. As long as I had the money to give the devil his due. Money that was not in my account right now. I would skin that man alive after I retrieved my money. He will scream in pain for days on end. He should have left well enough alone.

I had to keep my focus on the first part of the plan. The chemicals for the Chinese crops had already been dispersed but it would take anywhere from one to two months tops for the results to reach total fruition. The ones in China had already been dusted with poison producing excellent results but that was our small test batch. The chemicals for the wine vines would be tweaked, and the wheat, soy, and rice samples tested after the initial contamination were promising. The added benefit was the animals that grazed on anything infected with chemicals would die or any person ingesting it would hopefully die but if not become so ill they would want to die. My hope was the chemicals would leech into the nearby water streams and people or animals drinking from it would also become deathly ill. The populace would become afraid to eat any food from the region and famine along with starvation would set in. No other country would import their crops eventually leading to a global export ban. That's how I would start the rock to the roll of the stock markets finally leading to a global financial meltdown.

The bacterial infective was ready to be dispensed. It was already in place at the launching stations ready for me to tell my people where the product was located so they could disburse it. *Listeria* was at the ready to infect vegetables, along with *Vibrio* to infect shell fish, and *E. coli* ready to be spread in meat packing factories. A worldwide outbreak had to be perfectly timed. While they had their eye on the bacterial attack, I would deploy the spread of the viruses. I now had to rearrange the financing as that bastard Adrien Armond had interfered with my funding.

I finished my coffee and speed dialed Lozar, my intermediary to obtain whatever I needed, my fixer. As always, he picked up on the first ring no matter the eight-hour time difference.

"Good morning. How are we looking." I was careful never to use names or subject matter with him in the event a phone was on a conversation capture list.

"Ready, Az," he said.

And we disconnected.

Over the last two months, effective antibiotics had been substituted with fake ones at hospitals in large areas so when the bacterial infections from ingesting the bacteria on the crops became a pandemic nothing could stop my process. Properly manufactured antibiotics were stored in a warehouse in Armenia where it could be easily relocated by Lozar through Russian-controlled territories to earn the most on the black market when necessary. A win both ways.

Pharmaceutical stocks on the market were at an all-time high. As soon as the wave of bacteria and viruses hit I would need to time it perfectly when to dump the stock to create panic and void in the markets. This was neither a short-sell scheme nor a pump and dump. It was more a brilliant long-term manipulation of stock that was initiated two years ago, six months before the Easter attacks. Now it was time to cash in on my plan.

Marcello and I were not in agreement as to the release of viruses, but it was imperative to my plan. London, Paris, Barcelona, Istanbul, and several US hubs were at the forefront of the attack. However, to play even a small part he insisted Rome was spared. If the plan was discovered and Italy was involved in the fallout from the biologics the backlash from the mafia would be swift. The mafia was protective of all of Italy and we did not need a group of wild men on our tails. Probably one of the reasons ISIS had not inflicted their special brand of terror in Italy. No one wants to be hunted down by the mafia.

Specific biological and chemical agents would be used for Middle Eastern targets as there was already a bias who would launch such an attack. Consequently, an investigation would never lead back to us. I had mapped out the countries affected the worst by each type of bacterium and a virus based on population and culture. The major international airport hubs would do nicely for the spread of viruses along with cruise ships and intercontinental trains. No noroviruses for me. I wanted people bleeding from their eyeballs while at sea not able to reach port in time to save anyone.

The United States had more anti-money laundering laws than the EU and enforced them to the best of their ability. With that in mind, most of my money laundering took place in Europe. Europe did not take cybersecurity watch as seriously as the US. While I was in the US, I had to take an extra layer of caution.

Meeting with a group in the company's legal department gave me enough information to steer clear of certain landmines coming my way as I moved through my plans.

While at work, I had to use every mental resource to maintain focus on the work of the company while continuing to move my plans forward. I was almost to the end zone.

My job this week was to determine if the Financial Action Task Force standards were being adhered to in the company. Knowing how to exploit the information I was able to gather during my work allowed me to make my plan work to its maximum capacity. In particular, my findings helped me open a large number of fake accounts to move my money around. I was one step ahead of the game knowing that when a customer opens an account, a profile is compiled based on industry standard criteria. Financial institutions in a perfect world should be able to evidence how customer profiles are used to inform and interact with transaction monitoring systems, so financial analysts can effectively monitor and investigate. This knowledge has served me well in keeping my activities under the radar. Laws evolved. If I wasn't so involved with the ongoing changes of my nine-to-five work, I wouldn't know that in 2016, new laws were enacted. The laws addressed instruments I had used as trusts that now allowed financial institutions a closer look at the semi-legal investments I held. It forced me to find new ways to advance my agenda. I stayed personally engaged and employed a separate party to look back over my transactions to make certain I left no footprint to invite an investigation. I rarely, if ever, traded under my own name. And if I did it was a small amount and recorded as appropriate with the proper authorities. I knew the game and I played it well.

To keep in the good graces of my employer I encouraged the people I was evaluating to work as a well-oiled machine. This was always beneficial to me. Using the innovative tools available showed me where my plans could be weak. From this I learned, adapted, found loopholes and ways to avoid detection in my personal affairs. There was no way anyone would ever think I was anything other than a ballbuster whose main focus was to protect the company and make sure all the laws and regulations were met.

Weary from the day's activities, I returned to my temporary office to find a note on my desk, security was holding an item for me. The note described the item as twenty-four flowers in a vase that arrived by courier. Packages were not allowed past security for several reasons including potential explosives, hidden monitoring devices, and allergens that could affect the staff.

Flowers, my antenna went up. No one knew I had been assigned to this office. The company always kept these types of visits confidential. I had no family and Marcello would never do anything so reckless.

As I prepared to exit the building, I passed through the first set of doors that led to the security center. I handed my badge to the attendant and he swiped it for verification. Another uniformed man swiped my badge again and scanned a tag that he took with him and disappeared behind a metal door. A few minutes of small talk passed between the two of us at the desk when the other man returned with a huge assortment of black and white calla lilies. Resurrection and Rebirth. Death and Life. Adrien Armond had presented his intentions written on the card attached to the flower arrangement.

Game on.

Armond found my place of work. I could only assume he knew where I lived. I asked for a driver to take me home and no questions were ever asked of our requests. The drivers were trained in kidnap and hostage tactics and armed giving me the assurance I would survive any attack while in the vehicle. No more taxi's and certainly no public transportation for me until I was assured Adrien Armond was disposed of properly. In other words, dead and buried somewhere in an unmarked grave. The ride was quiet and gave me time to regroup my thoughts because they went to dark places that I tried not to visit.

The car pulled to the curb in front of my temporary home, and lights were illuminated in various rooms reminding me Marcello had arrived.

I stepped from the car mindful of my surroundings. Thinking about it, availing myself to personal gun protection would be a necessary precaution. I would raise that question with Marcello.

As Marcello opened the door and reached for the flowers, he lifted his eyebrow in question

"Odd choice of flowers for your company to bestow on you." Marcello, at six- foot-four presented a lean but rugged appearance. He punished his body daily with hours of training and thrived on the abuse his body took. There was no one quicker on his feet than Cello. Wild dark hair untamed by any product and a clean-shaven face save for the five-o'clock shadow gave him the aura of danger. That also brought him the attention of too many women. If the stupid women realized from the start they would only be around for a short time as his attention span was limited, I wondered how many would even dip their toe in that pond.

I handed the vase to him. "Adrien Armond, my guess. I didn't want to make a fuss at work. I checked for a tracking device, we're good. Just get rid of them."

We exchanged a quick kiss when I noticed the heavenly scent coming from my kitchen. I walked around him to sample what he had simmering on the stove. His culinary skills could rival the best chefs of Italy and he displayed those skills often. Before I had even removed my coat, I had a spoon of the sauce raised to my lips for a sample. I knew the sauce would taste like heaven and it didn't disappoint.

I heard the door close behind him and he returned minus the flowers. I didn't have to turn as I felt him behind me and his body immediately pressed up against my back as he enveloped me in an embrace that gave a sacred promise of more to come. If necessary I could mimic affection when needed, but Marcello understood me and accepted my limited ability to bestow affection. That didn't stop me from welcoming it when he bestowed it on me.

"Business or pleasure first?" he asked as his lips caressed the skin below my ear. I could feel a tickle of hot breath from his mouth as he softly skimmed closer to my ear.

"Business," I responded with a hint of hesitation. I wanted to savor the moment but there were pressing matters that required our attention. Matters that would interrupt my thoughts while making love, ruining our experience.

Apparently, a wrong decision in his estimation as I lost his warmth immediately and without warning.

"Then let's sit while the eggplant bakes," he suggested, and we moved to the kitchen table. He had already set the table with precision. Every food utensil in place like only an obsessive-compulsive person could execute with such perfection.

"Give me two minutes to change. Would you grab my computer from my briefcase and set everything up, so we can link and sync? Pour the wine and I'll be back in a moment," I said indicating where I'd left my briefcase.

The townhouse was an excellent size for me with minimal stairs to navigate and, as promised, I returned within ten minutes. Hair in a messy bun as he preferred it, dressed in a flowing robe, and smelling like rosewood citron. He had linked and synced our computers and was combing the new data. His eyes scanned the material as he pinched his lower lip in concentration.

"Your company has been pretty sloppy, and I think their overuse of the safe harbor protection at some point will send up a red flag." His brow furrowed as he studied the data. "The trial accounts we opened didn't even hit any suspicious activity radars. Good for us, bad when your company comes under intense scrutiny when we crash the markets."

"By then we'll be smoke." I had my exit strategy cleared long before I even started this plan. I was halfway to completion. Once we pulled the detonation pin we would move slowly toward the exit to avoid suspicion.

"Okay, let's just run through where we are at, then enjoy a pleasant evening," he said lounging back against the chair motioning me to sit on his lap. I obliged. Marcello embraced his Italian roots when it came to affection. Probably because he came from a large extended family that bestowed lots of love. I, on the other hand, was stolen from my Italian mother at five by my murderous father. When he became bored with me at seven years old, I was sent off to a Swiss boarding school. I was always the odd one out. Was it due to my father not teaching me how to integrate socially with others or was I born a sociopath? Nature versus nurture. Either way, I was tormented by people who found it fun to torment me at the expense of my mental health as a child. I had those people's names and I would hunt them down and kill them now that I had the resources I needed. I'd start with their families as I watched their grief and pain from afar. But when it came to them I would be close, present to enjoy watching them break knowing life as they'd come to know it would end by my hands. Who's laughing now, bitches?

"I know we discussed the choice of three samples of bacteria, but I think we should be over-prepared rather than good to go only. If something goes wrong with one strain or it is seized, we have others to depend upon. Small samples of the Crimean-Congo hemorrhagic fever, Lassa fever, MERS, SARS, Nipah, and Rift Valley fever specimens are on their way to the freeport. I am waiting on confirmation they arrived and are stored. Once you make a determination of exactly what you want, they will expect full payment before they ship your full requirement." He lifted his lips for a brief kiss. "I have isolated the mutant strains. The antibiotics are warehoused in a separate secure location."

"I have some good news as well. I procured smallpox. Here's my thought. I think we should use that in Somalia, the Emirates, Oman and Yemen. People are no longer routinely vaccinated anywhere since it was eradicated. Enough of the Muslim population disavows vaccinations that I think that will give us an open door to wider infection. The influenza virus is already spreading naturally in highly populated areas. The flu does this time of year and hasn't raised any alarm bells. Through a previously untapped back door I obtained a small batch of Ebola. Not as much as I would like, however, a little is better than nothing." I stood from his lap to stir the sauce and remove the eggplant from the oven.

"Antibiotics have been switched out and stored inside the warehouse of a family friend. The active antibiotics can be moved easily." He walked to the cabinet and reached for the diner plates. "I do have one bit of bad news."

I retrieved more wine from the refrigerator and filled the glasses. He went to the stove.

"The pesticide that we had procured to kill the wine vines in

Germany was not as potent as expected. We're still able to take out Burgundy and Napa but not the Rhine," he said as he ladled sauce onto the baked eggplant.

"We knew there would be some glitches." I reached for my phone to review the end-of-the-day market results. "I think we should start buying more pharmaceutical stock and if we release the bacteria and virus when we planned, it should hit a high exactly as I charted so we can sell it fast and begin the market rock. Carlos—is he on schedule for making sure the other crops are dusted, sprayed, and on schedule to for destruction?"

"He is." Marcello smiled, showcasing his bright white teeth.

"Then I believe we are on track to success," I said, stroking his unruly hair.

"Azar, the one thing that still concerns me is your emotional attachment to this plan. I think we need to have another discussion. Because there is no room for emotions," he said. We'd had this discussion many times and I understood his point, but not his concern.

"Cello, I won't go down this road again. Have I not performed beyond your expectations?" I asked, and he nodded. "My computer skills have moved money and merchandise around the world, has it not?" I asked, and he nodded. "My passion to complete this phase has only fueled this plan not disrupted it. I won't discuss it further."

"If I see your emotions start to interfere, you know I will step in," he warned.

"That day will never occur," I threw back at him.

"Brilliant and beautiful," he said grazing my lips with a kiss. "Now let's eat and plan the demise of Adrien Armond."

We sat, about to take the first forkful when his phone buzz and he excused himself. I could hear him yelling in Italian and when he returned he appeared furious. I gave him a moment to collect himself.

"Those idiots hired to move the unit to the freeport were careless and something may have broken inside during the move. I sent them specially designed hazmat suits to use so they wouldn't attract attention. They didn't use them. All the five contracted something in there and died within a day of their return home. Idiots," he yelled. I have never seen him so upset and out of control. Why did he care? The people at the freeport were collateral damage.

"No, no. That's great," I corrected him. "Think of all the people they interacted with on their way back to their respective places. From Luxembourg to Armenia with a connecting flight in Moscow and Paris. My God, we could never have planned this as well. Think of all the people they came in contact with, Marcello. This is working perfectly. And likely, they died fast. Before their illnesses could be properly diagnosed and treated. This is indeed fortunate," I said and clapped my hands together.

"Do you not see the problem here, Azar? A strain that invaded the blood brain barrier so quickly was not something we had planned for and did not order from the supplier. How did this happen? Did the Armenians switch out the specimens? Did the people we bought from switch them out? And if specimens were switched, how will that help us when we aren't prepared with treatments for those illnesses to sell the world?" he said pacing the floor and raking his hands through his hair.

He had a valid point. We had no idea what was in that container. Did something mutate? Or possibly two things broke and mixed together. The control of what we released was critical. Our control of the plan may have been altered. My body started to physically react as I realized I had to reclaim control not knowing how.

SIX

Jackson

OD KNOWS I LOVED ELOISE AND WOULD DO ANYTHING FOR THE woman. However, sleeping with the woman was like sleeping with a wild octopus. She was everywhere in bed. Since she'd moved in with me, my nights had been filled with no sleep and I prayed the new bed arriving today would end my torment. As if a sleepless night was not enough, my phone rang at 6:00 a.m.

"What could you possibly want at the ass crack of dawn?" I queried the person on the other end of the phone.

"Good morning to you too, Jackson." Emma was amused by my greeting.

"Sorry, Emma. I thought you were Cillian, but the question remains." This morning, the lack of sleep had manifested itself into nausea and a headache starting to filter through my head.

"We are on our way to drop off Aunt Mary for the week," she said with a touch a mischief in her voice.

That sure as hell got my attention.

"The hell you say," I bellowed back. I sat up immediately as if arisen from the zombie sleep of the dead. Eloise stirred and cracked her eyes open to determine what the commotion was all about.

"Mary?" Eloise said, part asking and part statement.

"Yes. I know who the hell Mary is, what about her?" I was in no mood for her antics. I turned my attention back to Emma on the phone.

"We are getting ready to go visit Cillian's brother for the week and you are babysitting Mary," she said with too much joy in her tone.

Kill. Me. Now.

"And when was this plan hatched?" I started to ask when Eloise suddenly grabbed the phone.

"Mornin', Em. I'm up and heading for the kitchen, bring her right over. I have a room made up for her. Tell her Jackson is thrilled she will be here for the week. Got to go." Eloise hung up the phone and turned to me. "We have a half hour before she gets here. She'll be here a few days and we won't have much alone time while she's here." She leaned into me and whispered, "You'd better make it fast."

Now that's what I like, a decisive woman and I wasn't giving up an offer of morning sex. Especially not for Mary.

At precisely seven, the doorbell rang, and I could see through the glass that Emma, Mary, and Cillian were on the other side. Yeah, it was a team effort to make sure I wouldn't try to throw her back at them.

Eloise slid across the wood floor in her socks in an attempt to beat me to the door. She wanted to make sure I didn't bar their entrance. As I tried to hold the door closed she tucked under my arm and pulled it open wide. With them pushing and her pulling it was a team effort so everyone could enter at once. It was a total fail for me to keep the devil out of my home. El gave Mary a quick embrace and Mary handed Eloise her bag in one flawless transfer.

"Jackson, I want to thank you for opening up your home to Mary for the week. We invited her along, but she insisted you needed her on this case you two are working on. And I know how dedicated you two are to each other." Cillian grinned and I wanted to remove it from his face. In response, I flipped him the bird where only he could see. He chuckled and shook his head.

"Mary is in good hands so you two can get a move on. I know you have a tight flight schedule," Eloise assured them. "I have a pot of coffee brewing and just put cinnamon rolls in the oven. We have a busy day planned. First the International Spy Museum and then the National Gallery."

"Ah. Learning a new trade, Mary?" Emma was just a bit too excited.

"Sorry, El, you should have checked with me first," Mary said with a bit of a tight grimace. "I'm on the list."

"The list?" El asked, stepping back on her left foot to brace for some convoluted story.

"The 'not allowed to enter the museum' list. There was an incident—" Mary started.

"Of course, there was." I shook my head and felt my mouth tighten. A week with Mary would be nothing less than a clusterfuck.

"Enough said, Mary." Eloise put her arm around her shoulder and gave her a warm hug. "You're still good at the Gallery, right?" she asked in a bit of a hushed tone. With Mary it was a crap-shoot.

"Yes, of course. And to be clear, it was just a slight misunderstanding at the Spy Museum," Mary said.

I decided to keep my mouth shut at this point. Instead, I shot her my knowing look.

"No need to explain," Eloise assured her. "Come, your coffee awaits."

"That sounds like a plan. We need to get back to the cab and head out. Call us if you need us," Cillian said. The women hugged, and they were gone.

According to mythology, ghosts, vampires, witches, and demons have to be invited into your home to effectuate any evildoing.

We'd just invited a demon in our home. I suppose when she left we would have to have it smudged and blessed.

Eloise embraced Mary again in a mother-daughter fashion. They took off to her appointed room to drop her luggage and then get her fueled up on caffeine.

As Eloise rounded the corner with Mary, she yelled back, "Coffee and rolls for Mary, Jax. Chop, chop."

"Thank you, Eloise. That will be lovely," Mary said to Eloise and threw me her evil grin.

Great. Just great.

Peace and quiet was mine while the dynamic duo took off for the museum while I made myself scarce in the café restaurant and bookstore. Two blissful hours passed, and then I received a text that Eloise and Mary were looking for me. I responded back that I would meet them in the lobby and threw a twenty-dollar bill down to pay the tab for the two cups of coffee and my sandwich.

This was the last place I wanted to spend a Saturday. If I wanted to see art at my leisure I could enter the evidence room of the FBI where stolen and forged art was stored. Forgeries were in themselves works of art. People like Beltracci had elevated the art of forgery to a new level.

I found a place to wait and observed the masses of people who passed me by. Who were these people and what did their daily life entail? Which people were foreigners, and who was here because it was a bucket list trip? How many people had felony records and how many deserved a felony record? As I lost patience, a cell phone was suddenly shoved practically under my nose to look at selfies of Eloise and Mary that I had no interest in. At all. As she swiped left I stilled. I took the phone from Eloise and swiped the photo right, swiped to the previous photo, and left again. A picture of a man behind them caught my attention. A man I was positive I recognized although his appearance appeared altered. He had the appearance of a hipster, but the face was that of a criminal.

"Who is this guy?" I asked pointing to the man directly behind them in the selfie.

"Oh, some guy that Mary struck up a conversation with. I think he said his name was Gabriel. Is that right, Mary?" Eloise asked, and Mary nodded.

"A nice young man. Very quiet and appeared quite knowledgeable about art," Mary offered. "I thought about humming a few bars of that Lady Marmalade song "voulez-vous coucher avec moir c'est soir" to offer a bit of enticement, but I felt it might be too tempting for him. Few men can escape my charms."

"French accent?" I used my fingers on the photo to enlarge it, attempting to ignore her commentary.

"Yes, how did you know?" Eloise asked as she leaned into my right shoulder to see what I was looking at.

"Was he still there when you left?" I asked.

"No. He and Mary argued about a painting and he kept insisting it was a fake, but Mary wouldn't let it go—" Eloise started.

"We weren't arguing. We were having a spirited discussion. There is no way that painting is a fake," Mary reported. "I couldn't get close enough, but those cracks have to be genuine."

"Mary, my dear. If he said it was fake I think you can take it to the bank that it is." I hit the several photos he was in and emailed them to Cillian and also to Ben from Europol. I didn't need to send an explanation with the email. They'd understand immediately.

Mary and Eloise stared at me as if I was speaking another language.

"Come. We need to get to security and see if he's still in the museum."

Mary and Eloise followed me to security.

Ben was the first to respond to my call. Considering the

five-hour difference I was surprise he responded so quickly.

"Tell me you are kidding," he said with a yawn.

"Nope, it appears Adrien Armond is in the United States. How did he slip past Immigration?" I asked.

"He must have a passport we missed," Ben said. "Where and when was this taken?"

"The National Gallery within the last fifteen minutes. I'm having security run the cameras and I've picked him up coming and going and he was only in here about forty minutes. He spent most of his time around three paintings. I'm going to shot them over to you and you tell me if they were on any of the lists," I said.

I sent photos of the three paintings that held his attention as we spoke and waited to hear the ping on his end indicating he had received them.

"Will do. I'll call you back." Ben hung up.

"Ladies, meet Dr. Adrien Armond. One of the most despicable human beings on earth." I meant every word.

"Oh my God. The London forgery case you and Cillian were involved with? Didn't he try to kill his wife? No, it can't be. How could he have the balls to step foot in the United States or the Gallery? Surely he is on some watch list?" Eloise asked without taking a breath.

"Probably entered under a false passport. But for what purpose? Between us and Europol we confiscated all the paintings from his art gallery. There is no way he is arrogant enough to think he can plan some job to reclaim them," I said more to myself than anyone in particular. "And to be honest, I don't know if he is on a list. I would imagine so, but he was cleared of the attempted murder of his wife. And because he was still married to her when he moved those paintings around, trying to sell them after his business partner shot his wife, it's hard to argue they weren't a marital asset. And he did have a court order giving him power over the business. It's a messy situation."

I could tell Mary wanted to ask questions in machine gun fashion. I held my hand up to signal her to wait.

"Give me a minute. My next call is to Immigration Control and Dulles to check if they captured him on the new facial biometric program," I thought for a moment to determine the best way to multitask. "Mary, since that is right up your alley I am putting you in charge of contacting them," I said.

"Copy that. But I was reading a memo the other day, the pilot program has only a one-in-twenty-five-person ability to detect facial fraud," she answered. I could tell she was all in. "Scratch that. You recognized him immediately, so he probably didn't have facial reconstructive surgery. But what if he came in through New York and took a domestic into Dulles."

"Let State run it through the passport data base. We can get pictures from the Paris police from when he was arrested. He changed his hair and has facial hair. However, I agree and don't think he had any facial surgery. It seems highly unlikely he is here for his art. That would be a fool's errand. Anyway, I'll get back with Ben about any open warrants from Europe," I said.

"I don't understand. If he's not on a watch list why can't he just move around as he pleases?" Eloise asked.

"I don't know if he's still on a list, he was. Like I said, there's a group of paintings that he tried to take possession of during his divorce. Some were fakes, some stolen, and some on the up-and-up. Because of international jurisdictional issues we confiscated the ones in the US and ceded jurisdiction of the case to Europe. I don't know what the outcome was. That's why I called Ben," I replied. "There was a particular group of his paintings that fell under Iranian control through Russian intervention and those were last in London. Maybe they made it over here and he's tracking them. Who knows what he's doing here."

"Okay. Do you want to stay here and work more with security or grab a cab home with us?" Eloise asked.

"I'll stay. And I am going to say something I never expected to come out of my mouth. Mary, get on the airport information and connect with Homeland Security after you go through State. Find out what you can about the paintings he was studying. Make sure when you talk to Homeland Cybersecurity you ask for Dave Cheznik. He knows that you're an albatross around my neck and won't make you jump through hoops. Check with them to see if there has been any unusual activity around art. There was a point where people were buying Chinese forgeries to send things through placement in the frames and on the canvas. Check out if they have any alerts out." I stopped to think if I was missing anything.

"No need for me to say those magic words, Jackie boy. I had lunch with Dave on Thursday when I asked him to get me into cybersecurity for a few days," she said with a smile. A malevolent smile.

"You did not," I challenged.

"Does he have a West Point ring on his right hand?" she asked. "And I might add no ring on his left?"

I had to think. Truth was, I didn't know about a ring, but I knew he graduated from the Point. And I knew he had recently divorced.

Eloise smiled slowly and patted Mary on the back. "Two points for you, Mary."

I squared my shoulders and turned to the door to reenter security.

"Anything else you need, Jax?" Mary asked in a sweet old lady voice buffing her nails on her shirt and admiring them.

I started to open my mouth but decided against it. Eloise and Mary laughed. They would be sorry. At least I could tell myself that to assuage my ego.

SEVEN

Adrien

I PROBABLY SHOULDN'T TORTURE MYSELF BY VISITING MY PAINTINGS AT museums—it was too much of a risk. How could I have let things spin so far out of control in Paris. Avigad was right. I should have killed Isabella when he told me to the first time. I had no excuse for not killing her after I had her institutionalized and the plans went to hell. Greed got in the way. That one more sale had to be made, one more euro collected. It became an out- of-control, full-blown obsession. Her suicide would have been believable, given the type and amount of drug I laced her food with and she ingested that weekend. What if they looked at me as a primary suspect? In the end there were plenty of drugs I could have used to kill that bitch before she ruined my life for good. Why couldn't she just cooperate? She would've gained financially, not lost. And because of her stilted sense of morals here I sat with the old woulda, coulda, shoulda dilemma.

As nonproductive as it was, I spent a great deal of time looking backward instead of forward. My fingers were useless for surgical procedures, that is, if I ever regained my medical license. From a cosmetic viewpoint, no one would know my index fingers had been amputated at the knuckle, but movement of small objects was a challenge. Months of exercise had been beneficial, but I would never hold a scalpel again. With effort I could pull a trigger and perform the routine functions in life. I owed the Roselovs punishment for their egregious action. I could only think of one thing at a time, but at some point, Ivan Roselov would have the pleasure of having his fingers removed.

Azar Abed was another matter. She deserved my full attention. If it weren't for her interference in my world I could have lived out a rather comfortable and normal life hiding in plain sight. I had the money to accomplish that plan. Until my money was stolen. I always wondered how she found out my identity so quickly. Was it the Iranians where the surgery was performed, and I took her kidney? Were they the ones who sold me out? Or was it the Russians who returned her kidney to her per my request. My guess would be the Russians. A debt for a debt. In returning the kidney at great speed, they were able to salvage it and return her to a normal life. She was in their debt, but honor among thieves' code likely nudged the Russians to give her my name. Ivan reminded me as he sliced my fingers off there was no love lost between us. His exact words were, "Avigad was a pain in the ass but he was our pain in the ass." And they did not appreciate me taking matters into my own hands and killing him. In the end, it was Avigad or me. That was for certain. I chose me.

Avigad, the man who enticed me into this mess and landed me into an abyss that broke and swallowed me. I had always felt there was more to his organ brokering activities than finding a match for his own kidney transplant. That alone was a higher plan with more people involved. Having plenty of time on my hands, I was able to put the puzzle pieces together. Not enough to make sense out of it as the picture portion still had too many voids. But if my theory was correct, Azar might be the only one left that could confirm it for me. However, if the group worked in compartmentalized cells no one would have the total answer. I could also be totally wrong. Maybe she wasn't part of his scheme and had her own design to steal money illegally. I had to stay focused and keep it simple. It all came back to money. She had it and I wanted it.

What did I know about Avigad's money laundering schemes and how Azar fit? Jude White, an American, forged the paintings and exported them to Dmitri Roselov. Roselov was the common connection between White and Avigad. Through my connection with Avigad, by association I was involved with Roselov. Roselov offered the paintings for sale at his gallery in London or exported them to sell at auction houses. Occasionally, Avigad requested I acquire paintings from Roselov and move them through our art gallery. If they were sold at the auction house, they were sold in a private pre-sale. If the paintings were good enough to pass intense inspection, they were sold for public auction under our gallery name. The name of the game was money laundering. Once sold, the paintings were whisked away to one of the four freeports they regularly used. I was dragged into the game without knowing the players or their rules.

Looking back, the worst thing I ever did was allow Avigad to become a silent partner for the financial investment. I ceded too much control and opened up a portal which I'm sure was what led Europol to our door. I should've been satisfied with the money I earned from the organ surgeries.

But what had been his ultimate plan for the use of the money we earned? He, unlike me, wasn't materialistic. He indeed appeared connected with the others for some type of cooperative scheme involving art and money laundering. But what was his end game?

Having nothing but time over the last two years I was able to determine he was one of the two men in charge of whatever operation was in place. Khalid Abdurrahman controlled the North and South American continents. Avigad Abed worked Europe, the Middle East, and Asia. Roselov appeared to swing play between the two. After putting the pieces together, his family was a pivotal force in the operation. He must have struck a deal that Russia was never to touch their master plan.

ONE

It appeared that when Abdurrahman and Roselov were arrested trying to leave the US, whatever plan was moving forward should have stopped. But it didn't. The pin had been pulled from the grenade and detonation was inevitable. The players in this scheme had a long reach. Although locked away in a maximum-security facility, someone was able to get to them in prison while awaiting trial. Abdurrahman was killed. Roselov now languished in a coma, presumed to die shortly. My theory—and it was only a theory—they had completed their part and were no longer assets and now disposable. Or they might have been considered a liability.

Avigad, although he recruited me for my surgical skills to organ harvest and transplant, also took advantage of Isabella's art gallery to move some of White's forgeries. Had she known that he was a silent financial partner she would have probably gone to the authorities. That would have produced a bigger headache than what was out there already. Avigad was right. I took too big a risk and should have disposed of her. Or as he had suggested, I should have let him dispose of her. Unfortunately, when he tried to kill her, even he couldn't complete the task correctly and she lived to bring us all down. After he gunned her down and placed me at risk, I should have stopped working with him. But he'd entangled himself so deeply in my life that it would have been impossible. Only in his death—the murder that I committed—did I free myself from him.

I was left alone to put the pieces together to save my life and regain my fortune. Avigad knew everything and shared nothing. He was so deep with the Roselovs they accommodated him with his kidney surgery in Russia. Take it one step further and Abdurrahman, a Qatar national with possible old ties with Iran, even from jail had been able to secure the initial surgery in Tehran. But where does Azar fit in? Obviously, she wasn't a willing participant to her father taking her kidney. But she plays some part in the overall plan, of that I'm sure.

Abdurrahman is dead, Avigad is dead, and that leaves Azar. Is she the last piece of the puzzle?

Things were too scattered. Did they all have a part in the Easter attacks? My gut said they did. If their plan was to rock the Western economy, they certainly accomplished that task. A year and a half after the Easter attacks the markets still hadn't fully recovered, and the European Union was unraveling as country states were in discord over the debts incurred to rebuild Paris and Rome. There was infighting amongst the European Union parliamentarians and more than random talk of dissolving the structure altogether—like Brexit on steroids. My God, if that happened how could they even think of going back to their financial systems? They would have to restructure each economy by country, print their own money. The thought was mind-boggling. Had this been a geopolitical move orchestrated by hostile governments or just some lone wolves acting together?

The thought of decentralizing Europe would be particularly harsh on the old Soviet states such as Latvia, Estonia, and Lithuania. Russia had been banging around their borders hungry to take back over for years. Would Russia make a play to recapture the Baltic states? Russia could cut off their natural gas supply as they did the Ukraine.

With no one to protect the small countries it would be a given they would fall to Russia. Russia would start piece by piece clawing back what they lost under Gorbachev and a new geopolitical landscape would be born. There was no doubt that the Roselovs would benefit being in Putin's pocket, and once again, there was that Roselov connection. Would the dissolution of the EU leave China, Russia, Eurasia, along with the US the new equal powers of the world? Without Europe to balance the power, civilization as we knew it would shift to an uncomfortable trade and financial balance.

In my mind it had now come down to one person, Azar Abed. Whatever Roselov and Abdurrahman's nefarious plan had been, she was the one left to execute it and bring it to its completion. Was she part of the original plan to set the global power shift in motion? Or was she now acting on her and in her own interest? In the end who or what would profit the most?

Azar. What an enigma. Working for a global investment firm and yet privately owned the wealth of a small country. Did she need more money? No. She had more than enough to live on for a lifetime. What was her endgame?

Look at what I'd become. Here I sat like a stalkerish creeper crouched in the bushes watching her home. Night-time gave excellent cover and she didn't close her curtains, giving me a peek into her life. Or was it a façade she wanted the world to see? Could she be so arrogant that she felt she was untouchable and didn't care who had an insight into her life?

Watching the man and Azar navigate the room I snatched my coat collar and brought it closer to my neck. Hiding amongst the bushes was not my finest hour, but as soon as Melzar, my highly skilled and highly secretive informant, had an identification on the man, I could leave for the evening.

Finally, my cell phone vibrated.

"What do you have?" I was glad my watch was coming to a close for the evening. I could see my breath as a light white fog in front of me.

"Ad, this is odd and probably important," he said in his robotic, clipped voice. "I ran through several algorithms and two databases to make certain I had the right person."

"Clearly, I am not interested in the how but only the who, so cut to the chase." I was freezing, and he was gesticulating. There wasn't time for this.

"Marcello Ghiaccio, thirty, resident of Rome, Italy. Never married. CEO of Fiamma, a pharma and biotech company traded publicly. He went to school with Azar and they have a personal and business connection. This is the man who has a business with Azar called Fire and Ice, their annual business income is half a billion dollars.

"His father is Marco Ghiaccio a high-ranking member of the Cosa Nostra. In spite of that connection or because of it, Marcello holds a high security clearance with the Italian government. That's a conundrum I haven't been able to unravel yet.

"I can review all his assets and tell you he holds no debt, but you can read that in the report I just sent over." The excitement of the robotic voice unquestionable. Unfortunately, he still hadn't mentioned why Marcello was here.

"Wait, isn't that Fire and Ice the company we invaded? The company that Azar and Ghiaccio own together? Why is he here?" I asked the obvious question.

"Yes, that is the joint company. A not so wild guess would be it coincides with the removal of the money from Azar's accounts by yours truly," he replied with a little too much glee. "However, that would be the simplistic answer and you may have thoughts there is more information to unravel. I scanned for anything to do with business holdings needing his direct attention in the US and found none."

"Yes, I think it's personal. They look very cozy, like lovers," I said.

"Odd because my information is that there is a woman he keeps in secret that I was led to believe is his wife. Who knows, rumors and all how reliable are they? I'll need to do some further digging. I'm keeping an eye on the money, but now she knows we are involved and no doubt has already hired someone to move her money around. With that said is there anything else I can do for you?" he asked.

"Any way to keep a tag on this Marcello?" I asked. I certainly did not need another party in my way.

"To what end? Do you want his every move? Or when he leaves?" he asked.

"I want a definitive answer as to why he is here for a start," I said.

"That, Ad, will take full surveillance," he responded.

"Did I stutter?" I thought I was clear.

"I'll report back when I have something. Are you ready for me to track the shipments moving around?" he asked.

"Of course. But your man on the inside said they are not art or artifact-related, right?" I was concerned what they were shipping.

"Absolutely not. From what I can tell something arrived at the freeport in Luxembourg in a refrigerated unit. You would think the freeports would be concerned about what needs refrigeration." His insinuation was clear.

"I would like to know myself," I muttered. That was quite a puzzle.

"For enough money—" he sniggered.

"I'll keep it in mind," I quickly replied.

"One more thing. Although I haven't been able to lock this down and I know you have investments in cryptocurrency, I thought I would share some inside information. Get rid of it, it's about to crash. That advice is free," Melzar said. If robotic voices could have an inflection of concern I believe I perceived a touch of it.

"Are you sure the information is reliable?" I reflected on that and my heart picked up speed. I had shifted a large amount of money into Bitcoin.

"I'm wounded at such a question," he responded sarcastically.

"When?" I asked.

"Less than a week," he responded.

"Got it, thanks for the heads-up," I said.

"Later, Ad," he said and disconnected our phone call.

That could have been a disaster. Cryptocurrency was easy to use and almost impossible to find and proved of great use to me while in hiding. That would be my first line of business. It was time to leave as I watched Azar and Marcello make their way to her bedroom. Lights out.

The Italian government was as corrupt as any country could

be and chaos was the order of the day. Why did Marcello Ghiaccio have security clearance with the government? He had close ties with the mafia. What the hell was in the refrigeration unit in the warehouse? I should have asked Melzar what made him certain it was a refrigeration unit and not a heat-incubation-type unit. And were they standard freezers or a super-cooled freezer?

My mind went to dark places and it stopped at bacteria. Stab and agar plates could be easily kept for a period. Viruses could also be kept with adequate refrigeration. No, it had to be something else.

My mind hit the brakes and I went back to formulating a plan to regain my fortune. Part of me was saying to stop now. That I'd obtained enough to live a comfortable life. That nothing was worth any further risk. The greedy half of my mind should have been tempered by the judgment portion. But my overpowering need to win at all costs outmaneuvered the good judgment portion and I pressed forward. I wanted not only to win the game but to crush Azar. Crush. Crush her head in and her soul. Leave her lingering between life and death.

Would the Abed family be my undoing, or would I put an end to their entire lineage and come out with all their money? That would be a risk worth taking.

EIGHT

Jackson

WORKING ON A SUNDAY WASN'T MY NORMAL SCHEDULE. However, Adrien Armond had popped up on our radar and that was troubling. Loath as I was to involve Mary in this three-way conversation between myself, Ben, and Cillian, I felt she had information that might be useful.

And here she was at 6:00 in the morning, dressed and ready for work. Even if we were working from my kitchen table. Here I sat, looking like I had partied all night and been dragged through the mud on the way home for good measure.

"Looking spry, Mary," I said with what I thought was a genuine smile.

"Dress for success, Jackie boy. You could take a lesson. You ever see the Pope in jeans or sweats? No. Leadership has its obligations. If you want to take a shower and change I can hold your place," she said pouring her coffee.

All I could do was shake my head and roll my eyes.

"Little boy, you better hope your eyes don't get stuck like that." She shrugged. "Just sayin.' It can happen."

I was about to give her a smart-ass answer when the video web channel kicked in and Ben's face appeared. A moment later, Cillian was on the call as well. Mary was introduced to Ben and everyone exchanged greetings.

"Okay, people, I will start," Ben said. "Since I've been out of the active loop these last few months, I touched base with Jillian my counter at Interpol. She said they had been keeping tabs on Armond, however, he went off the grid a few weeks ago. I guess we know why now. The only thing we can determine is that he either had an old fake passport hidden or a new one made," he said.

"Well, duh. My brain is calcifying here based on the obvious," Mary chirped in.

Both Cillian and I jumped on that, a competing "Mary" came out at once.

"Am I not saying what everyone is thinking?" she said with a shrug of a shoulder.

"Continue, Ben," Cillian said. "And, Mary, give our guest your best behavior."

"Needless to say, it's going to take a while to figure out when and where he flew out of through checking passports and biometrics. Now that everyone gets a generic-type passport in the EU it could take weeks. Or God forbid he's flying under another country like Mexico or Canada. But does it matter? Now we know where he is, isn't that the important part? And naturally the question on everyone's mind is, why he is there?" Ben asked.

"Not me. I have other questions," Mary interjected. "I thought you people said he was broke. That the reason he came after that Isabella woman was because he wanted his money. And that the money he'd hidden in their apartment had been confiscated. He had to have some traveling money squirreled away if he's here. Where did that come from? How did you miss that money? What other money is out there that he has access to? I'll bet the ex- Mrs. would like to know. If he provided fraudulent information the judge can overturn the ruling and grant her more. More to the point, he had access to money no one had found. Why is that?"

Everyone was quiet, dead silent.

"Mary has a point. Anyone want to take a stab at an answer?"

Ben asked.

"Of course, it's common sense, Ben. Misrepresentation and fraud are punishable everywhere," she said with the self-assurance of an attorney.

"Mary, I'm quite certain Isabella has moved on without his money. And even if it surfaced there's every indication it would be seized as part of a criminal operation," Ben said. "I'd say take Isabella out of the equation and focus on why he's there."

"Isabella? Sounds like you and she are familiar with each other. Care to share?" Her eyes were searching as if there would be a major revelation. Leave it to Mary to stir up the drama. Bad enough she inflicted it on me and I had to endure it, but to hook Ben in just wasn't right.

"All right, back to the main point. How did he get traveling money and a passport?" Cillian said to veer us back into the territory we needed to focus. "Mary, focus and filter."

"Thank you, Cillian," I said. "Let's not focus on the side issues. He's here. How he got here is interesting but the why he's here might be a national security issue. We know he's had interactions with Russians and Middle Eastern contacts through Abu Dhabi. Is he here on their behest?"

"I think it's personal," Mary said reaching for the coffee pot on the table to refresh her cup. And for good measure, she added a few cookies to her plate.

"Why?" Ben asked.

Yes, I wanted to know why as well. This was different. No conspiracy theory?

"No one came to help him when he was in prison. He has pretty much stayed under the radar. If he was doing anything as part of a group endeavor, why expose himself at a museum? I don't have his whole background but when I was talking to him, he didn't seem to be hiding. He was the one who engaged me in conversation by mumbling loud enough for me to hear. He could have just minded his own business and then he wouldn't have been memorable. I wouldn't know he was French for one. Or what art held his interest. I wouldn't have had him in the background of a selfie. I don't get the group vibe from him. You said he worked with one other person. Take it or leave it," she said stirring her coffee and then tapping her spoon on the rim just to annoy me. "But I am not channeling Russians or Middle Eastern people."

Because it was her theory I wanted to rail against her deductions. But I couldn't because it made sense.

"Okay, Mary. Give us your assessment," Cillian said. "And stay in your own lane; don't veer off into another. And for God's sake don't get off the exit ramp and then back on."

Mary met my eyes and then flashed them to the screen where the other two sat watching her.

"I have no assessment. I don't have enough information. I'm like you. I'm looking at this as some person or group is in possession of an asset he wants. Possibly he found his target and is proceeding with some type of action. I have no idea what his motivation is or what avenue he's going down. I don't have a clue as to what he can access, wants to access, or what path he'll follow to obtain it because it depends on the situation or goal. His methods and motives may vary.

"What I can tell you is, Eloise and I were talking about the artists and the paintings and he was the one who started a conversation by mumbling his disagreement. However, I found his information about the paintings we discussed to be lacking. His assessment was without merit, but he knew enough about art in general to say he knows art. I know you think he is some expert or brilliant art information guru, but I totally disagree. Maybe the man knows the monetary value of a painting and information enough to do a valuation. But how to assess a painting based on its beauty or aesthetics was lacking as far as I'm concerned," she said brushing her skirt. "He's a poser and uses his French accent to garner credibility."

"What you're saying, Mary, is that he talks a good game," I said.

"No, I didn't say that at all. Frankly, Ben, and I don't mean to step on your toes, but why would you buy anything from him. The man came across as an arrogant ass who knows dick about art. But engaging as a man," she said. "If that makes sense."

"Mary, you're catching me off guard here, but it was my job to buy something from him. Isabella was my target in what we believed was criminal activity. And your assessment of him being an arrogant ass is correct," Ben said. "Engaging as a man I don't see it. However, as a doctor he did get people to trust him, so you have a point. The man knows how to mimic a charismatic person and only us lucky rare ones were treated to his arrogant-ass side."

"People, I think in the end you are missing something here. I don't think this is about art. There was no passion in his speech. He hadn't studied art history, that was more than apparent. He must have picked his knowledge up along the way. I think you have to let the art angle go because there was a disconnect from him with the art he was viewing.

"What is the root of all evil? Money. Where did this man's money go? Not counting his real estate and property investments everyone seems to agree the money was there and then it was gone. I think he is on the trail of tracking down his money. If it were me, finding my money would be an obsession. It seems pretty evident he took great pains to be here in Washington. I would think he might think his target is here," she said. "Look, boys, we've been at this an hour and I would love to keep schooling you in the thoughts and inner mind of the criminal, but I have a breakfast date and I need to finish getting ready."

"Okay, I think we can finish this up, you go on, Mary," I said happy to be free of her for the day.

"I'll Uber it over so you can continue, Jackson. But expect a call for pickup. I'm not made of money," she said trying to engage me in an argument that would inevitably lead to her bogus settlement and cause my teeth to rattle.

"You take care, Cillian. Give my love to your family and Emmie Lou," she said and took her coffee with her to get ready. "Do you need me to visit with Lucy and Beelzebub?"

"No, thanks. My daughter has them well in hand. If she could have a dog full-time she would. She even has a soft spot for Sigmund. No need for you to travel to New York. Take those ear translation buds with you, Mary. You never know what you can pick up," Cillian said just to push my last nerve.

Mary left after placing her cup in the dishwasher. I could tell she continued to monitor the conversation.

"Back to Adrien. I hate to say it, but I think she might be right. I thought he wanted the paintings back to sell or possibly had hid some piece of technology in the frame or painting. I'll check with cyber to see if they have had any irregular activity. But I doubt it when I think about it. If he was moving chips in the frame, by now they would be deactivated or the information stale. Anything else?" I asked.

Everyone answered no.

"Oh, one thing. We've noticed some wobbles in the FTSE, DAX, and Euro Stoxx. And it had nothing to do with the Dow roller-coaster ride of correction last week. It was completely different sectors. Commodities of all things. The chatter level was the same as when we fought off mad cow disease in the late nineties that started in Britain," Ben said. "We've had reports we thought were vandalism by a rogue group doing damage to crops here. They're like some political faction but it's starting to gain some concern throughout the EU. If we have another widespread terror attack people will go nuts and I'm not sure that we could control a mass mob mentality for retaliation."

That got my attention.

"Commodities? Anything in particular?" I asked.

"Wheat and rice in particular," he said. "Why?"

"Hold on a minute," I said. "I want to check our markets for soybeans."

"Soy-beans? What the hell for?" Cillian asked. "And when did you start following the markets?"

"Long story involving Mary," I told him as I checked for the market report. "Okay, we had a wobble in soy."

"And?" Cillian asked getting a little irritated.

"Look, I have a theory brewing but I'm not going to trouble you with it. I'll talk to Josh and if it's anything I'll get back to you. Now have a good vacation, enjoy your family, and leave this to me," I said.

We disconnected, and my next call was to Josh. I hated breaking my rule of mixing government business and private, but before I started believing a conspiracy theory floated by Mary I needed an expert opinion.

It was early, and Josh was religious about his sleep. However, it could take him awhile to complete what I needed so I took the plunge and called him.

"What? Who died? Are you in a hospital?" he asked in a somewhat frantic voice as he picked up. I could actually hear the covers being thrown back as I pictured him bolting up in bed.

"No, for God's sake, calm down. I'm sorry to call so early but I need your help," I said a bit sheepishly. Was that a female voice I heard in the background asking who was calling. Oh God, if it is I am a dead man.

"Seriously, it can't wait a few hours? Last night was Saturday night, date night for the single people." I heard him apologize to whoever was there and told her to go back to sleep. "Hold on, you bastard."

After a few seconds I could hear him softly close the door and he was back.

"I need a quick course on stock market trading. Is wheat, soy, corn, and rice part of the stock market?" I asked.

"That's your emergency? That's what Google is for, dipshit. I should hang up on your ass," he said more than a little annoyed.

"I have raw data, but I don't know what to do with it and I think it might be important," I threw back.

"From Mary I would expect this. But you. No," he growled. "Give me a minute to pee."

Thank God he put it on mute.

"What do you want to know? And don't try my patience," he said shutting off the water.

"Nutshell version. And please don't put me to sleep or make my eyes glaze. Do the best you can to dump it." I was out of patience.

"In a nutshell, investing in grains provides exposure to an alternate asset class with different performance potential than stock and bond investment categories. Investment in agricultural commodities is a play on long-term population growth and the need for food products around the world. You can purchase individual grains through investing in futures contracts or get exposure to all three grains with an exchange-traded fund or ETF. Futures trading you need an account with a registered commodity futures broker and this provides leveraged action on the grain values. But ETF shares can be purchased through a brokerage account," he said.

I felt my eyes glazing and all I heard was noise. That was total gibberish to me. But I caught the terms alternate asset class and futures and ran with those two only because they sounded important.

"Why open a futures account? Isn't that risky?" I asked.

"Of course, that's the point. A grain futures contract can be traded with a minimum margin deposit of five to ten percent of the contract's value. As a result, the profits or losses from a futures position will be ten to twenty times the amount of the price change. It's best to start with an ETF; it's less risky. Both allow short selling," he said as if he was a commodities Wikipedia.

"Can you expand a bit, so I can catch some bits of information and decide what to ask?" I asked, knowing I was out of my depth.

And I knew at some point Mary would be ahead of me on this and I had to at least keep up with lingo.

"Agricultural commodities are subject to steady, though cyclical, demand. It's really a no-brainer. People have to eat, and as the population increases so does the need for food. Wheat, corn, and soy are a few of the most heavily traded futures and carry the most risk and reward. Corn is an international crop, but it is heavily grown in North America. If you have a drought, bug infestation, or an early winter, that can affect the price internationally. Rice is mostly a Northern Hemisphere crop that is grown extensively in East Asia and India, while sugar is grown in both hemispheres. Throw in the mix that prices of different crops can diverge based on time or specific events in the growing areas. And in today's political climate you have to be mindful of the political risks involved in countries that grow crops as well. Both India and China are major producers of rice. Widespread civil unrest or poor political policy there might have an impact on the price of rice around the globe. Future trading is an animal all its own and even has its own time schedule when it trades," he said, and I heard the bubbling of the automatic coffee machine in the background.

"How does that impact the stock market on the whole?" I asked. Still unsure of what I was putting together.

"You have to remember that when you say commodities it also includes oil, lumber, and metals. But if we were going to see a stock market crash in the United States we would probably see commodity prices begin to dip a few months ahead of time. When global economic activity slows down, demand for raw materials sinks and prices drop and then we spiral into a global meltdown." I could tell from his tone he was getting bored.

"One or two more questions. This one is more a statement— there is a difference in commodities metal, oil, and lumber may be one category, and agriculture another—" I started.

"No, lumber is part of agriculture," he interrupted.

"Good to know. If I understand correctly, two elements can affect the market, supply and demand. If supply decreases the prices elevate but that can cause a market stir. If the demand decreases prices plummet—"

"Jax, that's basic economics. What are you getting at? Could you get to the point, so we can end this tedious conversation and I can get back to my guest?" Now his irritation was unfiltered.

"I will cut to the chase. I want you to do an analysis and follow anything going on in the agriculture section of the markets for the last eighteen months," I'm sure he could hear me tapping my spoon on the counter, a nervous habit he detested.

"Jax, you have the government at your beck and call. If you think something is up, you can tap into them," he said.

"Mary—"

"Oh Jesus, all right. Stop there, enough said. I'll take a look. But I can only go so far, and I'll probably need to let Azar know because I don't want people to think I'm insider trading." He let that sink in and continued, "I'm going back to bed. Bother me again and remember I know where you live." Before I could thank him, our phone call disconnected.

It was embarrassing that I had no idea what to do with what I'd just learned, and Mary was putting puzzle pieces together and asking the experts relevant questions. I'd absorbed nothing I'd heard up until he outlined before a stock market crash the commodities market implodes. That was my take-away. Mary was so ahead of this game and she was meeting with people in the bureau that could help her stay one step ahead of me. Plus, damn it, she wasn't sharing her intel.

The Chinese men she overheard started this ball rolling and now Adrien Armond was thrown in the mix. Do the two intersect at some point or are we traveling down two completely different paths?

NINE

Azar

WAKING UP NEXT TO MARCELLO REMINDED ME OUR PLAN WAS in place and the countdown had started. I studied him. His beautiful face shadowed with dark hair across his cheeks and chin stirred a longing in me for more than just the few nights a month we shared with each other. Did I want commitment? How would I know? Was I capable of falling in love? It was impossible for me to trust anyone. I rejected anyone before they could reject me. Had I ever been loved unconditionally? That answer was easy, no. Trust was my enemy. Early in childhood I was taught to trust no one. Emotional, and yes, physical abandonment by a parent could ruin your life.

His eyes snapped open as if he knew I was studying him.

"I love you, Azar." He brushed his lips gently against mine. "You don't have to respond. Just know I do."

That empty, uncomfortable feeling came over me as it always did, reminding me of when my father first stole me from my mother. I was a possession. My father never said he loved me and his expectations were always so high I could never achieve them. I always failed in his eyes no matter what I did. If I had the love, nurturing, and tenderness of a mother, would I have taken another path in life? Could I have found love? Would I have had the capability to embrace love if it was on offer.

"As much as I would like to share a morning with you in bed, I have to meet with my associates," he shared as he enveloped me in his warmth.

"That's fine. I have a breakfast meeting with a little old lady that fascinates me." I returned his physical embrace. Sex was always good, and although it was unlikely I could ever place an emotional attachment to it, I always welcomed the physical release.

"Tell me about her," he encouraged as he rubbed his foot up my leg.

"She is the one that took Dmitri and Khalid down." I stopped and waited for the outburst. His explosive temper never disappointed.

"What the hell do you mean?" he yelled as the sudden warmth was gone and his expression turned glacial.

"That's all the information I have right now. That's why I'm meeting her, I want the full details about how those two betrayed themselves. The woman has a wealth of information and I need to tap into it," I responded.

He swung his legs to the side of the bed, leaned his elbows on his knees and scrubbed his face in frustration. I wanted to reach out and rub his back in an attempt at connecting. But when he was this angry any physical contact would be shunned, and I could become an unwitting target of his violence.

"Khalid. It was Khalid's fault. Paranoid, unstable, and volatile. Why your father brought him into it is beyond me—"

"Stop. I don't want to relive any of that. I do, however, want to know how things went wrong—what this woman picked up on and how I can avoid any detection," I said. "Khalid is dead. Murdered in prison. Dmitri is in a coma and as good as dead. Ivan must be furious, and the retribution may not be swift, but it will be certain. It would be good to know what danger is swirling around us."

"How did you meet this woman?" he demanded not lifting his head.

ONE

"It was quite a surprise. Josh, one of the department heads from work, invited me to lunch. The person I was supposed to have lunch with that day had to fly to Amsterdam. Josh's twin brother and a family friend were there. The information came out of her mouth totally unfiltered," I said. "I know it sounds incredulous. I have to follow up on this. I've read all the newspaper accounts and her name is never mentioned. But she has information and I want it," I said as I turned from my side of the bed to walk to the shower in the hall.

"Azar, be careful. There are too many variables floating around out there and one misstep will cause this carefully crafted plan to collapse. We already have Adrien Armond to deal with. Let's not court more obstacles," he said as he headed for the master bathroom. "We can meet back here for dinner. I want to go over the numbers again. I'm leaving with Lucas tomorrow. We're flying to Luxembourg to check on the bacteria and virus samples. I want an accurate account, I don't trust the Armenians. I want to make sure everything was accounted for before it left there and arrived at the freeport. With the deaths of the transport people I don't want it being traced back to the freeport if their last steps are traced. I may need to make arrangements to move the inventory. I am telling you this whole new level of bioterrorism still has me on edge. Doesn't it trouble you a bit that Nare and Davit Tavitian, the two Armenians swept up when Dmitri and Khalid at the airport and arrested at the same time, remain unharmed and breathing?"

I thought a moment and had to place their names and faces. "I hadn't thought about it. Why would anyone care about those two? They were just low-level players in a game they had no idea what it entailed."

"I know we are compartmentalized but Dmitri was at the center of everything. He recruited the Tavitians from Armenia. Sopia, the woman White married, he recruited her from Georgia. Or was it Azerbaijan? No, it was Georgia." He stroked his right side of his face with his hand in thought.

"Your point?" I was getting irritated.

"Ivan has a far reach into many surrounding countries and recruited a lot of people for Dmitri. I want to make sure no one has double-crossed us on his behest." His assumption made perfect sense.

"Are you moving the samples now or waiting for more information?" I asked as I leaned on the door-jamb.

"No," he said. "Yes. I don't know. You know I am a precise person. Was a vial broken by accident or did someone open the freight and release more than just the one specimen? There have been too many hands on this project. If you had taken my advice and just crashed the markets, the psychological tremor sent around the world would have had a ripple effect. You still have the time to complete the pesticide of the crops, kill the animals and disrupt world trade. We are at the point where if you pull the trigger now everything will work correctly."

"Have you reconsidered adding to the list of release cities? I think the list is far too restrictive." I ignored his attempt to change my mind. If it were up to me I wouldn't just unleash a virus that had people bleeding from their eyes and orifices, I would arrange for polonium to be spread generously around the world.

"Absolutely not. I know you are talking around me and ignoring my suggestion to alter the biochemicals or at least decrease their use. The circle you're traveling around with biologics is a world without end, but it could also turn into a world of pain without end," he said with a stare that I knew was brooking no argument from me. "I'm not in this to destroy all of humanity. I have carefully calculated this to be an adjunct to our supply and demand of market economics. Now don't bring it up again."

I absolutely despised relying on a car for pickup and deposit everywhere I needed to go. My independence is everything to me. Using a company driver had the benefit of protection, but it also allowed the company to keep track of me more than I would like. My safety came first.

After the driver dropped me off as close to the restaurant door as possible, I made my way to the hostess and waited.

"I'm meeting someone here and I'm a bit early. Can we have a booth away from the crowd and coffee," I instructed the hostess.

Tucked away in a corner booth fifteen minutes early, I checked for any updates. I placed my phone on the table so I could monitor incoming messages. I opened the menu to peruse what I could order for a light breakfast. From my observation Mary was a definite caffeine addict and if I plied her with coffee, that was my chance for her to open up.

As I was finished looking at the menu, a body slid in next to me on my right. Before I could move, he reached out and held my hand in place to stabilize my movements. Should I lurch across the table at him and push his eyeballs into his skull until they pop? Or would that bring cell phones out and we would be plastered all over the news. I calmed and planned in my head the ways I could escape and where punches would land if necessary.

"Azar, it's a pleasure to see you again." He smiled and patted my hand to avoid any unwanted attention.

"Adrien. Say what you want and get the hell out of here." Taking charge and going on the offensive was the play I found best in these situations.

"Ah, Azar. So ungrateful. No thank you for returning your kidney? Or for entertaining you at my trial?" he asked with a wicked glint in his eye.

When he realized I wasn't going to cause a scene he let go of my hand. I yanked it away and planted it on the seat.

"Again, Adrien. What do you want?" I demanded and scanned

the room for people watching and exits.

"What do I want? What I have always wanted—every bit of my money back, with interest. Plus, you'll agree I deserve some remuneration for the time taken to hunt you down," he stated with no qualifiers and no chance for negotiations.

"I see." I lifted my hand to rearrange the silverware, keeping my right hand close to the fork. "And what do I get in return?"

"You will continue to breathe," he sneered. "You won't have to worry about being jabbed with an umbrella tip laced with ricin as you walk down the street, or someone slipping puffer fish toxin into your food. I can think of hundreds of ways to kill you." Although my eyes were focused on the table, I knew his bore into the side of my head. "And, Azar, you will never see it coming."

"Do you have a number in mind?" Might as well see where this was heading.

"I think half a billion euros is an appropriate settlement." He seemed to relax more and more as I kept the conversation going.

"Cash or stocks?" I asked. As I was not inclined to either I decided to string him along.

As he was about to answer the cheerful hostess interrupted our conversation and announced, "Your party is here." And from behind her a head of white hair appeared, almost comical in appearance. Then the face with those ridiculous blank glasses.

Adrien and Mary exchanged a quizzical glance lasting but a moment.

"It looks like you've traded up, Azar. I guess this handsome gentleman's offer for breakfast was better than mine." Mary winked. "You snooze you lose."

"You are too kind, madame," Adrien said. "I was trying to interest this young lady to join me for breakfast as she was alone. However, my advances were struck down. I am devastated but not one to give up."

"Don't be silly. Why don't you join us?" Mary asked. "Everyone has to eat."

"Perhaps another time," Azar said. "Care to leave your number?"

"Ah, but no. This was a serendipitous meeting set in motion by fate. And I hope we may cross paths again." He slid out of the booth seat. With a smile, he bowed slightly and was gone.

As Mary slid in she turned to the hostess and said, "Frenchie. Probably married and that's why he wouldn't leave his number. Better off without him, Azar."

"Mary, I couldn't agree more." I turned to the hostess who was amused by the exchange. "If you could tell our server my guest is here. She can bring coffee for her and we'll order shortly."

After we ordered breakfast and I had plied her with three cups of coffee, she relayed the tale of how she had helped the FBI unravel the art forgery case that rocked the art world and lead to the capture of Dmitri and Khalid. Although I was certain she tried to claim far more credit than should be awarded, I got the answers I wanted. Khalid's obsessive need for vengeance against Jude White had led to a sloppy outcome.

Dmitri was another story. Had he not decided to kidnap the young forger and transport her overseas, he may have escaped without a trace. Both men made bad decisions that had put the whole mission in jeopardy. Dmitri's bad decision to exploit the girl when he could have returned to London. Stupid. It would have been easy to clean up his mess before the powers in Russia decided his gallery had to be destroyed to bury evidence. His bad decision created a domino effect that brought Isabella Armond too far into the game and threw the whole timeline off with her do-gooder attitude. One bad decision produced a lot of bad outcomes.

Back to my investigation. "What happened to the girl that was forging the paintings," I asked as if I had a voyeur's interest in the tale.

"I guess she went into some type of witness protection

program. I hope at some point she can reclaim her life. Her parents are dead and she's in hiding how can that child blossom?" Mary asked. "And that girl had a lot of talent."

"Yes, losing a parent can be devastating. But losing both must be too much to handle. And you said her mother had cancer?" I asked.

"That is what I was told. She never spoke about it." Mary seemed lost in the girl's story.

"What a story. Someone should write a book about it," I said offering another cup.

She threw a sly smile my way.

"No. Are you writing her story?" This wasn't what I wanted to hear. I plastered on my best fake smile. "Good for you."

Breakfast completed, I'd obtained the information I'd come for and it was time to depart.

"Mary, this has been lovely, and I hope we can visit the museum soon. I have some charts and reports I have to go over for a meeting early tomorrow, so I have to beg off and end this meeting. I've had such a lovely time. Can I offer you a lift home? I have a driver," I offered as I waved at our waitress to bring the check.

The waitress walked to our table and said, "Ma'am, the check was paid by the gentleman who was at the table earlier. He paid for breakfast and left a generous tip," the server offered.

"Did he? Thank you. Mary, would you care to stay and finish your coffee, or do you want to walk out with me?" Inside, I was fuming. He paid for my meal with my money, the money he stole from me. That indeed was a slap to my face.

"I'll finish up and call Jax to pick me up," she said. "And, Azar. Stay away from that man. I believe he's up to no good. I don't have a good vibe about him."

"Mary, count on it. I had the same thought." I smirked and winked at her. "Enjoy the rest of your day."

As I departed, I checked to see if Adrien was following me.

ONE

When I was sure he wasn't, I texted Marcello to meet me at home as soon as possible.

Approaching my home, I saw an object on the porch. As we came closer I realized what they were; canna lilies. The nerve of that man reminding me of Sir Percy's taunt in *The Scarlet Pimpernel*.

I wouldn't give him the satisfaction of showing any emotion if he was watching. I walked passed them and Cello could deal with the flowers later.

If Adrien thought this would rattle my cage, he was very wrong. This only fueled my fire to take that man out of the picture. If Marcello failed, I would certainly be up for the job. The bolder he became and the more he taunted, the deeper my hatred grew and the more severe his death would be. When I hated, I hated as deep as the black abyss.

TEN

Jackson

MARY. WHY HAD GOD CURSED ME WITH MARY? I TEXTED HER to meet me outside the front door. No response. Parking on the street was prohibited and I was not willing to pay what I considered extortion prices to park in a lot where leaving scrapes on a car was the norm. In her mind, I'm certain she thought it was my privilege to chauffeur her around for the day.

Her return text said, **Come in.**

The woman was grinding on my last nerve.

After struggling to find a lot open on Sunday and negotiating a parking spot for my tank of a car, I paid the attendant his ransom fee and lumbered through the door. A quick survey of the place prompted me to describe Mary to the hostess. She remembered Mary. Of course, who wouldn't.

The mafia queen sat in a booth by herself enjoying what looked like pastries from the remnants scattered on her discarded plate. Unfortunately, without anyone monitoring her she probably had consumed her seventh cup of coffee and her tapping finger syndrome would set in soon. One cup of coffee counted for every ring of hell she would put me through.

"Seriously?" I huffed out making certain to furrow my brow, so she'd understand my absolute annoyance with her.

"Cool your jets. Sit down and take a load off." She waved her hand at me and I subconsciously followed her order.

I waited and was forced to watch as she consumed another chocolate croissant and took a sip of her coffee. I raised my eyebrows high enough they touched my scalp. She finally decided to engage me.

"Did I tell you who I was having brunch with?" she asked carefully, placing her cup on her saucer.

"Oh my God, seriously? You brought me in for a chitchat? Get up, we are leaving." I leaned to slide out of the booth seat. Someone has to take this woman in hand.

"Not so fast, bucko," she said signaling me to sit down with her hand.

I sat. Why? Why did I willingly accept more torment?

She turned toward her enormous bottomless bag and reached inside. If I took the time to do a daily check, I am confident I would find it held several weapons. Some legal and some questionable. Finally, she located what she was rummaging around for, pulling out her phone the size of a tablet. She engaged her phone, held it about a foot from her face and tapped the photo app. With great dramatic flair, she placed the phone down on the table, twisted it and then straightened it in front of me. It took me a moment to focus and my brain to engage. I was so shocked at what I was looking at on the screen that I froze.

When my brain synapsis had a chance to catch up with my eyes she removed it from the table. Again, with all the drama she could muster, she moved her hand like she was performing magic, took her phone back, and started a video. Although the video was inaudible because of the restaurant chatter, the body language was clear. I watched what could only be described as a car wrecking in front of my eyes.

I hit replay six times so that I could absorb body language and facial gestures. Nuances appeared six times and I studied each one.

There was no reasonable explanation for what I was looking at on her phone. All I could do was sit back, absorb the video, and process through every explanation possible. None of them were good. Mary had moved across the table from me and we stared at each other waiting for the other to speak. She broke the silence.

"I was a cool cucumber and pulled out all my acting tricks," she said with a head nod.

"Mary, you aren't an actress," I interjected. Although with Mary, who knew.

She ignored my observation and continued. "I acted as if I didn't recognize him. But you know damn well I did. It was hard, but I think I pulled off the forgetful old woman. He wasn't alarmed. He studied me for a moment or two and I saw those wheels in his mind turning. But it worked. He started speaking again and gave no signal to Azar that he and I had crossed paths. Thinking about it, what difference would it make? Why would I have any reason to question if they had some underlying relationship?" she said as she poured another cup of coffee—ring of hell number eight. "Are you ready for more information?"

"There's more?" I pulled back involuntarily and place both palms on the table. My voice and heart rate rose simultaneously, and if I concentrated I could assess that hyperventilation was not far behind. "Start from the beginning."

"If I do, your hand will involuntarily hit the table in annoyance. Let me, as you say, cut to the chase." And just to annoy me she took another sip of coffee.

"During our chat, she was more than a little interested in Roselov and pumped me for information. I gave her the details that are in the public stream but nothing more. Jackson, for once I played down my role in the matter because the universe has turned on itself. What could those two have in common?" She tilted her head and swallowed loudly.

"At the probably-not-likely end of the spectrum, it was a chance meeting between two people. At the opposite end of the spectrum, they are working together on something." Somewhere in the middle lies the truth.

Adrien is not the guy I would label a player. Therefore, I am less inclined to go with the supposition he was trying to pick her up as he'd said. Azar has a great reputation and a job people envy. That information leads me away from them being in some type of conspiracy. Her body language said she was not receptive to what he was saying, and his body language projected that he was in control. "Where and how did their paths cross?" I asked more to myself than her.

"He sure is handsome, but he is arrogant. She sure is beautiful, but she is closed off. I don't see chemistry, or that this is about sex," the expert at love replied.

"Mary, I am going to forward your photos and video to Ben and Cillian. This is a whole new layer we had no idea existed. Please dear God in Heaven, do not tell me she is involved somehow in art and money laundering? What would be her reason? I suppose we could be jumping the gun. She's from London; he's from Paris. Maybe they met somewhere in business? No, I'm grasping at straws." I could not fathom what was going on and tried for the simple.

She placed her hand on my arm to stop the rhythmic tapping my hands were doing on the table, the noise was starting to garner attention. Getting wound up wouldn't help anyone.

"Jackson, start with the basics. Her body language wasn't that of a friend," she said, and I nodded. "From the ramblings you boys were having in your conversation or maybe it was something I read in reports—"

"Reports? What reports? Were you going through my stuff? I swear to God, Mary—Wait, I don't want to know. Plausible deniability. But if you went through Cillian's stuff that's his bad for not having it secured," I mused, and as if amused she nodded in agreement.

I strummed my fingers on the table again. She glanced at my

right hand and waited. When my fingers continued strumming, she stared at me until I consciously put an end to it. Then she restarted the conversation.

"Anyway, I remember something about that name Armond coming up in passing. Something about shady dealing and this person buying up Roselov's gallery after Roselov was detained. And I am pretty certain I read that the London police were all over this because the sale was presumed backdated." She stopped, and I watched her eyes move side to side as if walking through a mind palace looking for a clue. "Wait, it must have been a report because now I remember seeing the sale documents with scribbles of questions on several post-it-notes. Anyway, my point is that Roselov was spinning around in Armond's world, and Azar was pressing me about Roselov. Could she have known Roselov too?"

She pulled out her phone and I watched her Google *Roselov and Armond*. Nothing.

Oh, here we go. "Mary, I don't see how anything you have relayed to me so far indicates she was pressing you about Roselov. For all you or I know she was giving you your fifteen minutes of fame."

"Jax, if their body language had been different, I would have put some random facts together and made the following leap. He's into art. Although he wasn't arrested for money laundering, I'll presume it was due to lack of evidence. How they missed that mark I don't know. Or maybe they threw him back to follow it up the food chain? Personally, I think he looks sketchy and I wouldn't discount he might have been running money through the gallery. You know a front for money laundering. If you would give me access to all the documents—"

I hit the table lightly three times to bring her back to our conversation. Back to reality.

"Right. Azar's into investments, not only investments, but global investments and not only global investments but managing their risk. So, ipso facto she was advising him on the least risk to money laundering. I can't get down with that theory the way she was act-ing," she said reaching for the last pastry on the plate.

"Get down?" I chuckled. "Possibly they were quarrelling over some aspect. No, we have to stop the what-ifs. It's fruitless and will take us down the wrong path and waste time. I'll shoot this over to Ben and Cillian. This isn't my problem and I don't want to make it mine. I'll make the inquiry just because she's on our soil, but I'm not taking it to Nathaniel to open a case. Ben can do a lot more research on her from his end. Hopefully we can determine where their paths first crossed if it becomes an issue. I'll meet with Josh this afternoon and to get him on board. He can check Azar from the company end," I said and started to call Josh.

"I'm in on the meeting with your brother. If I'm going to put this puzzle together I'll need every bit of information available." She leaned in but reached for a napkin. She wrapped her remaining pastry, placed it in her bag, and swiped a few packets of sugar.

Loath that I was to agree to this, she had a point.

"Remember, Sherlock, this is not an actual investigation and I don't want you finding a reason to make it one," I reminded her as I helped her out.

"Too late." She walked briskly ahead of me.

The call was made, and we departed for Josh's place.

The reason for our visit was not well received. Had it been just me without Mary the drama llama, the conversation would have con-sisted of two paragraphs and a loud no from Josh. But the way Mary presented our story with the low voice of secrecy interspersed with the excited voice to induce drama, he sat, listened, and thought about what she said. With a strange hand gesture, she indicated she was finished.

Josh was torn, and I had placed him in an untenable position. I was asking him to spy on a coworker on behalf of the government.

He was conflicted and there was no easy decision for him. I didn't expect him to think about our proposal as long as he did. Personally, I would have kicked Mary and me out long ago. Something struck a chord with him and I could tell at times he wanted to sing from the same sheet of music as Mary.

Finally, he raised his bowed head and blew out a breath.

"I can't do it, Jax. This is my career and spying on Azar could ruin me. I have listened to every word you two have said but there is no reason to believe Azar is doing anything wrong at work. She is, from what I can tell, a brilliant woman and well thought of in the financial industry. What you are asking me to do is snoop on her through back channels. That will inevitably get back to her and my boss." He raked his fingers back through his hair, scraping his scalp.

"Can't you ask her out on a date. She's attractive... you're... well, despite being Jackson's twin, you're the better looking of you two," Mary stated with a flip of her hand. "Couldn't you obtain information over a romantic dinner?"

"I have to agree with your assessment of me being the better looking of the two," he said with a wink and crooked smile. "However, Azar is here to perform a risk assessment of certain sectors of the industry that we represent. If I try to charm her, we have these pesky things called sexual harassment laws. If I was to look into her more personally through back doors it could be taken as me trying to find some dirt on her to blackmail her. I don't see this coming out in my favor either way. Mary, you want some coffee?" Josh asked as he stood to get a cup for himself.

"No," I firmly answered for her. Surprisingly, she didn't give me the stink eye.

"I don't mind keeping an eye on the stocks. That type of activity will go undetected. It also might be a bonus if I get out ahead of something. However, this is a no-win situation for me." When he sat, he sloshed a bit of his coffee on the table.

"You boys. Thank God we didn't have to depend on you in the great war. Worried about your tails. Is there anything about her that is out there in the public realm of the company? Like bulletins about her accomplishments or her receiving awards? Or maybe a snapshot of her at a party with a date?" Mary walked toward his computer as if she knew that part he would agree to research.

She stood by his computer and waited.

"Right now, would be good." She titled her head at Josh.

He chuckled at her and gave me an eyeroll as he walked over to the computer and logged in.

"I'll type her name in the search bar and we can pull up everything you want to look at." That garnered a brilliant, toothy smile from Mary. Behind that smile I knew she thought she could work her way in through that tiny crack Josh showed, bringing him into her circle of trust.

"It's a start," she replied as Josh and I exchanged glances.

Azar was quite the superstar in her company. There were several hundred action lines and articles about her. She had as many pictures on their company site as any celebrity had published in the local rags. The printer kept spitting out the pages for us to take with us. I thought the stack should keep Mary busy for a few days.

Placing herself on the seat in front of the computer she maneuvered the mouse to the area titled Images and clicked.

"That woman is quite the dresser. Look at these gowns. They have to cost thousands of dollars. That gold material looks as if it was spun from pure gold. And I know that head dress of metal is fourteen-karat gold. That is definitely the real deal. This woman must be loaded." Mary drew out the last word for dramatic effect.

Every picture that flashed on the screen gave us a little more information about her. She liked her jewels and wasn't shy about showcasing them. Every now and then, Mary would make a comment about the dress or shoes, but even I had to admit the woman should have a bodyguard with her to guard her accessories.

"Now look here, you two clueless men," she snapped. And we inched toward the screen. "Lookie here. She appears to have the same guy escorting her to all the galas and parties. Who is he? No one seems to know. He is always described as a friend, no name, probably listed as a plus one. You think the biometric boys can run his face for identification? Maybe he's the money bags giving her all the bling," she said as if a revelation had just occurred.

"And under what case number and authority can we do that?" I threw back. And before she could make a case I said, "Considering we don't have a case open on her and no probable cause to open one up. The answer to the question you want to ask is no."

"What a Debbie Downer, Negative Nancy you are. Forget it. I'll use some of my government settlement funds and hire a private firm to do it. You can say I'm giving back to my country," she said studying the picture knowing that statement would rile me up. And it worked like a charm. I was now in full agitation mode.

"He is quite handsome. Almost A-list movie star quality and he has that exotic lover boy look about him. And look, his hands aren't small by anyone's measurement system. He's confident, attached to her, but she's not attached to him. He's educated, at ease in social settings unlike her. They are a pair but aren't." She stopped and tossed the picture she just printed out on the table in front of her.

"You got all that from looking at a few pictures? Impossible," I challenged.

She smiled, and it vanished as quick as it appeared. "Body language, Jackie boy, body language. You look these over and then you tell me I'm wrong. Either way, until we know who he is, we can't put the pieces together. But this we know, she is a cool flame. Him, he burns hot."

"Pardon?" Josh questioned.

"Cool flame, metro man. Google it," Mary threw back. And as he did she continued. "Here's how I see we approach this—"

"Oh no, there is no we in this plan. Josh already said he is out.

I am the captain of this ship and intend to keep it on course. I am not going to start chasing down wild ideas and conspiracy theories. I work from facts and logical conclusions. This meeting has run its course," I advised her. It was time to cut her off and take this back to my house. I picked up the papers, tapped them on the table to signal out meeting with Josh was over.

"Nonsense. Josh is not out. He just had to say that for plausible deniability. Right, Joshy?" she asked looking out from under the heavy weight of her Coke-bottle glasses.

Josh dropped his head into his hands and I could tell he wished he'd never answered his phone this morning. I knew that feeling well.

"Mary, what I'll do is keep alert to what is going on. I may be able to place a discrete call to a few people in London. You know, to ask about her under the pretext that I want gossip on her. But I'm not searching her office or cloning her phone," he said and put his hand up to emphasize the line was drawn.

"No need." Mary leaned back. She had no intention of leaving yet. "I have it under control."

"The hell you do. You aren't doing anything to her phone. You hear me?" I stood and walked toward her. "You're working with the government and there are laws against that type of behavior. This isn't some spy movie where you can go rogue on me. Azar is a citizen of another country and a guest in our country. We don't know who this other clown is in the picture. For all we know he's some government official with diplomatic immunity. So not only no, but hell no."

"Wake up, Jackie boy. There's telephone spyware out there that can be installed remotely. Google it," she demanded. "There are apps and people do it all the time. You don't think Eloise is keeping track of your ass?"

"No, she would never do that. We trust each other implicitly," I assured her.

But the possibility tickled around the edges, no one is immune to doubt.

Josh and I quickly retrieved our telephones, googled telephone spyware, and indeed it was possible. I was truly fucked. In my heart I knew Eloise trusted me, but she was just like Mary, a Nosy Nelly. I had to deal with that later. Even Eloise wouldn't tamper with my government phone because that action probably had felony written all over it as well as disbarment.

"Forget Eloise. If you are telling me you plan to commit a crime I have no choice but to terminate your access to the bureau," I threatened.

"I don't think so, as we're talking about a government issue in front of a private citizen. How would you explain that? And I made no admission against my interest." She smiled.

My head was ready to explode, and if I died it would be a relief.

I couldn't take anymore. I needed to go for a run, blow off steam, and think how bad it would be if someone found Mary's mouth duct taped by an agent.

"Come on. We're out of here," I demanded.

"Mary, wait," Josh said coming closer. "Um, are you saying anyone I date can spy on my phone?"

"Worried, player?" she asked with a raised eyebrow.

"Hell, yes. I have dated some real psychos in the past." He looked at me. "The best sex is with the crazy ones."

"I have heard enough. For the love of God and all that is holy, don't be talking about your sex life with Mary. It will not end well, that you can be sure of," I warned him.

"Now back to this spy thing—" he started ignoring my heartfelt warning.

"We're out of here. I have everything we need and if you come across anything else let me know." Papers in hand, I was ready to leave.

Mary would not be deterred and turned to continue a useless conversation with my brother.

"Have you checked for tracking devices on your car? If you're worried, take it to a mechanic and he'll find it. And if she's loco crazy she might have installed spyware on your computer when you were in the shower," she shared. "She could have taken over your computer remotely and is spying on you right now through your web cam. Or writing emails you don't know about to other women."

Josh's face suddenly showed a shocked look of recognition. "Thanks, Mary. I owe you."

"No, you don't want to owe Mary. Take that back… save yourself while you can," I warned. Mary was not amused.

"Always happy to help, dear." She gave him a sweet grandma kiss on his cheek. Then threw him the thumb and pinky to the ear "call me" sign.

She gave me a stern look and hitched her thumb toward the door indicating she was ready to go.

Once in the car and safely buckled in, she turned to me and said, "He'll have some good dirt for us in forty-eight hours. You'll see. Dollars to donuts that Polly girl he dumped two months ago is stalking him. She had wedding bells floating all around her. When he finds all the spyware she planted he will be forever grateful. Now you can move along, dear. I'm ready for my nap."

My poor brother, manipulated by the evil genius right under my nose.

ELEVEN

Azar

SOME DAYS THE PAIN IN MY HEAD BECAME SO UNBEARABLE THAT MY limbs responded with involuntary tremors. Today was one of those days that even the pain medication I took to take the edge off didn't help. This I had my father to thank for. It wasn't until he stole my kidney. Something must have occurred during surgery that forced my mind to start working against me. There were no words that could ever encompass the hatred that I had for that man and his accomplice who stole a decent life from me. The visceral emotions of anger and hatred were wasted on him as I had no one to punish because more than likely he was dead. But Adrien remained alive, and he must die, that was a given.

My hand tremored as I reached for another dose of the medication, unafraid of overdose or addiction. I just needed the blinding pain to subside and the overstimulation of my olfactory sense to make the smells that were heightened go away. The blurring normally subsided over a half-hour period, today I wasn't so fortunate.

I waited for Marcello all day. As the hours passed, my head throbbed more, and no medication could dull the pain. This was unacceptable, and I needed him. I craved his calm demeanor in times of crisis.

Could Cello be turning away from me? Did he feel I was overreaching our initial goal? He was treating me as if I'd become some

100

type of fanatic instead of a valued partner. It wasn't my idea to blow up the churches, that was Khalid's brain child. In theory it had sounded workable. Blow up some piles of rocks, people will be terrorized, and markets will crash. What he didn't tell anyone was he planned to do it when the buildings were filled with people in the middle of the day. It was supposed to be a night time strike, destroying symbols and frightening the populace. The strike was to be precise, only the churches. But something went wrong, very wrong.

He was never punished for his shock-and-awe shit show that started a multiagency governmental search for all involved and put my plan in jeopardy. He was arrested for murder and kidnaping and died awaiting trial in some Super Max prison. He was never condemned in an International Criminal Court. However, Marcello and I were left to clean up his mess without the proper strategy or tools and things unraveled fast. Only by pure luck was I able to stay one step ahead and avoided prison.

The Italians, for all their bravado of being lovers not fighters, were surprisingly the first to fight back, maintain a semblance of order, rebuild and restructure. But again, they had sustained the least damage as far as human casualties. The mafia and religious zealots were out in full force to hunt down and bring to bear their own justice against the perpetrators. To date they had failed. St. Peter's was the first to be repaired and within a six-month window the Mass schedule appeared back to normal as if nothing had occurred and was conducted again. Papal and mafia money were spent on repairs leaving Italy's country budget relatively untouched. Thus, the sting of that attack was lessened than in other areas. If Marcello knew I had a hand in any part of that, his father would have had me killed. But my hands weren't clean, and I could never confess that to him.

The British were next, rallying and rebuilding Westminster. However, it did leave their economy weakened and at times appeared to teeter to the point it disrupted my ability to fully execute the plans I had for them. Their populace having been through

World War II and then the IRA bombings seemed to rally, regroup, and move on almost as if it was a new normal. As Parliament was rebuilt they relocated to another area. Some said they hoped the location remained the new seat of government. The House of Lords was having no part of it. Of all the issues dividing the country this issue took forefront. Their economy did not wobble as much as I'd hoped. It was my guess their large Russian and Middle Eastern populace clandestinely pumped in money, so it wouldn't fail.

The French acted as predicted, scattered and emotional. Because *Notre-Dame de Paris* was a UNESCO site, funding poured in to repair the church from a number of nonprofit sources. People in the many parts of the city were terrified and Khalid had achieved his goal. Terror attacks had not been a part of their moral fiber and it appeared they took longer to recover psychologically. The city infrastructure sustained enormous damage, much worse than London because of the number of homes and businesses packed such a small area. However, after a year Paris began to rally cautiously.

Financially, his plan was a success. It interrupted both large and small businesses and forced the European Union to dig deep into their pockets to subsidize the economic fallout. However, the loss of life was more than anticipated and although factored into his original plan, I'm sure he felt it was within the bounds of acceptable loss. My part of the plan overlapped phase one and was now forced to address an issue I hadn't anticipated—the issue of higher than anticipated fallout and intense scrutiny. But as the twenty-four-hour news cycles became bored, something new always came along.

Initially, Khalid's part was to destabilize the world economies. As they recovered, my part was to hit the economy again. I studied and watched and waited as the recovering economy started building steam. Now it was my turn to rock their world.

I expected an outcome similar to the Plague of Justinian, the death of millions. If my plan unfolded to its true potential, twenty-five million would die from my portion plus the hundreds of thousands from phase one was only a drop in the bucket of the nine and a half billion people that populated the earth. Too many old people were living and becoming a drag on thriving economies. The people who were exposed to the biologic attack and became infected would surely be the first to go. Next would be the chronically ill—another group the economy did not need to be supporting. Where Khalid used the shotgun approach to kill, mine was a more handgun approach.

The grain and starvation plan plus hitting animal products should at best starve third world countries who didn't contribute to world economic growth but were parasitic barnacles. All in all, I thought it was a great plan. Marcello not so much. He was all for manipulating the agricultural markets but not a fan of my biological plan and certainly not in tune with my theory of which class of people should die and why. As close as Africa was to Italy his fear was that Italy would be caught up in the spread of disease and his family may suffer the harmful effects, it was always a possibility. After many nights of making love and heated discussions about the plan, we struck a compromise. Algeria and Libya would not be infected because the two countries were too close to Italy. We would center the attack around Chad, Nigeria, and Ethiopia. However, I planned to hit Egypt hard; that was non-negotiable. The biological weapon we would use in Africa was an ongoing negotiation, but I would do what I thought best with or without his permission.

I was pulled from my thoughts as I heard the alarm disengage and Marcello walked in with the flowers from the front door in his hand.

"This is out of control," he said placing the flowers on the counter.

"Armond followed me to my breakfast appointment," I started, and he went stone still.

"His number is half a billion euros to settle our dispute. If he hadn't aided and abetted my father to steal my body part, our paths would never have crossed. All things considered, I think he has more balls than a pool table. By committing such a transgression in my mind, the man assumed the risk of whatever fallout occurred. Something he didn't factor in was everyone has the right to revenge. Ivan Roselov meted out his justice by altering his index finger, so he can never use his surgical skills again. My justice of taking his money was more than fair," I said and believed a fair statement.

I motioned toward the flowers. "Get them out of here. I don't know if a listening device or a timer set to explode has been planted."

With that explanation and command, Cello took them to the bathtub, immersed everything in water and then took them to the trash. A quick phone call and I knew the flowers would be gone from the premises within minutes.

"All right. We need a plan for this problem. I don't need your thoughts diverted worrying about Armond. He knows where you live, and this place is not safe for you. Tomorrow you will be relocated to what I consider a safe house. Leave this vermin to me and my associates. His shelf life has now expired," Cello said. "Give me a moment to call Paulo to bring the car back and we can talk there until I am certain there is no chance of our conversation being overheard."

The car waited for us and once settled into the car he opened the conversation.

"I may be beating a dead horse, but I am still struggling with the bioweapon choices and I need you to hear me out and rethink this part of the plan," he said as he turned from me to gaze out the window.

"Once you unleash whatever you choose, it will be out of our control. You don't know if you are setting into motion a superbug that will mutate and continue to kill time and time again or if it will produce genetic mutations for future generations. But more importantly, what's the purpose? Is it to harm people? Cull the herd? Or give you edge and control over the pharmaceutical and health care industry financial outcomes? Is it to frighten the healthy people and keep them indoors and afraid to live their lives? Make people afraid to interact physically for fear of catching something?" he asked.

"That's a rhetorical question," I answered.

"No, it isn't because I see no reason for the size of your plan. The bacteria that would need antibiotics is a good plan and works along the supply-and-demand level. Even some viruses. I'm all in if it benefits us on a financial spectrum. Azar, I have to say I think this is an unworkable plan. If you insist on going apocalyptic with both virus and bacterium, use the United States as your ground zero," he said with a shrug of his shoulder as if this was a logical conclusion.

"Are you insane? They have the best health care and research facilities in the world," I snapped back. "My financial impact would be gutted."

"That might be so, but millions of Americans are without health care due to their health care system. Initially, they won't be able to seek care from a physician and privatized urgent care facilities will turn them away. Government-funded hospitals will become overwhelmed. While people wait in waiting areas, the already ill will become infected too. Some of the bacteria and viruses are so foreign to their shores that their doctors won't recognize the symptoms until it is too late. Let's not forget the drug treatments are so expensive that they'll probably be hesitant to treat them if they can't pinpoint the exact bug," he argued. "Panic will ensue, and your stocks will eventually rock and roller coaster to where you want them. I just think involving Europe is a bad idea."

"What exactly is your problem? When did you become such a bleeding heart?" I demanded.

"I was never on board with this from the start. Do I care if you wipe out third world countries? Hell no. I don't make money off of those people or their governments anyway. Other people, important people won't care either. They will attribute the spread of an epidemic to poor drinking water or people living in such squalor that it was inevitable. But spread it around the world in rich countries and they will come after us once they figure out the pattern," he argued, and I thought it was lame.

"Don't be ridiculous. Did they call the SARS virus in 2003 a conspiracy? Or that there's an outbreak of the coronavirus in the Middle East, yellow fever in Brazil, and cholera in Tanzania—did they call those a conspiracy? I can pull this off. Why are you backing out?" I had a right to know. "I have spent millions setting this up, planned it perfectly, and it is workable."

"When do you plan to pull the trigger?" he asked with a tone of defeat.

"Less than two weeks. I want the pesticides and poisons to take out the agriculture first," I leaned toward him to gauge his thoughts. "Once the bacteria and viruses hit and the food supply is destroyed, people will panic. Protests will erupt urging governments to do something. And if we do this right some countries might even spiral into anarchy. Venezuela, North Korea, and Cuba should be the first to fall."

"I would like to leave the geographic areas open for further discussion. And I need to have vaccinations in place for my family members." He kept his head turned. "Azar, I love you. I want us to marry and have children someday. I don't want us to be in hiding our whole lives. I recognize you are not there yet, but I hope the love I feel for you is enough for us both."

I neither agreed nor disagreed and I could not return his sentiment. My mind was made up. I wanted to wipe out as many people as possible in the third worlds. And I had some specific Middle Eastern targets tangential to the third world countries that would logistically be workable. I had my reasons and he wouldn't deter me. After my father murdered my mother and stole me, no one came looking for me. Anyone who should have cared left me in the hands of that mentally and physically abusive monster. And when even my physical being became a burden to him I was shipped off to boarding school to be tormented by schoolmates. Smaller than most classmates and with no social graces I was tormented and ostracized. No one came to save me from my tormenters. A family and children couldn't become part of my equation. Even I wanted such a unit.

He tapped the glass and instructed Paulo to return home.

When we pulled up to the curb, Paulo parked, came to my side of the car and opened the door.

"You're not coming in?" I was hurt by what I considered a rebuff.

"I have to put plans in motion to ferret out Armond. Marcus is on the doorstep waiting to help you pack. Azar, you know it isn't our place to impose a new world order. I was raised a strict Roman Catholic and God himself knows I don't believe any of the nonsense of that religion. However, I am a pragmatic man. I believe for every action there is a reaction. When something is set in motion it stays in motion until stopped. How will you stop it? There won't be enough medicine to even slow it down if it catches fire and spreads without barriers.

"Your idea about smallpox will harm all people. No one, not even wealthy countries, have been vaccinated in about sixty years. Some will die, but others will be left blind and deaf. Is that what you want? What financial gain is in that part of your plan?

"If you are targeting specific religions and banking on wiping out a large part of societies that reject vaccinations because the gelatin contains pork or fetal cells that might also back-fire on you." He waited for me to respond.

"Again, don't be absurd. Anti-vaccination proponents transgress all religions. Church of Christ, Dutch Reformed Church, Christian Scientists, and certain sects of Islam and Judaism reject vaccinations. I don't discriminate based on religion. I'm not targeting any group. The disease will go where it goes," I argued and found myself becoming embroiled in an argument I didn't need to engage in.

He leaned forward and scrubbed his face. "Again, what if these people don't die or seek help, but are left disabled and deformed, or with a life without hope? Pregnant women giving birth to children that are blind or deaf? Please tell me what you will have accomplished financially? What is your master plan here, Azar?"

"Control. I want to control it all." Surely, he could understand that. "People will understand my sense of justice, Cello, they will. Paris let me down. They didn't punish Adrien. Ivan Roselov understood justice when he took Adrien's fingers. The world will come to me for answers." I had it all figured out.

He studied me. His eyes traced every curve and dip of my face and stared into the windows to my soul. If I had a soul, as preached by the religion I was baptized, but my upbringing taught me I didn't.

"Get some rest and we will talk after you settle in." It should trouble me that he didn't kiss me goodbye. Our physical connection was always deep. But I understood he was laser focused on Adrien Armond, so I gave him a pass.

As promised, Marcus was waiting at the door and we spent the next hour packing what I had brought to this temporary residence. No more company drivers. A private driver handpicked by Marcello would come with the package.

After Cello killed Armond, he would home in on honoring our plan. And should he wish to back out, I had the resources to continue and would do so alone.

TWELVE

Adrien

THE PHONE RANG JOLTING ME FROM MY NIGHTMARE-RIDDLED SLEEP. Sleep would be a loose term to use for what occurred at night as my body involuntarily flipped from side to side. The cause? Azar Abed. The logical portion of my brain said I should move on, let go of this obsession with Azar and seek a new path in life. But what would that path be? I could no longer practice medicine; my license had been revoked. Art dealership was no longer an option. Who would deal with me after the notorious trial? Wherever I went, if I used my real name it would cause doors to slam in my face.

The emotionally damaged side of my brain demanded vengeance pure and simple. I would not rest until Azar was brought low and my money returned with interest. By all accounts, that should be today. Then I'll kill her. I had no other option.

The identification on the phone read Melzar. The man I relied upon and the only man I trusted. But trusted was a term used in the loosest sense of the word. Because of the disguised voice, I had no idea of the gender of the person, age, or where he or she lived. My relationship with Melzar was more a leap of faith.

"Hello." I was alert and ready to take information Melzar had for me.

"Ad, bad news," he said in his robotic voice, waiting for my prompt.

"Not what I want to hear," I threw back, annoyed. "What is it?"

"All the money we had readied for us to remove is now secured. There is no getting at that money and I doubt she'll move it, giving us the opportunity to grab it in transit. And if you want to know where she'll be after today you better get on the move. She is relocating," he said.

I bolted up and flipped the covers off. "What do you mean moving? Is she returning to England?"

"No. After your little stunt with the flowers yesterday she is relocating to a fortress secured by such high-end security even special forces couldn't break through. A place I'm sure won't have an option for surveillance."

"How do you know about the flowers?" Alarm did not even begin to cover the panic I felt as bile clawed up my throat. I took every precaution to remain anonymous and was certain my movements weren't monitored.

"Ad, you pay me an obscene amount of money to know everything that is going on in your world." I hated not knowing who was speaking. "It's my job to know everything that can affect you and I take my job seriously."

"And? What else have you found out?"

"Azar has bought up specimens of bacteria and viruses. As a man of medicine let's term them biologics," he replied. "Actually, there are some sitting in a freeport in Luxembourg. Others have been transported to additional holding areas waiting for her to give instructions when to release them."

"Come again?" I was shocked and sure I had not heard correctly. It was conceivable that she could acquire such a cadre on the black market and certainly had more than enough money to pay for them. But to what end?

"Azar Abed has made purchases of viral and bacterial specimens and is in negotiations right now to purchase smallpox. I know she is very close to completing a deal for the Marburg virus." He let that hang.

"Which bacterium and viruses in particular has she already acquired?" I had to know this information to assess what we were dealing with and try to determine her plan. This could be excellent extortion material. Or I could report her as a terrorist. I only needed to send the information to the right people and she would be killed by law enforcement as an active terrorist. But was that what I wanted? No. I wanted to carve her up into little bits piece by piece while she was conscious and aware of her pain. No anesthetic pain relief for her. And of course, there was still the issue of my money.

"Crimean-Congo hemorrhagic fever, MERS, SARS, Nipah, and Rift Valley fever all deadly. There are samples stored in the freeport and some are already in the country where they will be launched to spread," he reported with no inflection of his voice.

"The viruses—which ones are ready to go and are they already weaponized?" I asked as these were far more important as there were no antibiotics to treat viruses.

"I don't have that particular information. The information capture is ongoing," he said.

"And why are you sharing the information with me?" I wanted to know because Melzar always had an angle.

"Marcello Ghiaccio is coming to kill you." Just like that, without a hitch to his voice, I knew I would have an afternoon visitor. "You need to be ready. I don't want a dependable customer incapacitated with no need to procure further services."

I let that sink in and my stomach clenched. Who the hell was Marcello Ghiaccio? Was he someone I wronged in my practice? A hit man? Someone from my past dealing art?

"Who is he?" It came out as a scared tremor in my voice. And yes, I was scared. I hadn't come all this way to die in some foreign land with a bullet in my brain.

"That information is something for you to ruminate on and

once you've decided what to do, we can discuss it further. Perhaps we can amend our deal and prepare a novation to cover the cost of the new material I am providing to you and how it can be handled to accommodate you best," he said.

"How do I know this is even true and you are not just trying to extort money from me?" I leveled out my voice. Once the words came out of my mouth I wanted to claw them back. If you are in the hands of a surgeon, you don't insult them the night before surgery. This conversation was akin to that and a large error in my judgment.

A robotic voice laugh was quite unnerving.

"Although quiet insulting, I understand the place that question comes from, Ad. I am a merchant of information. If I was to misrepresent information to potential clients I believe my business would go down in flames rather quickly. Wouldn't you agree?" he asked. He had a valid point and the logic behind it calmed me.

"What should I do with this information?" I asked trying to elicit more information indirectly.

"Take a bit of time to determine what you want to do with the information and get back to me. We can determine a plan of action if the remuneration fee is acceptable. But, Ad, I wouldn't wait too long," his mechanical voice cautioned.

"I understand. How long do I have?"

"If you don't leave your hotel room for the next twenty-four hours, I don't anticipate a problem. However, that precludes you from observing Azar's movements today. Have a think and reach out to me."

"Come up with a number acceptable to you and call me back within the hour," I said. And we both disconnected.

Where to start? Where was Azar moving? I had overplayed my hand and she advanced instead of retreating. I had to know where and what my prospects were to get to her with this new information in place. Do I get my shit together and stake out Azar to see where she is relocating? I'd have to leave the hotel room. No, I need to strike a deal with Melzar for that job. He will find her. He's right, until I know what to be aware of I need to stand down. Would this Ghiaccio guy be on the internet? Is he some lone wolf or a public figure?

I tapped the computer to life and entered Marcello Ghiaccio. I raked my fingers through my hair waiting, waiting. As my foot tapped nervously, the screen displayed the man I saw with Azar the other night. My God he was already here to kill me and the two of them are plotting. It must be true.

My mind raced, and my heart wasn't that far behind. No, he can't be a hit man. Hit men stay hidden in the shadows. And look, you idiot, the man is a bit of an Italian celebrity. Different women all over him. My eyes scanned the education section. There it was— the connection to Azar through the London School of Business and Economics. Now my breathing could return to normal. Deep breath in, hold and release. After seven breaths my calm returned.

What else? He is the CEO of Fiamma, a pharma and biotech company whose company profile boasted research and development, took the original molecules to the final product of a marketable medicine. My eyes read as fast as the menu pages would open. And then I found it. Drug substances and drug products. Development and manufacturing. Small and large molecules.

I had to calm down and think logically. Put my medical brain to an accelerated use. If what Melzar said was correct, and I had no reason not to believe him. Azar was importing bacterial samples. Think, think. What can she do with them? She may be selling them to labs, so they can work on genetics. If Marcello knows ahead of time the bacteria it is, he will have enough antibiotics on hand to sell and market at an inflated price. Supply and demand. And if she was smart enough to mutate a bacterium and he was already working on an antibiotic in research and development, he would be the only one with the cure. He could sell the cure at any price. His company has a global reach. Scanning further I found the words to affirm my theory. Right there, he provided commercial-scale finished dosage forms, manufacturing compliant biologics and was heavily invested in pharmaceutical development.

He was in on it with her. But what did he have to do with me?

In a short amount of time, I had to find everything I could about this opponent. I must have read hundreds of articles until I found it. Buried in an obscure place and probably meant to be scrubbed but someone got careless, I found a nugget of information. His father Marco Ghiaccio was a major player in the Italian mob, the modernized mafia. It appeared there was a big investigation when Marcello initiated the process of starting his business and questions were raised about the structure of the organization because of his family background. It started out as a private corporation with minimal government interference but over time as the company did well, he took it public. I could only imagine the enormous amount of money that was invested to grease official palms to make that happen. But there it stood, and it prospered with an enormous global reach. No doubt a laundromat for mob money, but it appeared after various audits were performed. Nothing ever came of the investigations.

Shit. I was deep into a hole I might never get out of with this guy involved.

My head was spinning. Did this mean I had the mafia after me? That was assured death. However, from everything I read the man appeared a legitimate businessman whose company traded on the open market. No, this was making no sense, but there were pieces to the puzzle I couldn't ignore.

I had enough money to live and I could live comfortably. If it weren't for Azar stealing my money when I was in Russia, I never would have tried to extort money from Isabella and landed in jail. This was all her fault. Azar deserved to be punished and money was her weak spot. But if I couldn't get to her money as Melzar intimated, then maybe she just needed to die. No loose strings, and my final punishment could be exacted with no one left to guard her money. Possibly Melzar knew a man for the job. Yes, that was the best course to take. After all was said and done, it would be my death or hers.

THIRTEEN

Jackson

ONDAY MORNINGS WERE ALWAYS THE WORST. TRAFFIC WAS always a nightmare, but on Monday it was a nightmare on steroids. Road rage was more frequent, and accidents littered the highways.

Today was no different. The line to get in the Bureau building was backed up and whereas normally I would be angry that some questionable people were let through, today I just wanted the line to keep moving to get into the building.

People scrambled to get last-minute memos passed around before our weekly conference. Or in the alternative begged for a continuance which, save for a death of an immediate family member, was always declined. This morning was a particularly dreaded meeting. Hopefully, the good news that the first half of 2017 showed a decrease in crime would move the meeting along.

Good news always had to be balanced with bad news. The bad news was Mary had weaseled an invitation into the meeting, but on a scale of big pain in the ass to small, it was small. She would be swallowed up by the sheer volume of people attending the meeting. There she was at the opposite end of the table chatting up three young people too naive and wet behind the ears to know they should run. Run from the devil as she snapped at their heels. Did I have an obligation to warn them? No. Should I? Yes. Will I? No.

Maybe they can do her bidding and keep her off my back.

The meeting was about a half hour in, and oh my God, here we go. Her arm was lifted board straight in the air reminiscent of Hermione Granger from Harry Potter, begging to be called upon and recognized. Please help me keep control.

"Yes, Ms. Collier," Nathan acknowledged. Why would he even think to open up whatever can of worms she was about to spill all over our table.

"Since I am a neophyte and feeling my way around, might I ask a question about areas that we, you as the FBI, have control over? Two in particular." She was as sweet as she could be throwing in the little old lady head tilt and smile.

"Why of course, Ms. Collier. If you have a question then possibly the other new people may have a similar one but are too shy to ask," he said as helpful as he could be.

Even lowering my head so that my closed eyes rested on the heel of my palms could not blot out what was sure to make heads explode one by one. Or possibly in unison depending how outlandish the question. All that would remain would be puffs of smoke.

"Thank you, sir. It is several parts and if I overstep, feel free to shut me down." She stood and moved around to the back of her chair for support another ploy to draw attention. Here she goes, she's taking control of the room.

"It's my understanding that protecting vital assets falls within our purview of the counterintelligence department," she queried, and Nathanial nodded. "As well as terrorism." He nodded again.

She had the room's attention and the young people were hanging on her every word. The word terrorism and counterintelligence seemed to do that to people.

"I understand that back in 2013, a man was indicted for stealing corn seeds. Not just any corn but corn seeds that were considered intellectual property because they were cultivated for a specific purpose. That fell under FBI jurisdiction. And that same year, another man was indicted for stealing rice samples that were considered intellectual property.

"What if someone, other than the government-sanctioned grower, was lacing the crops and land with something that could either mutate the crops or kill them? Specifically, the seeds that were in research testing? Would that be considered interference with intellectual property or possibly theft as they would be destroyed. And would that fall under the FBI jurisdiction? Because if the underlying element of theft is depriving someone of their property, would that be a theft of intellectual property?"

The room was silent. I raised my head knowing where this was going. She was fishing for him to say it was part of Homeland Security and weasel her way into an invitation to talk to someone there.

"Ms. Collier, that is quite a conundrum as it may lie within the purview of Homeland Security or even the Department of Agriculture. I would have to get a legal opinion on that specific issue. The actus rea or act would be what the case would revolve around what the act was which is considered a crime. The question is if the act is the property being damaged or is it the fact that someone interfered with the intellectual property? Starting from the beginning you indeed have the valuable asset at stake. And as you pointed out it would be considered a taking or theft if you are considering that taking is depriving someone of their property. I'm going to jot that down and get an answer for you. And I'll make a leap that the question came from some concern you've run across." He leaned over to make a note.

"It does," she responded. Oh no. Please don't tell me she's going to take that one Chinese conversation she overheard and segue it into something the department should be aware of.

"Can you share a bit of the fact pattern?" he asked and took a seat himself settling in for what he even knew was going to be a convoluted hypothesis, spring boarding into a theory.

"I'm still collecting data. However, there are indicators that some irregular activity around soy-bean production is worth a look. Illinois, Iowa, Minnesota, and Nebraska are the biggest producers of soybeans, and early on were on target to have a stellar year. One might say a banner year. Mid-October everything was looking great. These last four weeks, production fell off dramatically, and I mean right off the cliff. Late November through early December, by all indications we should have had a blockbuster year. The production decrease put a wobble in the stock market but didn't totally rock it. Just enough to cause concern and have people looking how that might involve the export of it and its potential ramifications. Reading further bits and pieces, kids in various places in the farm areas noticed drone-like machines flying around at night. The ones that reported it, were recorded with precise accuracy. There might have been more that didn't report it because it was at night and they didn't want to get a lickin' for being out," she said as she leaned forward into her hands supported by the chair. A few people in the room had mentally dozed, but the younger ones held onto her every word and were scribbling notes as if they were at an International Money Fund seminar.

"If you look at other countries such as China to our wobble in soybeans they are having a wobble in rice. Brazil is having issues with coffee beans and they are having a bit more than a wobble. I guess I'm asking who's watching for patterns? And are the wobbles due to an issue caused by man? With so many government agencies in so many countries, is anyone tasked to watch this and integrate what is happening globally? And not that this is happening, but what if cows or farm animals are dying from possible bad grain here? Is it happening in other parts of the world at the same time? Would or could this be elevated to a terrorism threat?" She looked around the room for answers.

"Ms. Collier, I see your point. I'm going to get you access to the right people to talk your ideas and observations out, so everyone has the benefit of your research and thoughts. I assume you have a recordation of your findings?" he asked, and she tapped her marble composition book. "Was there another part of the question?" he asked because now he was all in on her lunacy.

"The second part has to do with pharmaceuticals, but I'm still working that one up. I'll need a touch more time," she said. "I've been collecting data. However, I can't classify it as empirical as yet. I'm concerned as everyone is that we weren't prepared for the flu and based on past experience deaths may rise beyond an acceptable level. If a new variation or strain hit on the heels of the one passing through now would that cause a pandemic? I believe the WHO or CDC probably has the answer, but I'm terribly afraid to trouble them with what might be just a silly what-if question."

He stopped and thought for more than a moment.

"You appear to have thought some issues through that I might not be giving you enough time to explore. Let me ask you this. Are the two areas you are thinking about linked together tangentially?" he asked as he stood to close the blinds with the stick attached to them.

Mary took her seat again, opened her marble composition book and thumbed through the pages.

"I hadn't come to that conclusion. I was going down another path," she offered. "If the grains were tainted and fed to animals, then yes, you could go down that path you are suggesting. However, I would think that might be a long endgame. I was thinking more of a quick buy quiet disruption, and a crash," she yelled and clapped her hands. Everyone jumped, even Nathanial. "I don't know enough to know what I don't know and should be asking. I just have theories floating around."

"Give the words a voice that are floating in your head, Ms. Collier," he said. Dear God, was the man insane?

"A commodities crash, you know. Such as soy, rice, and wheat, usually precedes a full market crash. But, what would cause the commodities to die or underperform? Blights and famine, terrorism, import-export implosion, and anarchy are just a few. Those are the words floating around in my mind that are bothering me," she said and tapped her pen on her paper.

"Do you have any soft data to support those words?" he questioned as his eyes laser focused on hers.

"Yes."

"After the meeting, you and Evans meet me in my office. I'll make some calls and set meetings up," he said. "Anyone else? If not, let's get onto the goals," Nathanial prompted. After that drama no one wanted to follow up with more questions. Truth be told it probably spooked half the room. Some of the nuts would go into survivalist mode after the meeting adjourned.

I was about to get Mary's attention and shoot her an "I'm going to kill you" look when I noticed a young guy I didn't know was ever so slightly lifting his phone. He appeared to be taking photos of Mary and sending them. These little dip wads better not be starting some bully campaign against her. Or put this on some social media forum to make fun of her as the butt of their humor. I'll catch the little bastard after the meeting and find what plans he had taking those pictures. That reminded me I needed to voice my opinion to Nathaniel again that I didn't think the interns should be at such high-level meetings. I didn't care if they were Harvard or Columbia students, it just wasn't appropriate.

The meeting droned on another two and a half-hours and at some point, I believe I fell asleep with my eyes open. It was about the time that everyone but me and another agent left that I noticed Mary had left for what I assumed was a bathroom break and had not returned. That was so unlike her. Her sweater remained but her enormous bag and the marble composition book she always guarded were gone.

I picked up her sweater and returned to the office. No Mary. I asked Paulette our administrative assistant if she had seen Mary. No Mary. I was becoming alarmed. We should already be in Nathaniel's office and she would never miss a meeting with the big boss. I retrieved my phone from my pocket and placed a call to her. It went to voicemail. I tried again, same thing. I sent a text to her and it hung. I waited for a response or at least the sign it was read. Nothing. This was not like Mary at all.

I turned to a female colleague and said, "I'm concerned about Mary. She left from the meeting and never returned. Would you check the ladies' room for me?" I asked.

"No problem at all. I think you should avoid checking it out." She gave me a wink.

Surely if she was ill someone would have found her in there already with all the foot traffic.

"Sorry, she's not in there," she said. "Let's check the break room, maybe she's having a cup of coffee."

Nothing.

Mary was not in the ladies' room nor in my office. She was not waiting for me at Nathaniel's office. That horrid feeling that something was very wrong clawed at my neck. Low-level panic was starting to set in. Several calls and texts later, it was clear I had to report this to someone. But one more stop to confirm before I pressed the panic button.

I walked past the steel double doors of building security and swiped my badge to enter the main area. Two older men in brown uniforms were monitoring the bank of screens from various parts of the building. Not every floor or hall was monitored on every screen, buy every camera in every hall fed into a server that captured the activity in the area.

My request was clear, run the tapes from when she left the room. The correct server was tapped into and the footage brought up on the monitor. We caught Mary leaving the conference room and entering the ladies' room. When she exited, it appeared someone was waiting for her. A woman. The woman was dressed as if she'd just come from outside or was preparing to leave. Her coat still buttoned, gloves on and a hat in place meant she wasn't planning to stay. She didn't appear to be an employee. Her cashmere coat was more of a fashion model style and texture than an agent or administrative assistant. And then the most bizarre thing occurred. After an exchange of a few words Mary retrieved her phone from her bag, powered it down and handed the woman her phone. She took the battery out and placed it in her handbag. The pair walked to the stairwell where we followed them to the parking garage. A few feet from the door a black car was idling. It appeared a man in a suit wearing no hat was driving. He didn't get out to open the door as Mary was rushed along to get inside. She slid into the back of the car followed by the woman and the car took off in smooth fashion as to not attract attention.

It was impossible to tell anything about the woman other than she had dark hair and a large hat that flopped over her forehead. Her coat was long, the collar turned up. I couldn't tell her age and barely could determine she was Caucasian. Hell, for all I knew it could have been a man dressed as a woman.

Then it hit me. Holy shit. Could Mary have been kidnapped right from an FBI building. Bile was clawing up my throat and I had to lean on the desk to take some controlled breaths to release my growing panic. My God, we are the people who find the kidnappers. One of our own had been kidnapped without a trace.

My next call was to Nathaniel. The security guard reviewing the tapes placed a similar call to his boss while trying to get a fix on the license plate of the car as it slid through the gate to pay and out onto the street. The car plate was purposefully blurred and once the car passed through the gates she was gone. No distinguishing marks on the car, no decals, nothing but a paper ticket that he had obtained when he came in.

The security department ran the footage of the person entering the building. All that could be discerned was that nothing stood out that would trigger a wand search, and no one remembered the person. A nondescript person leaving in a generic car kidnapping a person right under the eyes of security and anyone in the halls. Brilliant. Within an hour I hope a number of people would have their asses chewed and be on administrative leave, but that would not bring my friend home safe. I didn't believe in prayer, but I prayed.

FOURTEEN

Jackson

A S THE BUREAU PUT ALL SYSTEMS IN PLACE TO FIND MARY, I PLACED a call to Eloise and within minutes she was on her way to the building. Normally, a woman who thrived on drama, I knew I could count on her to keep a level head.

The next call was a call I didn't know how I was ever going to place. Cillian and Emma had to be notified. Before I placed that call, I spent an inordinate amount of time in the bathroom deciding whether to throw up or just keep splashing my face with cold water. How I found my way back to my office is still a mystery. I was working on autopilot.

I picked up my phone and placed the call. At first there was stunned silence, and then I heard a muffled scream and crying from Emma.

"Emma, I promise you we are doing everything in our power to find her," I started as Eloise entered my office and threw herself with dramatic flair on the couch.

"Put us on speaker, hon," Eloise said, and Cillian did the same on his end. "Now everyone just calm down. This is Mary we are talking about. If she didn't trust the person would she have walked out with them? She's in a goddamn FBI building for Christ's sake."

And that right there made it all the worse but made sense.

"What if that woman threatened her that they had one of us or

125

had a gun on her?" Emma sobbed.

"Emma, no one is getting past security with a gun," Eloise reminded her as she gave me a roll of the eyes.

"What about those 3-D printed plastic guns?" she asked as her breath hitched.

"Em, get a hold of yourself. If I was there with you, I might be forced to slap the stupid out of you. You can't get anything through that security system. One guy pulled me out to do a more thorough search. I told him I had a law degree and knew how to use it, and my fiancé was Special Agent Jackson Evans. 'Nuff said. Now here's what I know from Jackson. The woman took Mary's phone and she appeared to go willingly." Eloise moved to a chair, leaned back and placed her heels on my desk.

"But no coat, no stop at her office," Cillian reminded Eloise. Not helping things.

"Wait, people. How stupid are we?" she said pulling her feet from the desk and rummaged through her purse for her phone. "This is what happens when everyone goes into panic mode. No one is thinking correctly."

"What are you doing? We already tried to contact her by phone," I asked her, a bit agitated that she would think that wasn't our first route.

She looked at me with her annoyed face. "I sure as hell hope our children inherit my IQ because if they inherit yours we are truly and royally fucked," she said tapping on a phone app.

"Now hold on there. There's no need to get ugly about this," I said coming around the desk to see what she was doing.

"Em, remember I told you when I got her those ear-bud translators we also ordered that watch with the med alert?" Eloise asked, excitement in her voice as her fingers flew across the keys.

"Oh my God, yes. She didn't want the Apple watch, but you talked her into an elegant watch that all she had to do was twist the stem and it would send out an alert and GPS coordinates. Are you able to see anything? Give me a minute and I'll activate mine. God, what was the password, my mind is a blank," she said as the sobs now turned to breath hitches.

"Seriously? The password is Mary Rules," Eloise replied as she worked a grid that did not show any blinking dots. "People, she hasn't activated it. I don't know if that is a good or bad sign. I'm going with good because she could easily activate that without anyone knowing."

"Let's not jump to conclusions," I added before Emma started wailing again. "Let me see if our tech boys can somehow triangulate and lock into her even if she hasn't activated it."

"I'm booking the next plane out of here," Cillian said, and I was sure Emma was already packing. "You keep me posted and we will Uber it from the airport. If the app gets activated, Em should be able to pick it up on the plane so we can watch with you. What about any city or bank cameras?"

"We are all over this so just get yourselves to the airport. Remember this is Mary we're talking about. The bureau screeners probably missed about a half dozen of her makeshift weapons in her bag. I know she's gotten the pepper spray pen past them every day for a week. Eloise, stop me if I'm wrong but wasn't today the day she was going to test out getting the USB look-alike that's a stun gun on her keychain?"

"Yes, that's right, and if she didn't bitch about it being confiscated then she still has it and got it through," Eloise said. "She also has her earbuds with her because she said at lunch she was going to sit in the area where there were a lot of international financial people and try to listen in on Middle Eastern people."

"All right, El. You stay here. Cil, you get moving and I'm heading to central to see if they have any new feed," I said.

I walked down the hall toward the elevator when I saw the young guy from the meeting holding Mary's notebook, thumbing through it. What. The. Hell.

He lifted his eyes to mine as I invaded his personal space, but he didn't step back. Interesting.

"Where did you get that notebook?" I demanded, putting my hand out to retrieve it from him.

"It was on the table. I picked it up after the meeting," he said, looking me straight in my eyes as he lied to me.

"What's your name and what school are you from?" I demanded as I shifted my weight to my interrogation stance.

"Tyler Devonport from Columbia University." He mimicked my stance.

"Tyler Devonport, you're a liar. I swept that room as I left and there was nothing on the table. So, you want to try that again?" I challenged as I pulled my phone from my pocket.

"No," was his response and nothing more.

"No what?" I asked.

"No, I wouldn't like to rephrase my answer." His tone was indignant.

I called Nathaniel and he was quick to answer. "Any word?"

"No, but we may have a situation. Meet me in conference room 220, pull the file on a student Tyler Devonport, and get phone tech in on the meeting," I said, and we disconnected.

"Hand me your phone." I held my hand out to receive it.

"Not without a warrant," he replied stepping back on his left foot slightly.

"When you entered those front doors, you signed a waiver and released all your rights to privacy. Hand it over," I said through gritted teeth.

"Not without a lawyer," he threw back and placed his hands in his pockets.

"Hands out of your pockets," I said, and he complied. I placed another call to secure another agent to escort us to the conference room. Nathaniel arrived shortly after the call.

The three of us took a seat at the table. The temperature of the room was rising and not in a pleasant way.

"Let's talk again about how you came into possession of this book," I said tapping Mary's marble composition book.

"Don't you have to Mirandize me?" he asked crossing his arms with a certain confidence in his actions.

"You aren't under arrest." I sat back to study him. Well dressed, arrogant, impeccably groomed, and eyes like ice chips. Manicured nails and an expensive watch gave me pause, but Columbia screamed money.

"Then I'm free to go?" He started to stand.

"No, you're now part of an investigation and fact gathering mission, so sit your ass down," I ordered with my best authoritarian voice I could muster.

Nathaniel opened the door for the phone technician and entered the conversation.

"Son, you may be in some hot water here, so I advise you to cooperate with Agent Evans," he said to Tyler. Nathaniel then turned to me and asked, "What do you need from him?"

"His phone. I saw him taking photos of Mary during the conference and he may have videotaped her entire session. And now he is in possession of her property and has no reason to be," I said.

He turned to Tyler and held his hand out. "Phone."

"Warrant," Tyler threw back.

"Tyler Devonport, I'm placing you under arrest under 18 US Code 641. Now empty your pockets," Nathaniel ordered.

"Lawyer," he replied without following Nathaniel's orders.

"Cuff him and retrieve his phone," was Nathaniel's reply.

"Diplomatic immunity," Tyler responded.

"Son, I don't play games, and if you were here under any type of diplomatic immunity I would know."

"I'm not your son, and you're making an enormous mistake," he said as cool as could be.

After the phone was retrieved, the technician opened it and hit the photo app. Nathaniel's face turned from placid to concerned to angry all in quick succession. Photos populated the screen of Mary and there was a video of her portion of the conference.

"Why do you have all these pictures of Ms. Collier, and more importantly, why are you taking photos in a government building when that is strictly prohibited?" he asked.

"Lawyer," was his response as he tried to get comfortable in the seat with his hands cuffed.

Nathaniel opened the text messages and emails which he reported were encrypted. He handed the phone to the tech and gave him instructions to crack the encryption.

"Mr. Devonport, it appears you may be up to some nefarious acts other than the theft of government property—" Nathaniel advised.

"I didn't steal any government property," he said as he sat forward to make his point.

"You were in possession of Ms. Collier's book which is government property," I replied.

"I told you I found it on the table and was going to return it to her," he replied as cool as he could be. Who was this guy? A student would be ready to pee his pants under such scrutiny and arrest. "And I want it noted that I was not in possession of it to convert it to my own use. And by the way, did the government purchase that book or was it her own personal journal?"

"Son, with these photos and Ms. Collier's property, who I might add is now a missing person, you're in a world of trouble," Nathaniel told him as he lifted his hip to balance on the edge of the table.

"L-a-w-y-e-r," Tyler repeated, spelling it out for emphasis.

Nathaniel looked at me and as he stood ordered, "Mirandize him and take him to a holding cell after booking. He wants a lawyer, make the call."

"You don't know who you are dealing with." His voice was cold and steely.

"We're about to find out, aren't we, son?" Nathaniel said and left.

I called the duty agent and had him escort Tyler Devonport to be booked on three federal charges while I returned to my efforts to track down Mary.

Hoping to find Mary had activated the GPS on her watch, I was disappointed. Waiting for further news, I thumbed through her book to the last page that she made an entry. What appeared in bold black letters was the name Ivan Roselov. Nothing more.

FIFTEEN

Marcello

THE ONE THING I DESPISED ABOUT FLYING COMMERCIAL WAS HAVING no control over who would be assigned the seat next to you. Normally, I would welcome the flirtatious woman with the attractive face as a seat mate. Although I loved and cherished Azar, I was a man with a specific appetite that could only be fed by certain women. Normally, when one such person came along I made certain to take full advantage of what was on offer.

However, today my mind was cluttered with business activities. Mostly what to do with Azar. My bond with her was unbreakable on one level, but I knew I'd have to betray her. That was unchartered territory and I didn't know how she'd react. One thing was for certain, I knew there would be repercussions. Whether irreparable damage would be done was yet to be determined.

The way I assuaged my guilt was knowing she was betraying me as well. I was aware she had tried to obtain plutonium, neptunium, and mercury. I was forced to face the fact that I may have been deceived as to her expanded plans. Ricin, sarin, and VX, I was told were also within her reach.

What had started as a plan between Khalid, her father, and her years ago had morphed into what could only now be described as a declaration of war on humanity. In my estimation, part one— the Easter attacks—ended in disaster. The theory was workable with minimal blowback on them. To bring fear to certain parts of the world which would produce a panic in the financial sector. However, Khalid had unilaterally in a clandestine fashion advanced some changes. Each member's part was compartmentalized and that meant no one could stop the plan. Avigad's participation jeopardized the plan through his careless management of brokering organs and thus he'd taken his eye off the ball. The plan went unchecked, leading to arrests and deaths.

The execution of part two of the plan, crash the markets and cash in, was a plan Azar and myself could effectuate without Khalid or Avigad. Azar was a farsighted visionary who initially maintained a laser focus on the objective. I felt we had factored in the variables that could offset our plan, investors could be fickle, inflation was always a big worry for the stock market which could push the Fed to raise interest rates faster. We kept our eye on the US in particular as relatively few Americans actively trade or owned stocks, it was a risky proposition. But a ten percent drop in the markets could affect attitudes about the economy, even for those who didn't invest. When the stock market goes up, people typically spend more. This was the cornerstone of the plan.

The initial plan was pure economics, buy low and sell high. And with us manipulating the timing, the outcome was a no-brainer. Create panic over supply and increased demand and increased payment would follow. Throw a little controlled terrorism in there and our plan would follow where we led it.

Where the plan went out of control, or who set it on the course of the intensified destruction I don't know, but I had some inclination. I had minimal interactions with Khalid, but the man had the mind of a psychopath and the heart of a terrorist. He was passionate about his beliefs and that was always a bad thing. A very bad thing. Now Avigad, Azar's father, was another thing. He was tasked with one thing to accomplish; set up the best route to launder money for the plan. Midstream, he went off in a different direction. Although a master at brokering organs, that started as a small quid pro quo effort evolved into a killing machine with him at the switch. He became disassociated from the group's goals and that was a bad thing. A very bad thing.

Now Azar. She made this plan a puzzle. The woman I knew from school was calm and calculating. Her mind worked like a computer, always devising new algorithms and the beauty was she never let emotion enter her decisions. But recently, Azar had developed a glitch processing information and had allowed anger to enter her planning. There was no room for emotion in our plans but now the engine was fueled with fire and fury.

The biologics implantation was planned for a limited area, used as a fright tactic to drive up pharmaceutical sales and stock. When had Azar become obsessed with the actual spread of disease and pestilence? And God, when had her plan morphed into including weapons of mass destruction? I understood and supported the poisoning crops. Without crops people could potentially starve but it would not knock out civilizations or billions of people. How many first world countries could be relied upon to prop up third world countries indefinitely?

When had the plan been modified without my input? And how did I become implicit in it? If I had to pin down the time frame it would be after her father stole her kidney and she was on a multitude of drugs to help her avoid rejecting the replanted kidney. Her volatile rage was uncontrollable at times. The possibility that the drugs short- circuited her mind was a possibility I would have to face as a sobering reality. A reality that my Azar was gone and someone new had moved in to inhabit her mind.

How had I gotten sucked into the madness? Was it beyond the point of no return?

As we touched down at Rome's Fiumicino airport my seat mate asked for my number. Normally I would exchange her number for a burner phone number I kept just for this purpose, but today was not one of those days.

Passing through security and Immigration I was met by my father's driver who swiftly and safely negotiated the streets of Rome, depositing me at my father's home. He had summoned me, and I knew this would not be an easy conversation. To make a quick getaway my bag remained in the car so if my mother was home she couldn't guilt me into spending the night. My flight to Luxembourg after I left my father was going to be tight and the less excuses I had to not linger the better. My head was ready to explode over a problem I didn't cause, bringing Luxembourg front and center as another problem with no solution.

Walking up the old cobblestones to a home that held no happy memories caused a tightness in my throat. The memories within these walls were that of degradation, humiliation, and child abuse. I was the target of my father, allowed by my weak mother who turned a blind eye to his misdeeds. And to the world, we appeared that of a happy family. If someone questioned otherwise, the consequences were dire.

I was never rebellious. However, I was regarded as such for wanting to be my own person and forge my own path. The family business meant money and I was expected to participate and grow the business. I was expected to marry after university and by now should have populated the world with three children. An acceptable number would be one girl and two boys. I had lived up to bringing money to the family in what they considered an unorthodox fashion. Money was money. My reticence to start a family was troubling to my father and he was starting to put an uncomfortable squeeze on me.

My father was an old-school business man living in a modern world. If you met him would you recognize him as hard-boiled mafia? Absolutely not. The man was a true Italian to the core. And still he could easily pass for an A-list movie star both in the way he carried himself and his physical appearance. Never a hair out of place, trim waist because he was an exercise freak, and he still managed to eat two servings of pasta a day. He was king of his olive oil companies and vineyards. He ran neither, but in his name, with the sole purpose to launder money for the thriving black-market gun business he lorded over both. A brilliant businessman, horrid husband and father, and knew his way around firearms. In fact, the house was a virtual armory for his arsenal of weapons.

I entered through the thick wood and beveled-glass doors, walking carefully across the tile floor that he insisted was polished every day. I could smell the exotic spices emanating from the kitchen and followed my nose to where Maria the cook was putting the final touches on the main course, eggplant. Normally we would start with antipasto and an appetizer but due to my travel time constraints he agreed to forgo those formalities.

My father had a strict rule, no business at lunch. I knew I was under a timeline to meet him and leave, I offered to help Maria with the transportation of food to the dining room and was politely rebuffed.

My father found his way to the kitchen where Maria and I chatted about how lucky her son was to work for my father now. Although I gave the requisite smile to acknowledge yes, he was indeed fortunate to join the family, inside all I thought was what a poor bastard. I spied my father as he approached, we greeted each other with a small amount of chit-chat, and then quickly made our way to the dining area and consumed our lunch. After a third glass of wine we moved to the great study where he conducted his most serious business. Never a good sign. This was the place that orders were given and expected to be followed. Negotiations didn't take place in this room, he only accepted complete surrender.

The study was an odd name for this room. Noting was studied in here. This was the room where businesses were built or destroyed, and people's deaths planned. Today I was concerned that we would be discussing Azar's death as her refusal to abandon her plan infuriated my father. He was a horrid parent, and to most, an intolerable human being. But a necessary evil in the business world.

I crossed the white thick-piled carpet that sprang as I walked and took a seat bracing for the inevitable. My father closed the door to the soundproof room and stood a moment looking at me. Most likely he was assessing what a disappointment I was to him and trying to determine if he should try to resurrect the son he wanted.

"Are you comfortable, Marcello?" he asked, seating himself in the chair across from the sofa where I sat. He always chose that chair. It helped his back remain upright and gave him an authoritarian appearance. Plus, if action was required he could spring from the chair as opposed to rolling from the couch.

"I am," was all I offered because to offer more might open a door I didn't want to walk through.

"This plan of the Abed woman has risen to a level that should have never been allowed. The last conversation we had, you assured me you had this in hand. Now I find out not only have you not squashed this insanity, but the timeline has accelerated, and the apparatus is ready for release. This is not our way. This is the way of a terrorist and I will have no part in this action nor will any member of the family. Am I clear?" He crossed his right leg across his left knee leaving his obscenely expensive footwear on display. No foot twitching for this man. He had nerves of steel and a heart of ice.

"I understand, and I am leaving here to visit the warehouse in Luxembourg where a large amount of the samples are stored. Once I get there I'll inventory the stock and decide the best route to deal with it," I offered squirming a bit. "I will not lie to you. I believe because I have been so vocal about this plan being unacceptable she has staged other launching sites and not shared those with me."

"That is indeed unfortunate because fanatics make poor decisions," he said looking toward the window that led to his lush garden.

I couldn't disagree with that statement just with the context of it. I didn't believe Azar was a terrorist or fanatic, but her actions said otherwise.

"I don't believe Azar is a fanatic I think she is just a zealous advocate for her cause—" I started.

"Stop," he commanded leaning back. "Do not for one minute try to infer that she is anything else but an obsessed crazy woman with whatever mission she thinks she is tasked to carry out. And if I knew her exact motivation and if it was grounded in some type of physical longing such as more wealth or power I might understand. But her plan is a shotgun approach to hurt as many people as possible and we don't know why." He shook his head as if she was a petulant child.

"I have to argue with that statement. She is using this avenue in a two-step plan to motivate the money markets around the world to act in one direction for her personal financial gain." Even I couldn't swallow that whole idea.

"If you believe that, which I pray to God you are only stating for my benefit, then a further conversation is unnecessary," he replied with no emotion. "Because you, as the British say, have lost the plot."

I sat and thought about this and realized whatever way I went I was boxed in a small area with no escape. My father's reach was long and wide, and it was best to hear him out.

"What is your proposal?" I asked, careful to use the word proposal as if this somehow was open to negotiation which I was sure it was not.

"You have two days to destroy whatever surplus you can find. If I don't have confirmation in that time that this plan—which amounts to bioweapons being used for bioterrorism is completely eradicated, she will be killed. And, Marcello you will be the one tasked with that unenviable job." He leaned forward and studied my face. "This is not something I want, my boy. But not only is this the plan of a fanatic with an outcome that cannot benefit anyone, it also courts attention of the pharmaceutical industries who have the most to gain. I have worked hard to keep you under the radar and there you will stay. I don't want some European Union agency coming in to search our inventory. Do I make myself clear?"

"Crystal. I have a plan, and in three days I will report back to you that I have accomplished what I set out to do. Now I must go. My plane is on time, a miracle in Rome." I sat waiting for his approval and dismissal.

He studied me as if he were a human lie detector. Satisfied, he let me rise and walk toward the door unimpeded. Finally, a clean escape was in sight.

As he escorted me down the long marble hall floor to the door he said, "Enzo is waiting in the car and will accompany you. It's not that I don't trust you, he is there to keep you focused and aid your plan."

My body went still, and I could feel my blood pressure start to rise and my heart pounded against my rib cage.

"Don't play with me. This is you trying to control me." Where I had the courage no, the temerity to say that I have no idea. But I knew his intention was to keep me on a very short leash.

"Absolutely not. This is me making sure you think with your head and not your dick. That woman has always seemed to have a hold on you and I cannot understand why you are so mesmerized by her. By now you should be married with children, it's our way. Instead, you wait and hope that someday that cold heart of hers will thaw and she will love and want you. She never will, Marcello. The woman is a sociopath raised by a psychopath. I understand the physical attraction, but I see it ending in disaster," he warned putting his hand on my shoulder as he did when I was a boy. And the Pavlovian prompt worked. I hung my head and said nothing further.

I entered the car and sat next to Enzo whose measured gaze was to assess my temperature. If it was hot and I was about to blow he would handle it as he did since I was a child. When he was satisfied, he ordered, "Andiamo."

An uncomfortable flight to Luxembourg left questions between Enzo and me unanswered. I wanted to grill him as to my father's intentions and knew he would remain silent and loyal to him. A small private vehicle brought us to the freeport where the refrigerated samples were stored in a private room. After signing in, I left instructions that no one except Enzo or I was to have access for a week. It was critical that Azar be unaware of my plan. A motor cart retrieved us from the office and deposited us at the cold storage area. After the driver left we went about suiting up in biohazard suits that Enzo had shipped and stored ahead of time.

All he said was, "What the fuck were you thinking?" and left it hang.

After we completed the inventory we were satisfied that the Armenians had not kept any of the bacterium or virus samples. I found the damaged samples that had caused the death of the transporters and place them in a biohazard container. I only hoped that this room did its job and kept the ventilation contained within or more people would die before we removed the unit. We locked the refrigerated unit back up, secured the room and left the building.

"Your father will want to know your plans," Enzo stated. I knew how hard it must be for a man who knew me my whole life to intercede. He understood my father. Did he like him? Who knows. But if it meant enforcing my father's orders he would do it without hesitation.

This was worse than I thought. She had somehow struck a deal with someone to add more to the unit and hadn't told me. I couldn't let on that the number of specimens I inventoried were triple what she and I spoke of and I had no idea what was actually in the unit.

Had I not visited today, Armageddon could have been at hand. This was much worse than I thought. She had also been able to acquire some bacteria still in development that were not even labeled. Bacterium even I as a CEO could never legally acquire or develop. Azar must have paid an enormous amount for these specimens and I would wager there were no antidotes even in development for the new ones.

I scrubbed my face with my hands feeling the stubble scrape against the palms. God, I felt mentally and physically exhausted as I struggled to determine why I couldn't just retire and live off my investments. Step down and just dabble in the business and follow my own dreams. Dreams that did not involve the Ghiaccio family.

I couldn't run away from my reality. What the hell was I going to do? How could I explain to Azar that I was destroying millions of dollars' worth of product? Her money. Would it be possible to switch out what we had in time? Would she demand a third party sample the specimens along the way? I was in a mess. In theory, I absolutely agreed with my father but didn't want to disappoint Azar. No, this would not disappoint her, this would devastate her. It would be a betrayal she would never forgive nor forget. In for a penny, in for a pound.

"You can tell him that I'll have a new refrigeration unit sent over with false specimens within the week. I'll have someone pick this up tomorrow and bury it deep within the Namib desert where no one will ever find it," I replied and took a few moments to call the person for all things undoable.

Enzo left for Rome, and I went to Paris. I had people to meet that perform a specific line of work. In the event Azar came for me, I had to be prepared.

SIXTEEN

Azar

O NE WOULD THINK WITH ALL THE TECHNOLOGY AT HAND THAT the underworld of hackers and techno-savvy people would be replete with experts willing to help people such as myself for a price. Not so. There were very few willing to work one on one with limited information from a potential employer. Many enjoyed their rogue status.

In today's world, babies were introduced to technology in some form before they could walk. Toddlers were armed like soldiers with handheld technological weapons before they could speak. By the time most children entered first grade, Call of Duty was understood better than a simple reading assignment. When they reached middle school, they took part in virtual battles against virtual enemies in a virtual global war through online games. As teenagers, a large part of the population already owned weapons and knew how to use them. As young adults, a large majority took part in real war where they blew things up for the kick of it and got paid as a bonus to do it. Children were programmed from birth to embrace technology, violence, and war. It was as if artificial intelligence was being programmed in their brains from birth.

I was lucky to find Lozar, a treasure I could not afford to lose. A man, or maybe he was a woman, you couldn't tell from the modulated voice. Whoever he was he was a brilliant person who thought outside the box and always one step ahead with a solution. A person who chose his clients rather than the other way around.

Under his tutelage there were so many options open that I felt like a starving person at a smorgasbord. I wanted a little of everything. My original intent was to take a wide approach. But Lozar kept my mind into focus. He discounted that idea much like a double tap of the home button on the phone allowing one to flick away apps not useful.

When formulating my plan, I was open to a variety of options of how to manipulate systems to give me control over various resources. One such option involved the invasion of medical device networks that fed into the hospital networks and thus allowed me a passageway between life and death. However, Lozar at once pointed out the flaw in my plan and probably saved me half a billion dollars. In addition to being light years ahead in processing information he also provided information that wasn't available on any level to the general public. Although he joked about flying around with a team whose main function was to intercept signal intelligence, I believed that could be true. The idea gave me pause. However, if it were true it had proved a benefit to me.

Settled into my new fortress and not fearful of a breach, I was able to concentrate on my work. As the boring briefing droned on it gave me the opportunity to multitask my thoughts. Josh stepped to the front of the room and something looked off. He seemed different; more focused and not jovial as was his nature. It made me feel unsettled as if the room temperature had dropped ten degrees. He placed his notes on the small desk, engaged the projector and seemed to stare right at me. Or maybe it was over my head at something. I felt like I was in his sights. It took a moment for my mind to process what he was saying as his lips moved. And then my mind exploded when he said, "People, we may have a problem with commodities."

No, no, no, this could not be. It was impossible.

Years of anger management therapy and the tools from those sessions were the only things I had to rely upon to stop myself from leaping to my feet and pummeling him with my fists. It was impossible to effectuate the controlled breathing I needed while I listened to him. Did the people in the room notice me start to hyperventilate? What I heard was devastating. He hadn't put everything together, but he had a good start. How? How could he know? This wasn't even his area of expertise.

Suddenly people were engaged, and computers were clicking away while I sat and watched as years of planning was potentially being destroyed. Two hours later, the room which had been pulsating with excitement and exchange of ideas was now simmering at a low buzz. Teams were decided upon to research and monitor certain sectors and all I could do was sit there and assimilate their plans to make the proper changes in mine.

What a nightmare. My tight timeline and compact environment just exploded in my face. It wouldn't take long for someone to find global patterns now that they knew where to look. But would someone care enough to reach out globally and interlink with people in China, Brazil, and India? I had to reach out to Marcello. However, my gut told me I needed to step up the bioweapons plan. I had to keep that to myself and not share it with him.

"Azar—" My brain had gone on lockdown. I turned and found Josh studying me with concern. "You okay?"

"Sorry, Josh. What?"

"You okay? You looked a little spaced out. Maybe lunch would help? I'm meeting my brother and I'm sure he would love for you to join us," he offered.

Josh, a man with a metro look wore his suit well. Maybe it was his good looks that led me to underestimate him. Mistake. Big mistake. Huge.

"Thank you for the offer but I have some things to take care of," I replied as he continued to search my face for answers.

"If you change your mind we'll be at the same place as last time. Creatures of habit." He tilted his head. After a moment, I turned and left without offering a polite goodbye.

I forced out some necessary responses to emails and I was gone.

Whenever I called Marcello, his response was immediate. I never had to wait more than ten minutes for him to return my call. That was our understanding. When I called on a particular phone that meant it was an emergency and the response time was normally two minutes. Two hours had now passed. Was he purposefully ignoring me? Had he decided to run his own game? No, maybe he was in flight and unable to receive my call. Due to the elevated threat status of my plan, my mind was racing with horrible possibilities. I ran every scenario, and none brought me comfort.

The brain is an amazing processor unit. I could actually imagine the electricity snapping from synapse to synapse in my brain. Like a white electrical lightning storm snapping and retreating and spreading. It was quite the show. My thoughts were interrupted as the phone rang, the caller identification blank. I accepted the call anyway.

"Your funds have cleared." The voice was deep, calm, and unlike the obvious robotic nature of Lozar yet I could tell it was still scrambled. Precautions I understood were necessary.

"I want to hit India, Brazil, and China. I'll pull the trigger today. I've already performed successful test runs. And since we are on an accelerated timeline, boost the quantitative amount to hit another fifty percent," I said without a second thought. Although the fee was just a consult fee, it never occurred to me that he would turn down the job I was offering.

"Ma'am?"

"Did I stutter?" I opened the excel spreadsheet to track the numbers for his updated fee.

He was silent.

"Is there a problem?" If this was his reaction I'm not sure it would work.

"Yes. I have studied your plan and I understand your goals, resources, and timeline," he responded and blew out a frustrated breath. "I get it. Low tech, high impact. A successful attack could cause severe consequences. But the level of chemical spray you're talking about is going to bring the World Trade Organization and every version of Homeland Security for each country into play. That's a level of scrutiny you don't want. Stop me if I have misinterpreted anything but isn't the whole reason behind this deal to shake the population up so they feel the government can't protect them? Make them worry so they spend more money for food and drive up the stock market. Supply and demand. Or am I reading your intentions incorrectly? Because I have to say, this level you're suggesting feels like it is traveling into red zone terror attack territory." That came with a tone that went between questioning to one of judging and accusatory.

"My purpose isn't your concern. I need to know if you can handle the logistics. Can you get it done? Can you do it?" I asked keeping control of the conversation.

"I can do it, ma'am. But the question I need answered is why. Why are you doing this? What is the purpose? I'm walking down a nice level road here that's coming to a fork. At the fork coming up in front of me I have to decide if I want to go down the one marked safely staying out of jail or the one marked financial way. Because at the end of those roads there are two drastically different outcomes." His voice was low, and I could tell he had already made up his mind. "I'm not in the business of committing crimes against humanity much less the consequences of said crimes if I get caught."

This person was judging me. Me.

As my anger built, I could feel my right hand start to tremor.

More a constant twitch, but a sign of anxiety nonetheless. I forced my heart rate to remain steady and controlled my breathing. But that twitching hand wanted very much to break something, to throw something, to destroy something.

"Thank you for your time. I believe the consultation fee covers what I owe you." I disconnected before he did. I rejected him before he did me. I abandoned him before he did me.

Still no return call from Marcello.

I was alone and cut adrift. I had one other person I could reach out to despite knowing it would cost me big.

My next call was to Lozar. One ring and he answered. He always answered as if waiting for my call and I was the only person in the world that mattered.

"What can I do for you, Az?" he asked as was his routine.

I was angry, and now would prove to the world who was in charge. Their lives depended on my decisions.

"I want you to start the virus disbursements. I want Barcelona, Hong Kong, and Beijing hit Wednesday; London, Paris, and Rome Friday. Marburg and Ebola are the first to be released. It will take several weeks to reach prime infection levels. At the same time, I want the respiratory viruses released at airports, trains, and bus terminals. I want the water infected and the animas dying within two weeks." Those were my orders.

There was a silence on the other end that had me wondering if we had lost our connection.

"Az, I have to say the words I've never spoken before. That is too tall an order for me in such a short period of time. We haven't even discussed Marburg—"

"We have it in our inventory of specimens, do we not?" I snapped so he would see how serious I was at this point.

"Yes, but the—" he responded but I interrupted him.

"Don't give me the lecture it's too specific and the global communities will go after this as a unified force. No one will see it as a bioweapon and no one will link it to global markets. In 2008 there was an outbreak in Uganda, the Netherlands, and the US and not one peep about it on the news—"

"We are no longer in 2008. In 2008 the world was on the tip of a global depression and that meant more to the news cycle." His voice actually rose and if not for the modulator I would swear he was angry. "You'll be opening up Pandora's box pointing squarely at Russia as the perpetrator in this geopolitical climate. That will not sit well with Russia after their involvement with Syria. Russia will react and trust me they will come looking for you. And won't stop until you are neutralized."

"And? I have nothing to do with Russia. In fact, I have no idea where these biologics came from and don't want to either. In 2017 there was an outbreak in Uganda and Uganda boarders Kenya. What's to say that tourists visiting Kenya didn't pick it up from some infected person, carrying it to Europe? In 2012 Uganda had an Ebola outbreak, and 2013 there were deaths from Crimean-Congo which I might add is in our collection." Why did I have to educate this man? This was my project.

"Az, if I could refocus you for one moment. Wouldn't it benefit the plan to release just a limited number of bacteria? The ones that have an antidote. Wouldn't this drive your financial plan better? All you're doing with a virus is sentencing people to death with what benefit to your plan? People will panic but to what end?"

I was silent. Absorbing what he said and trying to wade through my options was giving me a headache of epic portions.

"Why not take some time and think this out. You have just implemented the pestilence test. What's the rush to add human destruction? I'm here to aide your plan and I think it's a good solid plan. But the word plan is the operative word. If you go off script, then the dominoes will not fall correctly. Please rethink what you are proposing. One change, one misplaced domino, everything stops," he explained as his voice returned to its normal modulation.

He had a point. Algorithms were run, dates decided, and people waited to do their jobs. But that damn Josh was onto something. Now that action plan was put into motion, where would it end? Could I keep ahead of it? Should I tell Lozar about what Josh had proposed?

"All right. Let things proceed as they are planned," I said.

"Are we good?" he asked with an inflection of concern if a robotic voice could have one.

"We're good," I responded and this time I was the first to say goodbye but waited for him to reply. Then we disconnected.

My next call was to the airlines to book a flight for tomorrow after work to Luxembourg. I wanted to get to the inventory before Marcello. I had to remove what he wasn't aware of and needed to stay on top of things. Marcello had taken too large a role in this and without him returning my calls it gave me pause if his head was still in my game. Or had he decided to abandon me and betray my trust.

SEVENTEEN

Jackson

A WHOLE TWENTY-FOUR HOURS HAD PASSED WITHOUT A WORD from Mary. It should have been a joyous time for Emma and Cillian who had just found out she was pregnant with twins. The distress and panic associated with the disappearance was a mess that only Eloise could manage.

Mary had not activated the medical alert in her watch. It was as if some alien force had snatched her from the planet. She'd vanished and even the NSA couldn't get a fix on her. What possible reason could motivate someone to snatch Mary from a government building.

I could barely continue working. More schemes to launder money popped up every day to feed an overwhelming population of criminal's work. All the life-filled air was sucked out of me and left me limp and deflated.

For the first time ever, I thought about jumping ship from the bureau and making the leap to the private sector. God knows the money was better and less pressure. I could take the cases I chose and the offer I received was to go in as a partner of a prestigious firm. Maybe the time was right. Eloise and I would be married in six months and we wanted a family, making this offer sound amenable for a new start. Mary getting presumably kidnapped made me realize how vulnerable we all are, time snatched without us seeing it coming.

I leaned back in my chair and took a power nap only to be stunned awake a few minutes later when my computer alerted me a meeting in Nathaniel's office was required immediately. Odd that he didn't ask for a specific file or report summary.

I shrugged on my jacket and walked down the hall fielding questions from my colleagues about Mary. For some reason, she was beloved by all and they expressed genuine concern. Even in the elevator people from other departments stopped me to ask if there was any word. My stomach clenched each time I had to say no. When I was within five feet of his office, his administrative assistant tilted her head giving the go-ahead to enter Nathaniel's office. The door to his office was open and he waved me in.

Nathaniel's domain appeared sterile and unwelcoming. I'd met with him here hundreds of times before, but it wasn't until today it struck me he hadn't invested himself personally in this job. Nathaniel was an excellent boss, an empathetic man, and model citizen. Today, for some reason I realized he wasn't truly anchored here and maybe he never had been. Were things missing all along or was I just more in tune that I wasn't as personally invested as I had been either. Maybe it was time to think about my other options in the private sector.

Nathaniel's face looked wrinkled and worn, and his normally clear blue eyes looked clouded and stormy. He'd shaved but had missed a patch. The look on his face portrayed defeat.

Another person was present in Nathaniel's office his polar opposite in every way. The man was young and almost glowed from all the products he had used on himself that morning. His white shirt was so crisp I was certain that if he removed it, it would stand upright on its own.

The man offered his hand. "Mark Blackwell, Counterintelligence."

"Sit, Jax. What I am about to tell you stays in the room. Cillian has been briefed but no one else is to have a whiff of this information." Nathaniel's voice was strong but low and solemn.

My mind spun in all directions. Mary, something had happened to Mary and they want to distance themselves from it. Christ, a cover-up and they wanted me to comply. Oh my God, I will never forgive myself. No one will ever forgive me. She was in my charge and now she's gone. I should have let her have her arsenal of weapons. I should have been kinder. But most of all I should have listened closer. If only—

"We know where Mary is—" His words broke through the gate of my rampant thoughts.

I looked to the other man who affirmed that was true.

"Jesus Christ! Have they asked for a ransom? Are they threatening to kill her? Oh no, please tell me they haven't killed her." I was on my feet raking my fingers through my hair to the point I was certain it stood on end.

"Sit down. The news is good," he said waving me back to my seat. "And get that hair under control, you look ridiculous."

Without thinking, I whipped my comb from my back pocket and the mundane action of easing it through my mop brought me some calm.

"I cannot tell you where she is, but I can say this was a governmental snafu. I was supposed to be alerted. However, somewhere the directive got misinterpreted or missed and that person will be dealt with properly." He looked at Blackwell who seemed unaffected.

"Why can't you tell me where Mary is? Cillian and Emma are wild with stress and Emma does not need that right now. Where is she and why is she there and not here?" I demanded.

"I repeat, she is fine and will be returned tomorrow after she is briefed, and the plan put into action. There is another government involved and no one, absolutely no one, is in on this except Mary. Now that's all I will say. The memo is going out that she had a family emergency and she regrets not letting anyone know. Now. Are we good?" he asked leaning forward.

"Of course we're not good. How the hell did Mary come onto another government's radar and why? I am not accepting this explanation. If anything happens to her—"

"Jackson, it will be fine. You have to trust me on this. Time is of the essence so get back to work and treat things as I've outlined them. Don't make a fuss and let her make the announcement at the meeting about a family emergency. This next week will be critical. If she asks you to do something, do it and know she is working under my direct authority. And, Jackson, Tyler Devonport was released and that's all I can say right now. Understood?" Nathaniel moved toward the door to open it.

"Mary's notebook—"

"Already back in her possession. Jackson, the arsenal she carries in that bag can't happen again. Clear?" he said without any humor to his tone.

"Clear," I responded.

The first call I placed when I returned to my office was to Eloise to let her know Aunt Mary was fine. I shouldn't have been surprised she already knew. And I had the distinct impression she had more relevant information than me, but I knew better than to ask. Especially on a government phone.

Second call was to Cillian who also appeared to be cautious about the conversation revealing nothing to me. We agreed to meet for lunch in one hour in the greenspace where we knew it was safe to talk.

I typed in Mark Blackwell's name in the FBI directory and he popped up under Counterproliferation of the Counterintelligence section. Wow, this guy was high up on the food chain with weapons of mass destruction. What the hell did Mary step in?

My blonde expresso with three equals in hand, I searched my memory banks for the time I drank plain black coffee. A mundane thought to give my mind a break from everything spinning wildly about.

Cillian slid a little too close for my comfort on the concrete bench but it was necessary. We both looked around to clock any people watching us meaning one of two things. They thought we were either lovers or spies.

"Where is she?" I asked desperate to know how I missed it.

"She's in country." He took a sip of his coffee and leaned forward with his elbows to his knees vigilant for anyone lurking too close.

"What the hell does that mean?" I twisted the top half of my body to study him.

"I don't have much more than you. It appears that a few weeks ago, Mary stumbled onto something that another country was monitoring. They scooped her up after the meeting to get her ready for the next phase and that government and ours are working with her right now. She'll be back tomorrow ready to execute whatever plan they have her involved in." Calm and cool as a cucumber. I knew he wasn't going to give me more.

"Wait, are you sitting here telling me that Mary is some type of double agent?" I sputtered. That idea was not only incredulous but would place national security at risk.

He, thank God, gave a full belly laugh and shook his head. "Hell no. From what I understand this other country has a target in sight. Mary appears to have made a positive connection with the person and they are using Mary to gain information about a series of events about to unfold. Apparently, she had treaded into unsanctioned territory that gave them additional information they needed."

"No fucking way. You know that she will fuck this up. There

is no way she can contain her need for drama and this will go sideways." Shaking my head, I could almost feel my brain rattle around.

Cillian didn't laugh. He stared straight ahead and focused on some distant object as he pulled his thoughts together.

"I know a lot more than what I am allowed to say. Trust me when I say Emma and I signed a shitload of documents this morning swearing us to secrecy. When I tell you, this is major shit and you cannot undermine anything she says or does, or the consequences could be dire. Take that to the bank. She is shaken up, but I know has mustered the resolve to bring this home." And with that drained his coffee.

"Can we play a little tap the cup game if I am close?" I needed to know, it was killing me.

"No. I have to run. I am taking Emma to lunch to celebrate." I knew he was diverting, but I played along.

"Oh my God. I'm sorry, man. I forgot. Congrats. When are the terror twins due?" I said as we exchanged the requisite man hug.

"We'll know more later today. I'll keep you posted but we wanted to share it with Mary first."

"Understood," I assured him clasping him on the back.

"It's big, man, like tidal wave big, so we have to be her support system. They have this covered and could probably do it without her but—"

"I get it but the not knowing is killing me. When we have some time, I wanted to share some thoughts I am having about making a transition to the private sector." The words were out there in the universe now ready to take flight. How totally inappropriate in the midst of chaos swirling around.

He didn't seem at all surprised and I knew he had dipped his toe in that pond as well.

"I totally hear you and I've been having similar thoughts with Tom and Jerry on the way now." He smirked.

I had to laugh at that.

"Good. Talk soon, yeah?" He obviously was offering no more and I knew the brakes had been put on the conversation. "My love to Emma."

He left from the west side of the entrance toward the train station and I went east to catch a cab. As I walked through the gates to the street, I caught sight of a figure walking in the opposite direction. That little punk Devonport. What was he doing here? I picked up my pace and was within ten feet of him when he had the temerity to turn his head slightly over his shoulder and give me a crooked smile. He opened the back door of a car with diplomatic plates, and once inside, the car slid away from the curb. He never looked back.

EIGHTEEN

Adrien

I HAD ONCE BEEN TOLD BY A STREET-WISE PATIENT I PATCHED UP AFTER A knife fight the best way to kill someone was to come at the other person in the open. Walk up to them nonchalantly, and at the last second, appear to bump into them. As soon as physical contact is made, take that time to plunge the blade into their lower abdomen. The best way to incapacitate your target he revealed was to stab in a forward upward thrust, then twist and remove. The key to the maneuver was calm resolve and to keep moving once the knife was removed.

Sneaking around or following the target somehow alerted people and an antenna went up. As primal beings we had a sixth sense of danger. The patient I treated advised to never wear a hoodie because it was too conspicuous; a low-pulled-down baseball cap was acceptable. By the time your target realized they had been stabbed, they would have gone into shock, bleeding profusely, losing too much blood to be saved. Panic would likely preclude them from reacting correctly and death would quickly follow.

Today would be the day. I was tired of waiting for Azar to answer my demands. I Had lost my ability to maintain my threats toward her. She was an unexpectedly formidable opponent. Although it was obvious she was not one step ahead of me, she was closing in on me.

By mid-afternoon I could not wait any longer. When she came

out of the office building my torment would end. She would die. I had a tiny window of opportunity. I had the knife I laid out on its velvet pouch ready to be placed in its leather holder around my waist. Long, sharp, and with a hook at the end to gut her.

How had this happened? How had I come to this place where a life meant nothing to me anymore? In medical school, I always felt I was damaged in some way. While others were hesitant to cut into cadavers and some even threw up, I always had a handle on my emotions. I never once thought of the body before me as someone's mother, father, or sibling. The cadaver on the table represented an opportunity to learn my craft much as an auto mechanic regards a car engine. My ability to distance myself continued when I started practicing medicine. I never saw the face, only the body part and the money I would earn from fixing the problem whether it was real or imagined.

And look at me now. Someone had to pay. Azar would pay for her sins and the sins of her father, a man who had transgressed against me.

I picked up the instrument of death and turned it over and over to test its balance. I flicked the tip and ran my thumb gently up the blade to test its sharpness. Probably a bad move as that maneuver may leave a bit of my DNA intermingled with hers.

My heart remained surprising steady and my breathing regular. In a sense I was a warrior prepared to do battle. I was not prepared for the Roselovs and their special brand of evil, but I was ready for Azar. I understood Azar. Both of us were children raised by heartless, controlling parents. We were now ready to release our anger on the world.

The choice had been difficult. Should I wait for her right outside her building and attack her as she exited? Or should I follow her as she walked to the private bank of cars and catch her off guard?

Before I could decide I saw her exit the building, my decision made for me. There she was, way too early for the end to her normal work day. What was she doing walking away from the company private car bay area toward the cab area? I was positioned to follow her until she threw me a curve ball. She raised her hand, summoning a black private cab parked behind the yellow city cabs. The driver engaged the engine and drove forward at her command. Amongst the other vehicles waiting for a fare he slid to the curb and parked. Azar, beautiful Azar, checked her surroundings as she waited for the man to open the heavy back door. Where was she headed? Hopefully home.

He navigated away from the parking spot past the public cab bay and I barely had time to catch the tail end of his car as it rounded the corner. Traffic in DC was normally a nightmare but today luck was on my side. Weaving in between the cars was doable. The slow-moving traffic worked in my favor to set the digital channel on my dash to catch any waves that came out of the car in front of me that contained my prey. Setting the digital frequency finder, I was barely able to intercept the message transmitted to the driver's base relaying the details of the passenger being transported. Perfect. Her destination was doable for me to follow, but unexpected.

Azar was on her way to the airport flying British Airways to Luxembourg. I had to be on that flight with her. What the hell was she going to Luxembourg for except to access a freeport. Evidently, she didn't want her company to know where she was heading, or she would have used a company vehicle. I engaged my phone to query a flight that matched hers. One British Airways flight was available, and no other flights available until the next morning. I secured a seat and booked it under my Canadian passport name no need to have questions under my Italian passport.

Although preferable, first class would be too close to Azar, so cattle call section it was. I groped around under my seat for the bag that contained my passport, glasses, hat, and other items I carried in my go bag. I wore my hair slicked back and a simple disguise; it had worked before and should now. Too many young girls mistook me for Jared Leto, catching their attention, but it would have to do.

It wasn't a race against time to secure the printed boarding pass from the desk. I took my time. And navigation to the gate past security gave me plenty of time to grab an espresso from Starbucks. I still had time to change my appearance again, now that I had passed passport control. I loved airports. They had everything. Like a little city all in an enclosed place. After securing a razor from the duty-free shop, I took a trip to the men's room and my facial hair was now gone.

People were people everywhere you went in the world. Especially at airports, their attitudes were hurry up and wait. Airports maintained that certain buzz that allowed people to notice you but not actually see you because they were bored. I took my position among the great unwashed of economy class in the enormous seating area and wasn't surprised Azar was not seated in any of the uncomfortable chairs specifically for economy class travelers. She was most likely in the first-class lounge enjoying snacks and wine. Something else she would pay for as a transgression while I waited here with the screaming children and obnoxious food smells.

Enchanted by the absurd behavior of the masses and trying to understand why people acted as such, I almost missed the vibration of my phone.

"Ad, why are you heading to Luxembourg?" the robotic voice of Melzar asked.

"How—?" I quickly twisted around to determine if someone was obviously watching me.

"I told you, always one step ahead, Ad, one step ahead," Melzar responded. "Why are you heading overseas?"

"Personal business," I responded. Clearly, I would not be able to determine who his scout was, so I settled back in and crossed my leg for balance.

"Care to elaborate?"

"No, I do not." I shifted in my seat again trying to see if I recognized someone in the area. I'd never met him or her so was impossible to tell exactly who he or she was. But maybe someone staring a little too long or a knowing smile would give the person away.

"Don't fuck with me, Ad, you are following Azar," he said with a bit of an edge.

"If I am remembering correctly, and I'm sure I am, you answer to me and not the other way around."

"I see. *Bon voyage* then," he replied and disconnected.

He's another one I would need to deal with eventually. He had grown too bold and that was never a good sign.

Do any of these people even think about turning over their lives to two perfect strangers in a cockpit? Who are those two pilots? Do they abuse substances or have mental health issues? Is there anyone on board harboring a communicable disease? Does anyone have plans to blow up the plane or try to take hostages? Does anyone give any actual consideration that they are hurling through space in a tin tube?

As I studied the crowd, I barely noticed the young man with silvery-white hair take a seat next to me. He settled in and didn't attempt to initiate conversation. Good. I hated when people started their incessant chitchat. I saw the pen roll from his pad and hit the floor. I heard the small curse murmured from his lips. I observed him bend forward to retrieve the pen from the corner of my eye. As I followed his head down I noticed no luggage, no briefcase, no electronic devises nothing but a pad and pen. Odd.

As he sat up, I felt what could only be described as a pin prick or spider bite. Christ, bugs in this place crawling up my leg, just great. Suddenly, my calf was tingly and warm. As he settled back in the chair my heart started to stutter and my head felt light. I never had a problem with atrial fibrillation before, it must be my nerves. My stomach was unsettled, churning, and nausea settled in for the long haul. My eyelids drooped, and I didn't realize I'd tipped forward. My equilibrium was off, and I leaned toward the silver-haired young man unable to hold my weight upright. As I leaned right he leaned left, taking my weight.

"Man, you all right? Let's get you to the restroom and splash some cold water on your face. You have any medical problems?" he asked concerned.

I responded with a head-shake no.

He maneuvered me away from the boarding area. What the hell? People were looking at me. Shaking their heads and rolling their eyes. The cretins were judging me. They thought I was a drunk or a drug user. It wasn't until after I was seated on a mobile airport people carrier that I felt my mind let go and was having difficulty breathing.

"Ad, you should have stayed on script," the young silver-haired person said in what could only be described as a scolding manner.

And then I was out.

NINETEEN

Azar

A S I WAS LEAVING THE SUITE FOR PLATINUM AND MEDALLION passengers I noticed a small commotion. A man was being taken away on a carrier. Was he ill? No. If he was ill emergency personnel would be on hand. What is wrong with people getting drunk before a flight? Good thing they removed him before he boarded. Drunks and unruly children ruined too many flights. If I had my way, no children would be able to procure a seat in first class, business class, or the first ten rows of economy. The only reason I chose to tolerate it now was their snotty little noses and coughs would spew bacteria and viruses into the recycled air and that was fine by me. The more documented cases of illness from airplanes, boats, and trains made my job all that much easier.

The flight was filled to capacity, and despite the one stopover, we did fairly well time-wise. After I did a sweep of the freeport, I'd fly back to US soil within forty-eight hours, travel time included. I didn't want a hitch in my plans and the less time I spent away from my original focus the better.

I maneuvered my way through Luxembourg's Immigration and Customs at this frankly uninspiring airport without any problem and continued quickly to the arrival area. I had arranged for the car that awaited my arrival although it was unnecessary.

The building that held my treasures, my plans, and specimens wasn't a bad- looking facility for a building that was nothing more than a secured warehouse. Designed by Portuguese, American, and Italian designers it had a pleasant appearance but not decadent. The inside was nothing short of stunning. It provided the ultimate in security and I would wager if a bomb hit the building the content inside would remain intact. Amazing how a group or conglomerate can keep the treasures of the world safe, but nothing was safe from my father and Khalid. In one fell swoop they'd destroyed buildings that had stood for centuries representing years of hope and fear and God. Battles and wars fought on the soil near the buildings could not withstand the mayhem and madness my father and Khalid had inflicted on them.

The few times in the last year I had walked through these iron and glass front doors, always brought an unsettled feeling to me. The building although aesthetically pleasing could drown you. Like you were entering a building resembling the pyramids in Egypt where people were buried with their treasures. The building was secured with the highest technology known to man yet impossible to detect.

Gaining entrance beyond the doors was much like gaining an audience with the Pope or Queen, nearly impossible unless specifically invited. Except I had the magic credentials. Or so I thought.

After the preliminaries of identification and verifications were exchanged, I was escorted to the director's office. That had never happened before and didn't portend anything good. Pleasantries were exchanged, and I was offered a beverage and declined.

Once I was seated, the director removed a burgundy leather folder with a number of white and pink papers from his desk drawer. He typed in the floor and number of the vault room into the computer. A red dot appeared at the upper right corner of the computer screen. He leaned back in his bulky leather chair making what could only be considered a dramatic gesture. He tapped his long, well-manicured finger against his closed thin lips.

ONE

He swiveled his chair to face me, opened the folder in front of him and leaned forward.

"I am sorry, Ms. Abed, but your name has been removed from the access list of this particular vault," the pretentious little man said in French.

"Don't be ridiculous. I have been a co-owner of that vault with Mr. Ghiaccio for two years. Let me see your computer screen," I demanded starting to come around to see the screen better.

He raised his hand to stop me from coming any closer and then lowered his hand much in the same gesture as you do when teaching a dog to sit. And for some odd reason I obeyed.

"As you know, Mr. Ghiaccio is the registered owner of the room as well as the annexed refrigerated unit. You were added as an authorized attendee to both, and now that has been rescinded. There is a note that for this week no one but he and one other person may enter the room. I'm sorry, Ms. Abed, but those are my instructions." He shrugged as if that was that.

"Does it specifically bar me from the room?" I demanded sliding forward on the chair.

"The exact language is barring all others. I am taking the instruction to mean all is all. Except for the other person listed as having specific admittance," he stated checking his watch.

Leaning back in the soft leather chair, I took my phone from my handbag and placed a call to Marcello. No answer. Next call was to his office and he wasn't there.

"I could avoid a complete waste of a trip if you permitted me entrance to my room," I snapped.

"Of course. Can I call the mobile transport server, or would you prefer the in-ground person mover?" He responded with a smile.

"Call that golf cart you call a mobile transport server." I wouldn't return a smile. He was a mere employee and I would have his job before the day was over.

165

"As you wish. He will be here in three minutes. Your driver is Luke." He stood and had the good grace not to offer a hand but walked me to the door to wait for Luke.

As I waited for the golf cart to arrive, I called Marcello again on both my phone and the emergency phone. I texted and still there was no response. I called his main office and received a curt response from his assistant that he was away and could not be reached. This was outrageous and unacceptable. He wanted to play this game of cards? Fine, I had a few cards up my sleeve too.

Luke arrived dressed for the part of a high-end driver in his crisp white shirt and black pants that hugged him in all the right places. However, I didn't like that he wore a watch and tie clasp that probably cost over a hundred thousand euro. I certainly hoped he was not stealing from the vaults. I should check on my jewels.

The trip was quick, and the building empty. I waited for him to depart, then entered the code, watched for the green light to flash. I placed my chin on the plate for retinal recognition, the heavy metal door popped open with a depressurized whoosh and I pushed forward.

The small space accommodated the few priceless objects I needed to store. Paintings, jewels, Faberge eggs, my fabulous gold headdress, and slave bracelets. I opened each box that held my priceless belongings and took photographs. Everything appeared in order. I quickly uncrated the two paintings: one Van Gogh and a Gauguin. After checking them, I took a moment to admire the beauty of the colors used in both paintings. At some point, I could display these beauties in a home when I no longer lived in the real world where possessing them could possibly lead to an investigation. An investigation I had no plan to participate in.

I tapped in the code for the annexed refrigerated area. I believe I was correct to follow my gut and keep these from Marcello. Trust and total commitment were words not firmly cemented in my mind or heart. I carefully removed the box that held what I hadn't planned to collect today. However, the contents of the box was an insurance policy should Marcello have some underhanded plan ready to execute. I had only myself to rely upon.

The box and contents safely in my handbag I summoned that odious man at the front to send his golf cart back for me. As I waited, I booked the next flight to Paris where it would take about an hour for me to accomplish my agenda. From there I'd take a flight to Rome with a half hour window to accomplish what I needed, and next Barcelona, ending in London. Once I was certain that Heathrow was well and truly infected, I could return to the States. I would arrive at JFK and fly to Dulles last.

The beauty of this was the original specimens had been modified and converted by a team of the best and brightest Germany had on offer. After purchasing a small luggage piece from a boutique store at the terminal, I placed them in the luggage wrapped with clothes I purchased for that very reason. My checked luggage contained biologics in oversized lotions and shampoos. They would pass through any type of security easier because they were inside checked luggage. Marcello should not have shown such utter disrespect to me. Now his precious Rome would be infected with the rest of Europe. The first wave would be the viruses. The next wave the bacteria.

TWENTY

Jackson

THE NIGHT PROVIDED NO REST DUE TO ELOISE AND EMMA SPENDING every minute they had checking out baby items, and at times devolving into small whispers about Mary. There was no chance of getting any sleep. The next day would be a killer between no rest and stress.

Cillian had been smart, he stayed at home and was able to sleep through the night. I should have sent the girls his way, but it was too late now. He'd received the call from headquarters and he called us to advise Mary was to be returned shortly. Since everyone was at my house that was where she would be returned. When Cillian arrived, we were all there gathered for what was certain to be her dramatic entrance.

Eloise had prepared an enormous pot of coffee and the six boxes of pastries Cillian brought with him were placed strategically on the table. The table was so well appointed it was certain the Queen was arriving, and in a sense, she was.

"I don't want Mary inundated with questions. And the minute she walks in, I'm taking her to the bedroom to tell her about the pregnancy in private. I want to start this off on a happy, positive note before you start your shenanigans, Jackson. Understand?" she ordered and who was I to argue with a pregnant woman?

But I did.

"I beg to differ, Emma. I am the levelheaded one in the group. Just because I disagree, strongly disagree with her crazy theories does not make what I do fall under the category of shenanigans." I shook my head and leaned forward on my elbows. "I believe what I engage in are spirited discussions."

"Call it what you want but I get first dibs," she said.

Cillian stood by the window where he had the curtains pulled slightly back like some creeper spying on a neighbor. Without any announcement he walked to the door and opened it. There she stood. The woman of the hour. A new coat, shoes, and hat, fresh manicure, the works. She turned to the person next to her and gave two air kisses to a young, dark-haired gentleman and said, "I'm free Saturday if you are. Now don't be shy."

"Mary, I will be six thousand miles away on Saturday, but next weekend I'm free," he said. Dear God, not again.

"You want to introduce your friend to us, Mary?" Cillian asked with a chuckle.

"Can't," was all she replied.

She threw him the "call me" sign and he promised he would.

She was barely inside the door when Emma raced toward her and grabbed her so tightly they'd merged into one.

"I'm pregnant with twins and you had me worried to death," Emma cried.

Mary went silent and rigid. Her face softened, and she smiled so wide I thought it would split.

"What? My God, Em. I thought you wanted your private moment. If I knew you were going to pull that shit I would have beat you to the punch," Eloise scolded and ran to join the group hug.

I tried to say something and was quickly cut off by Eloise grabbing Mary in a hug. "Coat off, coffee and cake in the kitchen. Let's go."

"Now you're talking." Mary straightened her shoulders. She kissed Emma on the cheek and headed toward the kitchen with her entourage in tow.

When everyone was seated, Mary opened up the conversation.

"I want to say that I don't want to talk about this blissful event around the kitchen table. I need to get my Emmie Lou in my arms in private where we can talk alone. I love you all, you know. But this is a blessed event that I want to savor with the one person that means the world to me," she said.

"Yeah, yeah. You ladies can do all your crying and hugging in private. I want to know what the hell happened when you left the conference room," I said filling my cup.

Eloise filled two cups for her and Mary, then sat and hung on Mary's every word as she admired her manicure.

"Jackie boy, no can do. I'm working for two governments and had to sign some important papers. And that other government, they don't play, at all," she said quickly tapping her hand twice on the table.

"No. I know who it is. Israel," Eloise said with a gasp, throwing herself back in the chair. "Am I right? How exciting."

The way Mary's eyebrows flew to her scalp and her mouth tightened I knew Eloise was spot on, but Mary refused to give anything away.

"Israel. Jesus, Mary how—" I started.

"Don't even, because I can't say a word. If you people would listen to me more, you would be lock step with me. That said, let's eat this cake and that coffee isn't going to drink itself." She reached for her cup. "Just know there are other government agencies that know how to treat a lady. They arm all their women with nice firearms and I was promised my pick of the litter. That's all I'm saying."

"Answer me this," Emma started, "did you leave the country?"

"No, their country came to me," she said with a coy smile and head nod.

"Oh, give me a break. You probably just met a few of their low-level intelligence agents," I chided.

ONE

"I can neither admit nor deny that statement. However, hypothetically if I did come in contact with any such people they may have been anywhere from eighteen to thirty-five years old," she said and lifted her cruller to her lips. "And again, hypothetically, brilliant people who will scare the bee geebers out of you. Very focused, dedicated, and visionaries. Part of an elite team. That is, hypothetically speaking."

As I was about to push her further, Cillian's phone rang. We waited for him to acknowledge who was on the other end.

"Nick Marino. One of Maine's finest. How's it hanging, buddy?" Cillian said with a smile that quickly dropped after a response came from the other end. "Let me put you on speaker if that's okay. Everyone is here."

"Good morning, everyone. It's Marino and Chavez here—" first Detective Marino announced and then Chavez chimed in.

"Oh, it truly is my lucky day. Detective Chavez, it's so good to know you're on the other end," Mary started. "I have so much to share with you."

I had to take control of this before it spun out of control.

"Mary, save it. The detectives are calling for a reason," I said but she wasn't done.

"And, Detective Marino, I'm so pleased that you're calling." She sounded as sweet as could be but threw him the middle finger, that he of course could not see. Cillian had purposefully not put it on FaceTime, with good reason.

"Right," Marino started with a throat clear. "Emma and Cillian, I need you to hop a flight up here because we found more artwork associated with White. I think this is the real deal, Chavez is not so sure. Now, before you say it's criminal forfeiture and not your problem, deal with the court, this just came into our possession in the last two days. On advice from the DA it falls outside that case right now and we are treating it as a new report. Between us, I believe they plan to consolidate them at some point, but we need to

171

get on this to start the case rolling. Legalities aside, apparently there was a storage facility in White's name we hadn't been aware of, an old run-down separate building on someone's property. He hadn't paid the renewal bill. Well, um, probably because he's dead. Before they auctioned off the contents, they decided to call us because they thought the paintings were real and were afraid they were in possession of stolen property."

Everyone around the table was dead silent. A real treat to be savored.

"I don't know, I don't want to go back there," Emma said. "Can't I just sign some documents?"

"No, because it gets better. Someone had accessed this storage facility, not White, and there are eight new paintings that have been stored there within the last year. After looking at the artwork, I believe they might be part of that Armond mess you people were dealing with the last time I talked to you. Possibly these are paintings reported missing after he had his wife declared incompetent," Chavez interjected.

"Do you have photos of the paintings?" Cillian asked. "And have you run them through the database?"

"Sending them over to you now. The description in the database is a little sketchy. I think the Europol guy might be the one that would have better intel since I strongly believe these were from the lot you guys were chasing down. Can you get them to him?" Marino asked. I heard the ping and we both opened our emails.

"Why do you need Emma?" Cillian asked.

"I can answer that one. Because the probate matter is still open, and Emma's name is all over the documents and trust," Eloise said. "Because his son is in England and Emma is the registered owner of all the property until the judge signs a final order and they are still sorting through that entire mess."

"Right, but I thought the forfeiture and seizure took care of that," Emma said getting herself some decaf tea.

"No, the forfeiture was federal, the probate is a state matter. And this new property was not part of either so it's up for grabs. We can fly there. When do you need us?" Eloise asked.

"And what is this we?" I asked. "Your ass isn't going anywhere near that case again."

"Sorry to overrule you, Jax, but my name as Emma's attorney is all over those documents and I am still the attorney of record. Detective Marino, from what you're saying, this opens a new matter but still under the probate, is that correct?" Eloise asked taking my phone to view the paintings.

"Spot on," Chavez said. "I'm going to say what everyone is thinking. This is another Roselov connection. Because from what I vaguely remember from the reports, the unresolved paintings from London sent here were from his gallery. Even in a coma that man still resurfaces. I suggest you bite the bullet, come on up, and let's search these paintings. Maybe with Eloise representing Emma, and Cillian representing the Bureau we can get this place on the seizure list. We just don't have the authority to do it."

"If you're there you aren't leaving me here with the sour patch kid. I'm coming too. Pizza for everyone on me. And a five-star hotel. I have to spend all that government money I won," Mary shouted as she slapped the table.

"No." I shook my head. "Emphatically, no. And don't you have some crisis you are attending to or creating some drama-filled right here? Although with you, they aren't mutually exclusive."

Everyone seemed to be ignoring me. Great.

"I'll forward these to Ben and he can have Isabella look at them. My guess is you want them to fly over too?" Cillian said.

"Thank you, that is what I'd hoped you would say. I just didn't want to put any pressure on you," Chavez responded. "But if she doesn't recognize them there's no need."

"We'll be there within the next forty-eight hours. I have time off because we had to cut our vacation short, but we have a doctor's appointment tomorrow," Cillian said rubbing Emma's arm.

"Emmie is pregnant with twins," Mary popped out.

I leaned back and shook my head, so she could see my displeasure.

"I just found out myself. We don't know the sex yet," Mary said as if it was my fault.

Marino and Chavez conveyed their congratulations from the other end of the call. We ended the call.

Cillian offered to phone Ben from Europol and they would be up to Maine as soon as possible.

"Looks like I need to get with Jarica from the Feds and Marvin from the State seizure departments. I'll alert the probate judge's clerk of what's going on so when we get these we can at least have a unified video conference. We may have to alert the attorney for White's son because the storage unit is technically White's. Em, I need you to sign a few documents, and, Cillian add me to your tickets you're purchasing, and I'll pay you back," Eloise said.

"Nonsense, we'll pay for your ticket. It's the least we can do," Cillian said.

"All right, Mary and I need to have a short conference. How about you all scatter so we can have the room to ourselves. Give us an hour," I said getting up to pour her a refresher of coffee which should keep her from arguing. "But she isn't going. We have a matter of national security happening here. The way I see it she would have to have Nathaniel's permission to leave the state. Think of yourself as a national treasure, Mary."

"Jackie boy, I do every day. But nice of you to acknowledge it," she said.

"Em. Eloise. You're with me. Let's go into the office and coordinate," Cillian said and the three took the last of the coffee in the large silver pot and migrated away from the area.

"Spill," I said. I was having none of her nonsense.

"Jackson, I'm an integral part of an operation and was

instructed not to speak about it. However, I can tell you it involves an elite cyber department akin to our NSA but without the leaks. And should anyone leak in that country they would be in jail forever. Or worse."

"Who was that woman outside the bathroom?" I quirked an eyebrow at her.

"My handler," she replied.

"Your what? You have got to be kidding me?" I stood and the only place my hands could find a place to rest were on my hips.

"Jackie boy, I am an international super-star. I wouldn't doubt if at the end of the road I get a Nobel peace prize—" she replied with a wide sweep of her hand.

"Fat chance, unless they give them for quackery and bullshit." I was done here. Seriously done.

"All I can say is you had a chance to get on the Mary-go-round and you were afraid to jump on board. Others were watching. Now my lips are sealed. Can I be excused to visit with my Emmie and share in some happiness?" Before I could answer, she was up and her back was to me as she made tracks out of the room.

I piled the plates and cups in the dishwasher. As I started the wash cycle, I received a text from Tyler Devonport. "We have to meet. Starbucks down the block. Twenty minutes."

Why that little punk. I'd be there in ten and packing heat. I replied with a thumbs-up emoji although my finger hovered over the middle finger emoji.

The place was crowded. As a couple stood to leave, it was a race between me and two teenage girls to claim their table. I was in it for the win. My coffee in hand I waited for that smug jerk to come walking in and as expected he made an entrance as if he owned the world. He arrived exactly to the minute and glided into the chair. I found it difficult not to uncap my coffee and heave it at him.

"Mary is now in my charge and I don't want any trouble from you." That's all he said, and he got up to leave.

I was stunned into silence. That is the last thing I ever expected him to say.

"No, you sit your ass back down there," I ordered. This kid couldn't be more than twenty-one years old and he thought he was going to give me orders? Hardly.

"This is not up for discussion, and I don't want Mary put under stress. If you have any other questions, you talk to Nathaniel," he replied and then he was on the move.

Now I understood why he wanted to meet at Starbucks—a quick in and out. I waited a few minutes after he left to ascertain if anyone was watching me for more than my good looks, and then left.

When I reached an area with less of a crowd, I called Nathaniel.

"This isn't going to work," I snapped.

"Make it work," was all he said. "We're up against a tight time-line and things are already in play. Suck it up. If all goes well this problem will wrap up by next week. If not, then your new friend Devonport will be in it for the long haul. Show him a little respect. He received his PhDs in biochemistry and computer science as well as a high rank in his government at a very young age. Yes, the man is a genius and connected. Play nice."

I was definitely taking a private sector job.

TWENTY-ONE

Adrien

I WAS ENVELOPED IN BLACKNESS AS IF I WAS IN A BLACK HOLE IN SPACE. My pupils hadn't expanded to adapt to my surroundings. There wasn't even a sliver of light in the room, not even for a door. There was no offensive or pleasant odor noticeable. Although I attempted to identify any smells or whiff of cooking odors, there were none. The temperature appeared to be regulated by some central air system as I could hear it shut on and off, but the air in the room was stagnant.

I exerted every effort possible to hear something. There was nothing but silence. All I could hear was my own regulated breathing. I had an awful taste in my mouth; my tongue stuck to the roof of my mouth, but I wasn't thirsty or hungry. I didn't feel dehydrated; my mouth was just dry. My eyes felt dry as I blinked them, but they weren't crusted.

It felt as if there was something like a stiff mattress underneath me, but it could very well have been a table. All I knew, something was beneath me holding my weight, but I had no sensation if it was soft or hard. I must be covered with something because I felt pressure against my skin. I was unable to move but had the sensation that neither my hands nor feet were bound. If I had the physical ability to move about I believe there wouldn't have been any physical constraints preventing me from standing. Whatever drug I was given had essentially paralyzed me but allowed for unimpeded breathing, possibly something akin to Anectine. So, this is what it felt like to be alive trapped in your body with no control over anything. What a terrifying sensation.

"Welcome back, Adrien," the voice said. A man with no particular accent. There was no gravel or damage to the voice as sometimes happens to smokers, and no nasal tone from chronic allergies. A very deep baritone quality that could lull a person into submission.

"Where am I?" I was unable to turn toward the voice as my neck muscles were still stiff and not at all under my control. What a horrid feeling. My mind was present, but I lacked control over my body. I could glide my eyes toward him but to what avail? The room was void of any light and my eyes had not accommodated to it fully.

"That's not relevant. You have an intravenous fluid bag attached to you for hydration and as soon as the drug wears off in an hour or so, I'll offer you some food. Right now, you're my chemical prisoner. If you cooperate, I'll see to it that your sentence will reflect reward for good behavior," he advised.

"My sentence? What for? Are you insane? I was acquitted of all formal charges in a Paris court. I demand you tell me under what authority you kidnapped me and have the audacity to sentence me for some false crime I'm not aware of," I shouted. The frustration of my paralysis was beyond compare to any experience I could draw upon. I couldn't wiggle my toes and wouldn't have known I had an IV in my arm if I hadn't been told. I had no sensation at all anywhere.

"Ah, Adrien. The world may not be fully aware of your crimes, but I am," he said. I could hear his pant cloth moving against the fabric of the chair but could not discern if he stood or just repositioned himself.

I remained silent.

"What I'm unable to comprehend is why. Why you made the

choices you did when you had a wonderful life. A bounty any man would find enviable. You yourself must agree that you amassed a fortune trading on your greed. Now look at where you are. Can you partake in the abundance? You slink around cities unable to enjoy any semblance of a normal life. So, I think not. You are with me today, not an enviable position." Again, the room went silent.

I wouldn't grace him with an answer.

"I'm your judge and executioner. The International Criminal Court, and more specifically, the Rome Statute sets forth eleven crimes as crimes against humanity. I charge you with the crime of murder against a civilian population and I also charge you with other inhumane acts intentionally causing great suffering, serious injury to a body and to the mental or physical health of that population," he said and again went silent. I could hear nothing.

"You're out of your mind, I've never murdered anyone nor was I ever involved with an act against a civilian population," I yelled struggling in my mind to move but was unable to do so.

"Silence," he yelled, and I heard him stand. The acuity of one sense heightens when there's a deficit in another. "You don't think I know how you and Avigad Abed butchered refugee families for their organs. Taking body parts as payment for transport to a new life that never materialized. Taking their organs and paying them pennies on the dollars you made. You don't think I know about the mass murder in Cairo? Think again. I was forced to bide my time and now you' re mine."

"Ah. You fancy yourself a member of some type like from the movie *Star Chamber*. A member of some medieval court of inquisition. You think you have some type of criminal jurisdiction without a jury and are comfortable using arbitrary investigation methods to impose some non-sanctioned brand of punishment. You have no right to judge me," I spit back at him.

"It appears you have no remorse Dr. Adrien Armond. And that will count heavily against you. You have already been judged and now you can await your punishment," he said without missing a beat. He didn't wait for more questions. "In an hour or so, the drug will wear off and I will be back."

I heard him walk toward a door and he stopped before saying, "Dr. Armond, you will be judged in accordance with your crimes."

I waited patiently as the drug began to wear off. I gained full mobility within a forty-five-minute window, but the time lapsed slowly. As the drug wore off the IV in my arm produced a pinching sensation. The taut pulling of the tape and discomfort where the needle was inserted in my vein about drove me crazy. I had no ability to ease my pain, and no control over anything. Soon after I became aware of an ache in my penis area and realized a catheter to collect urine was attached and taped to my leg. The pulling of the leg hair was only made worse by the humiliation I felt for its presence. I was a helpless blob of need and the lack of control I could exert over my body was unbearable. I heard the door open and could see an imposing figure different from the previous man—enter and watched him take a seat in the nearby chair.

"And whom might I have the pleasure of speaking to?" I asked with as much sarcasm as my humiliating position granted me.

He sat in silence. As I focused his way, his right ankle was balanced on his left knee, his hands gripping the arms of the chair. It was an angry position but one of an authoritative man in control of the situation.

Finally, he spoke.

"Dr. Armond, it doesn't matter who I am. I'm a man and I'm every man. My time with you is for a specific purpose. It's to advise you how we have decided to impose your sentence." His tone was that of quiet moderation, far more threatening than if he yelled or cursed.

I should have held my tongue and waited to hear him out. However, I couldn't hold onto my temper.

"Who are you or any of you irrational lunatics to judge or pass sentence on me? What proof do you have of these crimes you people say I've committed?" I hissed out. Who were these people to judge me? No judicial body would sanction this transgression of the law.

"Dr. Armond, I know about every kidney you stole, every heart you ripped from someone's chest, and every section of liver you removed under a contract of distress—"

"If you were so appalled and offended by my alleged actions then why didn't you stop the procedures? Why allow them to progress? You're just as guilty of the crimes you accuse me of, I believe. You're an offender accessory before and after the fact." I was grateful to finally feel my skin now fully sensitized.

"I don't answer to you, Dr. Armond. Someone will remove the intravenous needle and urine catheter shortly. You'll be fed and given access to a shower. You'll move to another room where you will spend the rest of your days."

At those last words, I trembled at the certainty of his tone.

"And?" I asked. But did I really want to know the answer.

"Then you will be carved up just as your victims were. The victims that you judged not worthy of a decent life, damning them to a life of despair or death for money. As the need arises for a body part or organ we will call upon you to offer it up. We will be more humane than you, you will be properly anesthetized and helped to recover until the next donation is needed. Once your kidneys are removed we will keep you alive on dialysis. If skin or tissue is needed you will be treated and cared for. Your offering of blood will occur as frequently as medically reasonable to sustain your life. A portion of a lung might be needed, and we will take it. Or if a heart-lung transplant is needed then that will be the end of your time with us. I want you to ponder upon how it will feel not to have control of your life," he reported to me.

I was stunned, scared, and panic set in. I had no control of my feelings. My heart pounded to a cadence of over a hundred twenty beats per minute and hyperventilation was setting in. I wanted to cry, beg for my life, and curse him all at once.

"How long? How long do I have?" I asked not really wanting to know.

"That isn't a question I can answer. We will be selective as to who receives your body parts. It could be weeks or months. I don't think more than six months. When you have expired we will strip the skin from your body and the corneas from your eyes. Does that about cover it?" He walked toward me and bent down by my ear. "I'm not your judge, you're correct. I'm just the man who is to execute the sentence you bestowed on yourself. Dr. Armond, I'll be the one operating on you and removing your body parts. Believe me it will give me great pleasure. You are a monster and evil incarnate. You used the gifts God gave you to butcher the innocent and helpless. 2 Corinthians 11:15, Dr. Armond. It is not surprising, then, if his servants masquerade as servants of righteousness. Their end will correspond to their actions."

Then he was gone.

TWENTY-TWO

Azar

I ABSOLUTELY DESPISE CHARLES DE GAULLE AIRPORT. IT'S THE embodiment of the word rude and it is first on my hit list. Despite having flown first class, once I left the plane and merged with others I felt the absolute chaos that only the French could deal with and navigate with grace.

I determined what carousel my baggage would be deposited to and I walked there amongst all the other passengers trying to get there first to hurry up and wait. I stood and watched as the bags went around and around and after a half hour it was apparent that my bag wasn't coming down the shoot. Panic struck me and it took me a few moments to gather my thoughts. I found my way to lost baggage only to encounter an insolent little man.

"Here are my baggage claim receipts. Where is my luggage?" I demanded. I placed my palms face down on the counter and leaned in for emphasis.

He removed the claim tickets from the counter and stepped toward the computer to input the data.

"It's at carousel three, madame," he replied in a bored tone and handed me pieces of paper.

"It most certainly is not. I was just there, and it isn't on the carousel. What do you take me for, an idiot? You think I can't find my own luggage? I demand someone escort me back and show me that the piece is there," I said.

The man looked at me with a quizzical look, picked up the phone and spoke in a low hushed tone. "Alan will be here in a moment to escort you to the carousel and will assist you. Please have a seat for you comfort."

I continued to stand.

More than ten minutes later Alan arrived to escort me to the baggage claim. Ready to engage in an all-out war, I was stunned into silence. There was my suitcase. Sitting on the belt waiting for me.

"Would that be it, madame?" he asked ready to return to his important job probably napping in the back.

"Yes, thank you," I replied.

I grabbed the handle of the bag and yanked it off the belt. I pulled up the periscope handle and wheeled the case around toward the ladies' rest-room. The disabled person's cubicle was available and had a chair in the corner, perfect. I placed the bag on the chair, locked the door and unzipped the bag catching the zipper slightly. With excitement, I threw open the lid and jumped with a start. My heart thudded, and my mouth was dry.

On top of my clothes was a thick cream-colored envelope with my name in bold black lettering. I opened it quickly and my eyes skidded across the message inside.

The specimens are safe. You can return to the States. You will not be spreading your particularly cruel brand of death here.

I turned to the commode and threw up.

I must have sat on the floor contemplating my options too long because someone knocked on the stall door and asked if I needed assistance. I gathered my luggage and handbag, opened the door, and walked past her. I leaned over the sink, washed my hands, and held a cold paper towel to my face.

A few deep breaths and I left the bathroom and walked to the ticket counter to renegotiate the tickets which would no longer be useful. I was now on a flight back to DC.

ONE

As I waited in the lounge for the call to board, my phone rang—must be Marcello.

"You have a lot of fucking nerve calling me. What do you want?" I gritted out through my teeth.

"Ms. Abed, this is Marcello's father. We have not met," he said with an authority that caused me pause. I was confused because the caller ID on my phone displayed M. Ghiaccio.

"I will make this brief. From what I am aware, your plan that my son agreed to with my blessing has greatly veered off its original course—" he started.

"My plan has nothing to do with you, so I don't see why I should carry on with this conversation any further, Mr. Ghiaccio." That should put an end to this intrusion.

"On the contrary, Ms. Abed. I am a major shareholder in the company that you would have partnered with in your plan. Now, up to a point where there was a profit to me I was in agreement with the overall plan. However, now it appears that you are bringing in new specimens that were not agreed upon and can do serious damage to ecosystems—plant and human alike—and ultimately, have long-lasting implications on the geopolitical stage. And that isn't acceptable to the company or me personally," he said. I heard a door open in the background and he muted the phone a moment and was back.

"And?" I asked in a clipped tone.

"We'll continue to participate if you fall back to your original position. If you don't and continue down this road you've chosen, we will withdraw from the operation completely. There are billions at stake on our end and any hint of recklessness can throw an unnecessary light on us. What's your decision?" he calmly asked.

"Is Marcello there with you?" I asked.

"He is not," he responded giving nothing away.

"I cannot make a decision until I speak with him," I said trying to buy more time and hoping when I spoke with Marcello I could sway him back to my side.

"Ms. Abed, I'm confident my son will be in touch with you, but we stand a united front. I must warn you I am prepared to take any and all action to stop you. I may not be a terribly religious man, but I do believe in God. What you're proposing to do may lead to the extermination of millions," he said. "And, Ms. Abed there is no room in the world for fanatics."

"First, Mr. Ghiaccio, I owe you no explanation about my life. Second, I owe no duty to you as you may be a silent partner of Marcello's, but you aren't a partner to me. Third and most importantly, my plan leaves it serendipitously up to your God to determine who lives and who dies. I'm only his tool to facilitate his wishes. How long do you think the world can sustain enough food to feed everyone with our growing population? Animals under man's hands have gone extinct and plants now have to be genetically mutated to produce enough to feed the world, biodiversity, Mr. Ghiaccio." I observed the people around me in the first-class lounge, wondering which of these people would be alive in a month.

"I see, Ms. Abed. Please tell me, in your new agenda how did your plan to morph from how my son and I could make a profit to you being the person to solely control the world as we know it?" he asked with an angry calm to his voice.

"Of course, the financial aspect is very important. However, there's the second benefit to my plan," I said.

"Yes, and what if the health care industry throws a dither your way and decides it's too expensive to treat people and makes their decision on who to treat. They'll run the numbers and decide that the healthiest should be treated to make sure they return to optimum health. Others will be left to die after some actuarial runs his numbers and a bean counter decides a number-only determination. Your original plan of infecting people with known biologics that we could treat with a known antibiotic we're ready to provide was a solid plan. We would have had deaths that were statistically acceptable, however, most of the people would survive if they paid our fee. People understand supply and demand. It would be a win-win for everyone. But the biologics you're now trying to introduce have no antidote stored in enough quantities to contain it and we don't have it either. So, what do I get out of this new plan of yours?" he asked as he tapped his pen on something.

"Mr. Ghiaccio, I don't need you and Marcello to run my plan. I alone am in charge of the end result. If he wants to jump ship under your orders, so be it. I will carry out my plan to its fruition. Without either of you," I said with determination in my voice he could not miss.

There was an extended period of silence, an eerie stillness, as I waited for his further argument.

"Then we understand each other's position, Ms. Abed. I will caution you to rethink yours, you don't live in a vacuum. Stay focused on the end game. Ms. Abed. Profit."

"Mr. Ghiaccio, I'm neither your employee nor business partner and have given you enough of my time already. Good day," I said and hung up. Ending the connection with him before he could from me. I had to maintain the upper hand.

I heard the call to start boarding my plane. Shit. I dialed the number, and as always, he picked up.

"Az, what can I do for you?" he asked.

"The new specimens, I need them. When I get back to the US, I'll send you my new address. Marcello can no longer be trusted." I stood and gathered my belongings to leave the lounge to board.

"Leave it to me," he said, and we ended our call.

I stood in a short line and as the line progressed a young man about my age maybe younger slipped in behind me. As I turned to make certain he gave me enough personal space, he smiled at me as if he understood. I passed the check-in terminal desk, boarded the plane, and seated myself in the first-class area. I turned to my right and saw the same silver-haired man that stood behind me settle into his seat the next row over. I had a niggling feeling I had seen him before but couldn't conjure up where and had other things to deal with after that phone call. But something pulled at me as if I needed to take a closer notice of him. The man was sexy with an aura of glamour. Maybe he was a celebrity or model? Either way, not relevant to me right now.

As I sat back and waited for the remainder of people to board, I typed instructions to the first contact located in India and texted the word **Release**. I immediately received the thumbs- up emoji. With my genetically modified Ebola dispensed, blood would be running from people's eyes very soon.

My next instructions went to my second contact in Greece, the gateway between continents. I texted the word **Release**, and immediately received a thumbs-up emoji. My genetically modified Marburg was on its way. Soon there would be people all over Greece with organ failure and internal bleeding.

I opened up five more text message boxes and wrote the same for each and from each I received the same response, a thumbs-up emoji.

In a matter of five minutes I'd ordered the death of millions. And the ones that didn't die would be in the tens of millions needing medication only I could supply. Some might say I was the embodiment of the four horsemen of the apocalypse.

TWENTY-THREE

Jackson

I HAD TO GIVE IT TO MARY, SHE WAS AS SNEAKY AS THEY COME. HAD IT not been for the debriefing I never would have known that she had stealthily installed some type of sophisticated software remotely on Azar's phone when she had breakfast with her. Software so sophisticated only one country in the world had developed it and was not sharing it. That is until they discovered Mary's breakfast plans with Azar and brought her into the operation the night before. How the hell Mary held that under wraps boggled the mind. It also explained why she left with the woman at the Bureau without a care.

Tyler, Mary, Nathaniel, and I sat around a wood table in the heavily secured room on the eighth floor. When the first buzz came in from the text alert, Mary and I twitched. Tyler did not.

As we watched each text repeat the same message, Tyler returned the response with a thumbs-up emoji. Mary appeared mesmerized by the ability of Tyler to remain so cool and in control. I disliked the little punk with his cocky attitude, but internally, I was surprised by him.

"Can I do one?" she asked getting ready to turn the phone her way.

"No," he replied.

"What's your real name?" she asked trying to distract him.

"David." He lifted only his eyebrows to see her. "But that does not leave this room, Mary. Okay, that's all of them. She's put her phone away and the flight is ready to take off. One more disaster averted."

"You say it as if you were able to catch some eggs before they cracked. You probably saved millions of lives." Mary leaned back to study Tyler.

"Mary, these people have had these plans in motion for years. We have no idea how many people are actually involved. There are probably couriers planted in countries we still have no idea about. We don't know if they are in physical possession of the biologicals or if they are just ready to take instructions how to access them. With the access you got us to her phone we were able to determine how to intercept the contacts on her list that she had hired to work with her. However, if we hadn't intercepted those messages there could have been a global pandemic." Tyler spoke directly to Mary.

"But what about the crops and agriculture?" I needed answers.

"That is a twisted and difficult answer. Drones are involved, and these chemicals can be manufactured in each country, making it a country by country problem. We are able to monitor through interconnected sources drone swarms—and try to get there before the poison takes effect, applying palliative treatment. But we have no ability to assess the actual poison used on the spot. We can test if it is alkaline or acidic and at least try to mitigate the uptake initially using that information. There is always the worry of starvation in rural areas, and in the short-term global trade will be interrupted. Are the chemicals carcinogenic enough to mutate cells and cause cancer? I am not a doctor, but our people are concerned. They are definitely poisonous. But how will anyone know which ones are being exported worldwide?" Tyler responded.

"What will you do with the perpetrators?" I asked. We had made a deal with the devil to allow their government to coordinate the take-down of all involved and I didn't like it much.

"Jackson, you know that is impossible for me to disclose," he said.

"Are you letting Azar back into the country to return to work?" Mary asked.

"Yes, we need to see who she contacts next to pull the trigger on blowing out the commodities and agriculture component," Tyler said.

After concluding Azar was in the air, our meeting adjourned.

We exchanged goodbyes and went about our work, mundane as it appeared now.

I was preparing for my two o'clock meeting when Cillian's call came through.

"I'm just checking in to let you know these paintings were not part of the grouping we were trying to track down. Where's Mary? I have something—" he started.

As if she had her ear to the door she knocked and walked into my office. I gave her a questioning look.

"I have been told I have the second sight, a sixth sense, a third eye," she knowingly replied to my look.

"Cut it out, Mary. I know Eloise just called you and told you to head over to Jackson's office," Cillian said over the speaker-phone.

"Okay, blabber mouth. Why am I here and not basking in the glory of my young fan club?" she asked.

"Christ. Just out with it, Cillian. Her head is so big it can barely fit through the door anymore," I complained as I slouched in my chair.

"I assume you both can hear me so let's move this along. The paintings in the storage were absolute fakes and not Diana fakes. Their main and only purpose was to be placed in a custom frame that held small compartments built inside the frame. The only way we discovered this was when we put them through the scanners, you could barely discern their placement. The kicker is they were wired internally with an explosive so if the frame was not dismantled correctly to remove the object they would explode, destroying the painting. Don't even ask, they are being taken care of as we speak. However, we have no idea what is in the frames and won't know until the devices are neutralized. First guess is they contain scan discs," he said.

"Where did the paintings originate?" I asked.

"Don't know but when we get access to the discs I'm certain we'll have the answers."

"You three heading back? Or am I stuck with the duchess?"

"We need one more day. Chavez asked Emma to go through the studio one more time with a few officers and imaging machines to make sure there is nothing hidden in the walls," he said.

"Why do they need Emma's permission? Don't they have ownership subsequent to the forfeiture and seizure?" I asked twirling my pen between my fingers.

"You have the Fed, State, and probate involved, and to go through every channel to get everyone signed off would take forever. Eloise was able to get a consent order from the probate judge, so they are taking advantage of it tomorrow. Then we'll head back," he said.

"Thank God, because between Mary, your monstrosity of a dog Lucy, and that demon spawn of a cat, I find myself in need of numerous shots of brown liquor when I get home," I shared with him knowing he hated Sigmund as much as me.

"Ah, suck it up, buttercup. Put your big boy pants on. Now, Cillian," Mary interjected giving me a dismissive wave of her hand.

"Yes, Mary," he chuckled and acknowledge her.

"I've been giving this some thought." She tapped her chin with her finger.

"Christ, what else is new?" That garnered a stink eye.

"I was watching Sherlock the other night—" she started.

"Oh no. I'm not wasting my time talking about that moronic show. This call is over," I announced.

"Not that one, the BBC version with Benedict Cumberbatch. Keep up or leave the room and let the investigators investigate, Jackie boy. Anyway—"

"Hey, Mary," Eloise interrupted as she must have just entered the room. "What did I miss?"

"Just getting there, Eloise, my love. If someone had hidden something that he knew he had to come back for but presumed the house would be searched, if I was him I would hide it somewhere outside and easy to get to. My suggestion is to start at the dock and see if there have been any signs the wood on the dock posts had been cut. Like the top of the post taken off and hollowed out to drop something inside. If it was me I would hide it near the dock, so I could get in and out quick and easy by boat," Mary said.

"Wait. Are you talking about the person who left the paintings in the warehouse or the people who had Armond's paintings now?" I asked.

"Either. How do we know how many people were in on the scheme from the start? We know the common denominator was Roselov, and we know he has family that remains active in the art theft world. I'm only saying with the house abandoned right now it would be the perfect place to continue storing and swapping paintings out. Not quite a dead drop but along those lines. But don't listen to the old lady. Do what you want," she said. "Now I've given you all the pearls of wisdom I intend to give." She stood to leave. However, not before flipping me the bird.

"I know this will flip your switch, Jackson, but she has a point. Would that not beat all if they were able to continue their ring by using the same damn dock?" Cillian asked.

"Except they wouldn't have that master forger she's somewhere in WITSEC," I said.

"Or they could be using it for stolen property," Eloise piped in.

"Nah, there's not enough market for that purpose," I answered. "If there were any Diana forgeries around that we hadn't found that would be the only reason to continue to use it," I said.

"You know," Cillian started. "Not necessarily. What if they were using the place as a drop-off and pick-up for something involving drugs, guns, biochemical, or transfer of state secrets?"

"Please. Somebody kill me. You are channeling Mary and she has left the room. I am done with this conversation. Call me when something turns up. Or better yet, El, why not make a visit to your tarot card reader friend?" I laughed.

"You think I haven't already done that while I was here?" she stated without a laugh to follow.

"Nope, I'm not getting sucked into this nonsense. I have a meeting to break into, I'll talk to you later," I said as Cillian laughed. I heard Emma asking, "What?" in the background before Cillian hung up the phone.

TWENTY-FOUR

Azar

THE WAVE OF RELIEF THAT SWEPT OVER ME KNOWING MY PLAN WAS now in motion allowed a brief nap that lasted about six hours. I was close to the US now and would soon be able to execute the next phase of the release: smallpox, measles, and polio. One final payment and the deal was sealed.

People who don't vaccinate tend to fall into one of three categories. First are individuals who take the stance that they have an individual right to decide what they put in their body. The second arise out of various religious standpoints and vaccine objections. The third groups have a suspicion and mistrust of vaccines among global cultures and communities. In all, there were millions of people who didn't get vaccinated globally. Perfect. Once the bodies started stacking up, panic would ensue. My plan was to hit Africa hard, and then Central America and India. Pockets of the US like the Amish population and Middle Eastern cities would be last.

As I made my last few notes and reviewed my checklist, the captain was giving directions that we were on for our final descent into Dulles and to buckle up and stow all items. The landing was smooth and the deplaning a bit chaotic. What is wrong with people? The silver-haired man who sat across from me must have lost his balance and tipped forward invading my space. I wanted to scream at him when he touched my shoulder and it felt as if it had been stung by a bee. Apologies were offered, but I was offended by him touching me and let him know it.

As we all walked into the open area I started to feel a bit woozy and it was then that Mr. Silver Hair took my arm to steady me. Suddenly, I was more and more dizzy and right before I passed out I was guided to a mobile device.

I have no idea how long I was out cold, but when I woke, I felt as if someone had beaten me, although there was no physical evidence to sustain such a conclusion. I couldn't feel any wet or dry blood and no knots or bumps. The room was black, and I couldn't see anyone, but I thought I could smell a hint of aftershave.

"Good afternoon," the voice said.

I immediately turned my head to where the voice came from. Somewhere to the left of me but I couldn't even make out a shadow.

"Where am I?" I asked sitting up but unable to sit completely. My arms felt numb and it was hard to sustain my weight.

"Not relevant," he advised.

"Of course it's relevant. You've drugged and kidnapped me," I shouted. "I demand to know who you are, where I am, and why have you kidnapped me?"

"The why is easy. Because you are on a mission to destroy innocent people for no tenable reason. We need to put a stop to that plan," he said.

I remained silent.

"What I'm unable to comprehend is why. What could prompt you to devise and now try to execute such a plan?" His question echoed in the empty room and the room was silent again.

I refused to answer because I answered to nobody.

"The plan you have devised is more than just a plan of terrorism. It is a plan of eradication. And that, Ms. Abed, is unacceptable.

The terms mass atrocity, dehumanization, and crimes against humanity come to mind," he said and again went silent. I could hear nothing.

"You know nothing of my plans," I calmly maintained.

"I see," he said, and I heard him stand. "You don't think people with power and money have a reach far and wide, my dear?"

Thinking a bit and cataloguing those involved and loyal to me I found it impossible to believe anyone would betray me. The circle was limited, and it was a circle of trust that I vetted completely.

"I think you may know part of my plan but not all of it," I said back to him, confident he was bluffing. But if Josh had put the pieces together about the commodities portion maybe someone else had put together the biologics portion. Suddenly, the reality of what had happened came crashing down around me as the fog of the drug wore off. Someone had stolen the biologics from my luggage, of course someone knew.

"It seems you have underestimated me, Ms. Abed. And that will count heavily against you. I'm here to dispense your punishment," he said. "In a half hour or so the drug will wear off completely."

He walked toward a door, stopped and I could see he was a tall man. "Ms. Abed, you will be judged in accordance to your deeds and plans."

I waited patiently. The door finally opened, and I heard someone come in and take a seat in the nearby chair.

"Who the hell are you?" I asked now able to stand but took the route of being cautious and waited.

He sat silently. My hearing was so acute that I could hear him physically constrain his breathing.

Finally, he spoke.

"Ms. Abed, it does not matter who I am. I'm a man and I'm

every man. My time with you is to accomplish one thing. It is to advise you how we have decided to dispense your punishment," he said, a line I felt he'd practiced and said many times before.

"I have committed no crime and therefore you have no right to impose a sentence upon me."

"Ms. Abed, I know of the biologicals you have illegally acquired and lands you have poisoned in the name of money and revenge. Someone will be in shortly. You will be fed and taken to shower. You will be moved to another room." He didn't wait for me to respond. "Then you will be used as a human bacterial test site. We will inject you with certain bacteria and see how it progresses. We will take your blood and use it to procure a cure for others," he advised.

"You wouldn't dare," I said.

"Ah, you are so wrong. I'm the man who will execute the sentence you bestowed upon yourself. You used the gifts God gave you to devise a plan to hurt the innocent and helpless. 2 Corinthians 11:15, Ms. Abed. It is not surprising, then, if his servants masquerade as servants of righteousness. Their end will correspond to their actions."

TWENTY-FIVE

Jackson

66 **I**'M NOT CLEAR WHY WE ARE INVOLVED IN THIS, IT'S CLEARLY A Homeland Securities issue," I said at the meeting that droned on and on. "I don't want to sound like I am not a team player, but we are stretched pretty thin helping the DEA with the influx of drugs from Afghanistan and the massive number of weapons that the ATF is picking up. I have hundreds of open money laundering schemes that I need to investigate on my desk.

"I am wrapping up that online vehicle fraud and business e mail scheme that mushroomed into us being able to shut down an unlicensed hawala system. I think thirteen indictments internationally says we have been busy. And again, not wanting to sound like a whiner but sports bribery is up as well as trafficking in counterfeit goods; the general population doesn't get behind either because they don't feel they are affected personally. But we still have to investigate the hundreds of reports in addition to the thousand emails and wire fraud cases. And God knows if ICE didn't overlap us with drug trafficking, exploitation of children, and alien smuggling, we would never leave this building. And that's just our department—organized crime."

"Jackson, if we don't keep this within a tight circle and it gets out, global panic will ensue. Investors will leave the stock market, people may start pulling money from their bank accounts, and banks could fail.

"If you need to put it in a little box that would warrant our resources, then think of it this way. Although Azar is not a US citizen she is on our soil, making this a transnational problem. Azar's scheme clearly fits under the RICO statute, Title 18 of the United States Code, Section 1961(4), the Continuing Criminal Enterprise statute, Title 21 of the United States Code, Section 848(c)(2). American lives are at risk as well as our economy.

"People will panic. The news with their vulture mentality of 'if it bleeds it leads' will play on a constant loop. We have our work cut out for us. Congress has shifted funds to address the immigration issue and fiscal tightening across the Defense Department also had an impact on military programs that develop chemical and biological countermeasures for civilians. Right now, with this imminent threat it's us, DHS, Health and Human Services, Defense Department, and the U.S. Agency for International Development working together. We are behind the eight ball as we are only now ready to test bio-detection systems in train stations but nowhere near ready to combat it. I think that answers your question," Nathaniel said wearily. In my opinion he was hanging on by a thread.

"Why not just kill the bitch?" Matt asked, and the room erupted in a sound affirmation.

"Because, idiot, if she's the mastermind and the only one that has a blueprint of the operation, who knows if she has people ready to go on her command or if she's on a detonation schedule. She may be the only one who knows everything. Or it could be cut the head of the snake off and she has someone ready to spring into action. If she's been planning this for years, the world is truly fucked." Mike's last comment was met with silence as people absorbed his information.

"People, I have advanced degrees in biology and it doesn't take a person with an education to tell you that synthetic biology and genetic engineering technology could be misused for nefarious purposes and we should have a system for ongoing monitoring and assessment of synthetic biology risks in place. It's now possible to synthesize viruses from scratch. We're beginning to find ways to create life artificially from the genetic code. If this lady slipped through global monitoring systems and has the ability to weaponize smallpox for example, then life as we know it is over. Can we move on here? We need to devise a plan to get this monster off the street, find her supply, and not quibble over jurisdictional issues," Larry said with such calmness it was almost frightening.

Waiting for Nathaniel to give us further information and instructions, his head bent reading a text. The room was silent with all eyes upon him as we watched him toss his phone onto the table and scrubbed his head with his hands.

"Apparently while the French were waiting for her in Paris, she switched her plans and now she's disappeared. She arrived at Dulles and she was last seen on airport security tapes with a man who helped her onto a cart and then they were gone. Perfect. We may have lost her for good."

I turned to see Mary raise her hand in that annoying Hermione Granger way where her arm was so stiff she could use it as a tennis racket.

"Yes, Mary," Nathaniel said smiling her way. The way that man coddled her you would thing he had a crush on her. As he acknowledged her, all eyes in the room swept her way.

"If you'll recall I have her phone cloned. Even if it's powered down we may be able to find her," she said waving her phone around.

Tyler looked a bit uncomfortable. Shifting in his seat he tried to catch Mary's eye. Finally, as she visually swept the room, I saw him give her a slight shake of his head and she took her seat.

After several minutes of thinking and a room so silent it could be taken for a mausoleum, he finally responded.

"Jackson, I want you to liaise with cybersecurity, NSA, and

everyone necessary. You will be in conference room 866 in one hour. Now let's move. And need I remind that everything in the room is classified information, and under 18 US Code 798, disclosure of classified information holds a ten-year prison sentence. I'll find a few more statutes to lock someone up for life if anything leaves this room," he threatened. "Jackson and Mary, a moment."

After everyone left, it was me, Mary, Tyler, and Nathaniel.

"How are we going to get around once a battery is removed it is useless because you need radio waves to track it," Nathaniel asked.

"I can answer that but that will be giving away state secrets. I can assure you I am all over this problem and will have a report back to you in less than an hour. I'll answer your concern in generalities under an understanding this is all hypothetical," Tyler said. "There are several possibilities that the guys who helped Mary get access to Azar's phone might have used. These guys may have remotely modified the firmware in Azar's phone. Obviously, Mary could not attach a chip to the battery physically but maybe the wonks attached a virtual chip to the phone. Even when some modified phones are switched off, there is a baseband processor that powers up every ten minutes or so to retrieve SMS messages, but not phone calls, so a Geo Spatial Intelligence agency could track it. Not many, but some phones are equipped with two batteries used by your drug traffickers and arms dealers, so they never lose juice. It's not obvious the second is installed but it's there. I have reason to believe that Azar's phone has such a secondary battery. If the person who has her is not aware she has a second battery for backup then the second one might still be transmitting, or Mary's cloned phone might pick up on it similar to the Find My Phone app. But of course, this is purely speculation and no way represents any information I may or may not have available to me."

"Thank you, Tyler," I said making certain he understood the disdain in my voice.

"Enough, Jackson," Nathaniel said in a clipped voice. I had not heard that tone before and by his facial expression I saw a bit of panic in his face. "I have to alert the White House. I have better things to do than watch you have a pissing contest with Tyler. You will lose every day of the week and Sunday. Now, everyone move. Tyler and Mary, my office."

All I could say was, "Right boss," and I moved.

An hour later to the minute, we were all gathered in the conference room reserved for the highest security available.

"Azar indeed has a second battery in her phone that is undisturbed," Tyler advised, and this was confirmed by the other security geeks. "It's got plenty of juice, good for us. Now the question becomes once you geolocate her who takes charge?"

"I believe that question needs no answer," Nathaniel stated, looking at him as if he had two heads. "We do that, as in the DOJ."

"I see. Then might I have Mary with me to observe?" he asked.

"I don't see why not," Nathaniel responded. "That taken care of, here are the coordinates that Tyler's faction has given us for the takedown. We have two hours to mount up and then we are moving, it's get in and out. We don't want any casualties, and at all costs, we need her alive."

TWENTY-SIX

Mary

I WAS RATHER SURPRISED THAT NATHANIEL ALLOWED ME TO PARTNER UP with Tyler—or David, probably wasn't his name either. It never got old and I never tired of him calling me a national treasure. He was overinflating things a bit but who was I to argue?

"Mary, unlike Jackson, I want you to take every weapon you have available. I want you armed to the teeth," he said. "We won't be needing them once we get where we're going. However, you never know what hostiles you will encounter along the way."

"Tyler, we are singing from the same hymnal," I said and sorted through every make-shift weapon I had managed to sneak into the building and had hidden in my desk. "My bag is large enough to hold a five-pound fire extinguisher, but I've been putting off toting it around. Your thought?"

He shook his head no.

"Locking carabiner as a knuckle duster?" I asked.

He shook his head no.

"Aluminum water bottle as a blunt force object?"

He nodded.

"I have my pepper spray in a pen, but how about some hornet spray?" I asked continuing to rummage through my bottom draw.

"No, your pepper spray pen should be fine," he said. I was pleased he was taking my weapons seriously.

"That should do it. I already have my sock full of coils. I can use my bag as a shield, I have my pepper spray pen, taser, hair pin, and umbrella," I reported as I carefully placed my weapons in my bag. "And don't forget I am licensed to pack heat."

"Then let's roll," he said.

"Tyler, how old are you?"

"Just turned twenty-one. But don't let that fool you. Mary. I've been training for missions like this my whole life," he said with seriousness, but managed to break in a smirk.

"Call of Duty and Metal Gear don't count, Tyler, I can whip Jackson's ass at both. Keeps me sharp and him humble," I told him letting him know I was up for the challenge.

"Mary, you are a wise and humorous woman and that is why when this mission is over I will miss you. Now a few ground rules. You have to wear protective gear and I'll let you use my country's body armor. It's lighter and provides better protection than yours. When I tell you to pull back, you pull back. I don't anticipate any issues but those are the instructions. Are you able to comply?" he asked as he texted and hit send on his phone.

I nodded.

"Then let's go," he said.

The man drove like an absolute maniac and I wasn't sure if it was because of his age or background. I suppose he saw me gripping the side handle for dear life and stomping my foot for the invisible brake. It made him smile. He assured me he was trained in counter-attack driving and never had an accident yet, despite the fact he had been driving since twelve. He emphasized that twelve was an acceptable age to drive in his country.

"Call me crazy, but aren't we completely off target to where you indicated Azar's cell phone is located?" I asked an hour into the drive.

I was all for joy riding and taking scenic routes, but I did have my heart set of seeing some action in this mission. After spending hours that probably added up to months reading about the stock market and all the sectors, my eyes at the end started glazing over and my brain became oversaturated.

"I was truthful in giving Azar's phone location. However, maybe not so much truth in where she is being held," he said and gave me a side smile.

My God, the boy was my kindred spirit. "Couldn't you be charged with obstruction?"

"Diplomatic immunity covers a lot of things, Mary. And as I said, I have no doubt her phone will be found at those coordinates," he replied.

"Where is she?" I asked, and unlike Jackson, he answered.

"In a safe place in Virginia. Buckle up because we're now getting ready to book," he said. As we entered the highway he exceeded the traffic limit by twenty miles. At the very least.

"Tyler, the only speed above this is speed of sound," I told him. Now braced with my left hand on the console between us and my right straight out in the event of impact. We were booking.

"Where are we heading exactly? No flim-flam or coordinates, just the name of a town or identifiable location," I asked again not expecting to receive an answer.

"An area between Monongahela Forrest, and Washington and Jefferson National Forrest."

"That sounds about three hours away. Won't the rest of the team become suspicious when they show up and we aren't there," I asked. I was all for adventure, but I was not up for being booted from the Bureau for insubordination. Of course, Tyler was in charge here with high-level clearance so who was I to argue with him. Yep, I was up for this free ride.

I decided to relax and let the hum of the speeding roadway carry me away for a minute.

The crackle of gravel woke me, and I saw us surrounded by forest. To gain a better perspective, I sat up, did a bit of a stretch, and reached in my bag for a tic tac.

"Welcome back." Tyler smiled.

"Did your boring chatter put me to sleep?" I asked a bit embarrassed I had dosed off.

"That must be it, Mary" He smiled. Such a sweet boy. "See that building over there? It has a crematory and that's where we're heading."

"Why?" I asked a bit confused and frankly a bit uneasy.

"As the magician says, all will be revealed," he said and smiled again.

"Have you been in contact with Jackson?" With Jackson you never know if he will be concerned or angry when he is not in full control. But either way, I would get a chewing out for not being in contact. At least this time I could tell the truth I had dosed off.

"No, but they'll know where we are in about an hour. You and I have some loose ends to tidy up. Are you up for saving the world, Mary?" he asked as he put the car into park and turned the car off.

"Is the Pope Catholic, Tyler? Let's get a move on," I said grabbing my bag. "Are there friendlies in there or do I need a weapon?"

"Friendlies except to the bad guys. One minute. I'm sure they saw us coming but let me text them." We waited until a young silver-haired man opened the door and waited for us to approach.

Tyler didn't introduce us, and I didn't question it but thought it was in the name of plausible deniability.

The place appeared as if at some point it was a funeral parlor, built around the early 1900s and abandoned in the 1970s or around that time based on the style. There was dust on the few tables along the wall and debris littered the hall. A few prints were hung on the walls, dust coating the frames. It was cold. A cold that chilled you to the core.

We proceeded down the hall to a large room. If I had to guess, it had been a viewing room at one time. The large area was heated and had electricity. What the source of the heat was, who knew? Maybe a generator. Not a puzzle I wanted to tax my mind to figure out. All I knew was it was warm, lit, and had furniture that appeared to have been uncovered after being hidden away for quite a while. The sheets that had covered it were tossed haphazardly to the side.

"Please, have a seat," the silver-haired man who had let us in said. "I'll be right back." Tyler directed us to two high-back chairs made of leather and looked medieval next to three others placed behind a long wood table that faced three seats.

"Mary, you have to remain totally quiet and as a spectator unless asked a direct question," Tyler advised. "If there is something pressing, lift your right hand at your wrist slightly and I will lean over. Do we have an agreement?" he asked. And I nodded.

As he finished speaking and I was just getting comfortable, two men in black robes entered and sat next to us. The robes were similar to what judges or British lawyers wore. Pretty cheesy and dramatic if you asked me. Neither man made eye contact and we waited in silence.

I tapped my fingers on the table—a habit that reflected my anxiety level—earning a side glance from Tyler. As I was repositioning myself in the chair, the silver-haired man led another man I recognized from the pictures with Azar. He was her plus one. Silver-hair guided him toward a seat in front of the table facing us at the right of me. Young and even more handsome than his pictures his body language relayed fear mixed with annoyance. He was instructed to remain seated and not to speak. His eyes moved slowly to each of us, assessing and studying us. To avoid the tension, I felt as he held my gaze I clasped my hands together in front of me and averted my eyes.

The man left the room and returned with Adrien Armond who

was clearly annoyed, making threats and speaking in French like a machine gun going off. He was led to a seat. After exchanging looks with the first man, he refused to sit. The silver-haired man whipped out a tactical periscope baton and slammed the backs of his knees producing a yelp from him and a forced seating.

Once again, he left the room. This time he returned with Azar, who entered with dignity tinged with anger. Surprisingly, she didn't say a word but was clearly shocked that the other two were present and gave me only a glance. She sat without incident.

Everyone was seated and settled. The silver-haired man moved to the last chair at the table. He started the conversation.

"Welcome, Ms. Abed, Mr. Ghiaccio, and Dr. Armond. Each of you have met the two gentlemen to my left. Ms. Abed, you know me as Lozar, and Dr. Armond, you know me as Melzar," the silver-haired man said. The room erupted in surprised chatter by the captives that quickly elevated to personal threats against the man and personal epithets not of a kind nature.

The man to Tyler's right slammed his hand on the table and demanded silence. The noise died down.

"Now that we all know the players in this game, I'm confident you understand why you're here. You have each been judged and sentenced and now is your time to convince us to mitigate your punishment. At the end of your appeal, the five of us at the table will discuss and determine if you should be offered anything less than the punishment we've already discussed with you," he said.

"Mr. Ghiaccio, please stand," the silver-haired man said, and he complied.

"Mr. Ghiaccio, it's my understanding after a thorough sifting of the facts that your part in this plan was limited to acquiring specimens and when it became necessary for an antibiotic to be utilized after the attacks your firm would be the firm to dispense those," the man to Tyler's immediate right stated.

Ghiaccio remained silent neither admitting nor denying.

"No need to answer. We have further information that you had abandoned the plan, and had the specimens moved from storage and disposed of in the desert this week."

This brought Azar to complete attention with a look of unfiltered shock on her face. She turned her head to the left to study him, but he wouldn't return her look.

The man continued. "As a result of you placing the specimens in a facility some were damaged and caused the deaths of the men moving it which we deem an accident from their carelessness. You participated in a plan to crush the world economy and didn't pull back from that venture. Land was fouled, and animals fell sick. However, that is only money. From your account with Ms. Abed—your Fire & Ice account—we have wired an amount to several banks set up to recompense the people whose property was involved. Call it restitution. The legal system can be so tedious, and it may take years for you to get to trial and those people shouldn't lose everything while bureaucrats work through the logistics. At the end of the meeting, you'll receive several doses of ketamine. You'll live in flashbacks and a daydream-like state for a period of twenty-four to forty-eight hours, so no one will be able to determine if any information you give them when questioned is real or drug induced. You'll be transferred to the proper authorities. But before that, you'll witness the sentencing of these two. You'll never speak to your father or his organization about this, understood? Our reach is long."

Mr. Ghiaccio nodded his head. He now tried to make eye contact with Azar, but she refused to look at him.

The man next to the silver-haired man spoke.

"Dr. Armond, you and I have already chatted. Do you have any idea how many lives and families you've ruined? How many futures you've stolen?"

Adrien just stared at him.

"I have a number for you. You have stolen six-hundred-seventy-two futures. That's six-hundred-seventy-two lives. And multiply by the families and it's unthinkable the misery you've caused," the man said as he peered over his glasses at Adrien. "For money, for your greed."

"I never took anything from those people that wasn't on offer for sale. And besides, Avigad Abed did the negotiating. It's the same as if someone wanted to sell their blood. It's yours to give away or sell. I saved lives. For every healthy person who had an organ to sell, there was a life that benefited from that transaction.

"In the past, passage to another country was procured by owing someone money or indentured servitude for years. How many people had to be drug mules or prostitutes to pay off a debt. Years and years of misery. Everyone wants something in life, gentlemen. How you pay for it is your own business. In Iran, it's perfectly legal to sell an organ. In every country, it's legal to sell sperm and eggs, so what's the difference?" Adrien replied. He made a valid point but the way it was procured, the organs in question, wasn't accepted in civilized countries.

"Do you have any idea of how people were treated after you operated on them?" the robed man asked angrily.

"Not my job. I removed the kidney or liver or lung. Once my part was completed, another person took responsibility. If that person did a piss-poor job, then blame them. If you are building a car and I put in the engine and later the chassis cracks, should I get blamed? No, I did my job. Someone else didn't do theirs. I only see me sitting here taking the blame for other people's wrongs. What about the people who lived and prospered because of me? Your judgment seems skewed to me," Adrien stated.

"The money—"

"Again, not my end of the business. The deal was struck with Avigad. If you went to a restaurant and I prepared your meal, I was the cook. If the owner bought the meat from a vendor and paid that vendor ten dollars a pound but after it was prepared charged the customer thirty dollars for a half a pound of the meat, would it be my problem the meat was overpriced? No. I just prepared the meat and had nothing to do with the transaction," Armond argued, leaning back.

The man studied him as he took in his argument. "You as the captain of the ship take no responsibility for the heinous nature of this business you participated in. You left it up to Avigad to broker the deal and plan the event?" the man asked.

"Captain of the ship in the operating theater not the ship builder nor financier," he responded without hesitation.

"Egypt?" the man threw at him.

"Ah, there were several times we staged the operation in Egypt, but I won't waste your time acting as if I don't know which time. It was a blood bath and travesty. Avigad's greed, pure and simple. Was I a willing participant to the initial agreement? Yes. Had I thought about the welfare of those people? No. When things devolved into the death of ten people could I have saved anyone? At that point no. Nor when Avigad killed the staff. That was a mess and I had no power to change it," he said.

What had happened in Egypt that had involved the death of ten people?

"Now we will address the art forgeries—" the man began holding a folder.

"Business pure and simple. Did I sell forgeries? Of course. Did I sell stolen paintings? Without a doubt. Was it for profit? I'd be a fool not to, I wasn't in business for the loss. If you are charging me with business decisions outside the law, then I plead guilty. However, the people buying the product either knew it was a forgery or assumed the risk if they didn't have an expert verify it. Greed begets greed," he said with a hand wave of dismissiveness.

"The proceeds were used to arm people who should not be armed or used to buy biochemical weapons. Does that not trouble you?" the man asked.

"Not one bit. If I am a producer of fertilizer and sell it to a store, and that store sells it to a man who uses it to make a bomb, am I responsible? No," Adrien said pure and simple.

I had to admit on one level of logic his arguments were effective. But what about the moral component? Had his thought process veered so far afield that morals no longer entered the equation?

"Dr. Armond, you have no remorse that you participated in the Easter attacks?" the robed man asked.

"I have no direct knowledge that anything I did had anything to do with the Easter attacks," he said.

"Your connection with Roselov as an active participant? That doesn't trouble you?"

"A business transaction. He sold, I bought. When you buy eggs from the store, do you ask where the proceeds of the sale will go or what it will be used for?" Adrien asked.

"Anything else you wish to add?" the robed man inquired.

"Yes. You are trying to punish me for participating in a free market, capitalism if you will. I had a service someone wished to utilize. Is it morally corrupt? No. The person had free will whether or not to sell their body part; no one stole it from them. If you tell me Avigad did not pay them for their organ, then that was a breach of a contract between him and them. I was paid to perform a service. I was paid to purchase a product. What you are trying to hold me accountable for is conducting business where you didn't like the outcome of my participation," he said.

"Let me ask you this, Dr. Armond. Would you be willing to donate the money in your investments to the families that limited power to negotiate with you?" the interrogator asked.

He thought for a while. I took that as a sign that maybe this back and forth had forced him to reflect on his bad deeds.

"I believe that what occurred was a business transaction that you are asking me to enter into a novation of sort. Or maybe a refund when the contract on both sides has already been fulfilled. So, no," he said.

I was disappointed.

"If there is nothing more, we will discuss your arguments amongst ourselves. However, that money has already been transferred so the point is moot. Now to you, Ms. Abed," the man said.

Azar stared at the robed man with disdain.

"You are the worst of all. Your plan involved mass murder of animals and people alike. We can all understand the underlying component of the market crash, financial gain. And if that was the only portion then it would not be so compelling. The wealthy people who are able to invest in the market are the ones who suffer the most and working people through their pensions and savings. In time, the global crash could lead to wars because each country would point the finger at another. In time, the world would recover. You would make your money and there would be limited risk of permanent damage.

"But the weaponization of bacterium and viruses that had the potential to kill and maim millions not to mention future generations from potential DNA and RNA mutations is beyond anyone's understanding," the robed man said.

"We live in a world that has outgrown its ability to sustain itself. At some point, Earth will run out of food to be able to feed the populace. We live in a world where the population lives longer, and old people are now a drain on the economy. They have outlived their usefulness. We live in a world where the physically infirmed are rewarded monetarily for their infliction. They cannot contribute or be productive, and they are a drain on society too. We live in a world where the poor and unhealthy are draining the live blood from productive people. The world economy can't sustain itself. Health care systems are imploding.

"You are bleeding hearts who weep for the poor and infirmed and you curse the rich. These people who would die from my plan, while tragic, probably will save other lives. And my existence and my plan to make this world a better, stronger place while

incongruous to you, will make this world better for future generations. The strong will survive and the weak will perish. Darwin's
theory at work. Deep down in places you don't want to admit, you
agree with me you just can't verbalize it without worrying about
being judged. And thus, I have no inclination to explain myself, so
move on," Azar spit out looking from person to person.

"Let me clarify. You're saying this is clearly a case of eugenics
and nothing to do with financial manipulation?" he asked.

"Don't be absurd. Money is what turns the world. In this case,
we would supply an antidote, an antibiotic, to the deserving for financial benefit," she said and Mr. Ghiaccio visibly winced hearing it
out loud.

"And you would determine who was worthy of the antidote?"
he asked.

"Don't be ridiculous. I couldn't do that on a case-by-case basis.
Millions would be touched by my plan. The highest bidder would
obtain it and then they would determine who receives it. The supply of course is not endless—"

"Especially since you'd planned to switch out the drug for nothing more than a placebo. You would resell the real medication again,
am I right?" he asked.

"The details hadn't been finalized." Azar shrugged.

"Is that your complete statement?" he asked.

"It is," she responded.

The two robed men sat back and appeared to be thinking. Was
this the point they would remove the three and we would discuss
their destiny. I thought their explanations plausible in their minds
and the words financial transaction sounded better than butcher or
mass murder. I had decided I would abstain from the proceedings. I
would be no better than Azar if I decided someone's fate based on
limited information.

"Ms. Abed, tell me. How does your system work? Is there a
predetermined time to set the plan in motion or is it just on your

orders?" he asked. That's a useless question, she'll just clam up.

"I'm in control. No one knows where the product is located except me and everyone is paid upfront to be at the ready," she said in a bored tone.

"You understand the man you know as Lozar understands your finances and where they're located?" the robed man asked.

"Yes." She annunciated the entire word.

"Can he have your permission to destroy the biologicals in the general stream of where we find them to terminate your plan?" he asked.

"Absolutely not," she replied, squaring her shoulders as if she believed she was in charge. I gave her more credit than she deserved.

"I see. Then can I have your permission for him to invade the corpus of your investments and use that money to compensate the agricultural sector of people whose crops you have destroyed?"

"Are you high? Certainly not," she said. In my eyes this was not going well. It was as if she had a shovel in her hands and with each question and answer she dug her grave a little deeper.

"I understand. Let me ask you one final question. Would you consider making an investment with your money into the markets to give back for the chaos already in play?"

"Now you're just being ridiculous," she said.

Well that wasn't a smart answer.

"Dr. Armond and Ms. Abed, I believe that you both are without remorse and you are capable of understanding the severity of your deeds. I think we've heard your arguments clearly.

"Do you know why we call the gentleman at the end Melzar?" he asked and they all shook their heads.

"Because Melzar means the overseer and steward. He oversaw all your financial interactions and by now you must have pieced together that the questions I asked were rhetorical. He has already disbursed your funds as restitution anonymously, and in some places a contribution anonymously. In effect, you are bankrupt and destitute.

And, Ms. Abed, we will sell your jewels and accessories, contributing that money to a worthy women and children's cause."

Both Azar and Adrien looked stunned.

"Do you know why the gentleman at the end is Lozar?" he asked and again no response.

"Because Lozar is a bit of a wizard. Through Mary's help he has been able to find all the biologics and pesticides you have amassed and made them disappear. Very clever boy, wouldn't you say?"

"Impossible," Azar shouted. "How?"

"By you underestimating her," was all he gave her.

"I don't believe you," she said with a shake of her head.

"Lozar, please hand Ms. Abed the sheet of paper with the locations," he instructed.

Lozar or Melzar, whoever he was called, slowly walked past the other two and handed Azar a paper. After she read the paper, she visibly paled. The sheet started shaking in her hands. I couldn't tell if it was anger or fear. Lozar returned to his seat.

"Why this waste of time? You already determined and carried out your punishment. A punishment I might add, I reject," Azar added.

"Sometimes one just has to firm up in their minds that they've made a correct judgment call," he said. "I believe we've seen an adequate glimpse into your damaged souls."

Lozar stood to take them back to their rooms, stepping behind Adrien. And before I even knew what had occurred I heard a bang and saw Adrien's head explode. Blood splattered everywhere, and brain matter and skull fragments landed on the table.

He then stepped behind Azar. She was still in shock. Again, I heard a bang and watched her brains splattered. Her long black hair drenched in blood and bits of brain. I looked toward Mr. Ghiaccio; he must have urinated on himself because I could smell the strong odor of pee.

As the bodies slumped forward I would have thought that

gravity would have brought them to the ground immediately, but it didn't. It took a short time for the body to slump and land on the floor.

Tyler turned to me and said, "Why don't we step into the other room." He reached to help me from the chair.

My mind couldn't process what I'd watched upfold. It was as if I had shut down completely and was working on autopilot. My body moved but it wasn't under my conscious control.

"Why? Clean up on aisle three?" I asked unfiltered and just spewing what popped into my head. Even years of therapy would not wipe this from my mind.

"Something like that," he said somberly as I watched the two robed men leave and six more entered.

As I turned to leave the room I saw the men spreading two tarps and my imagination filled in the rest. Crematorium. They were going to burn the bodies.

"What about the other one?" I asked, too weak to come up with any smartass remarks.

"He'll be drugged and returned home. He has no idea where we are, and it will remain that way. Now I need to explain something. This operation has been coordinated with both governments. I want you to feel comfortable with that knowledge. There will be fanfare about being sent on a wild goose chase and it's all part of the operation. Play along and everything will work out just fine," Tyler spoke as he reviewed text messages and returned them.

"What's you exit strategy?" I asked hoping for an oversimplified answer.

"As soon as my three people are ready to leave, we'll depart for home. We'll drop you close to DC and call Jackson to come get you. There is nothing to fear Mary. You've been an invaluable asset to us and our governments have the story working already," he said rubbing my arm.

One of the six men walked into the room and said, "Done."

Tyler acknowledged him with a quick tip of his chin.

"We're ready to leave. Here comes the other three, so let's move out," he said. "You still have your arsenal?"

"Never leave home without it," I replied clutching my bag. "Any chance of a Starbucks run on the way back?"

My mind had shut down completely and must've blocked everything. PTSD is what I was experiencing. How could I possibly be thinking of Starbucks after watching two people being executed at point-blank range in front of me. It was shock.

"Afraid not, we're going via helicopter and I don't know of many Starbucks locations with landing pads." He smiled and pulled me closer to him searching my eyes. He looked worried.

I was about to spew more nonsense when I became aware I was surrounded by the other three men and they indicated it was time to leave. I guess we would have a bit of a drive to clear the trees for a safe place to depart.

"Can I use the bathroom before we go?" I asked.

"Of course, we'll be right outside. The bathroom is right there." He pointed.

I truly was uncertain if I would throw up or have massive diarrhea, but I about made it to the stall and my body decided for me. As I was cleaning up and washing my hands I heard the unmistakable sound of gunfire and yelling outside. Then dead silence. Considering my heaviest protection was my taser and hair spray, I decided to remain inside until I heard all clear from one of the men.

The signal never came.

Before I could make any further decision, the door was thrown open. I stood stone still outside the bathroom door as three men walked in and sized me up.

"Marcello Ghiaccio. Where is he?" an older man asked. He was clearly in charge.

"Back there getting ready to get dosed with Special K," I said, pointing to the room we just came from.

He walked past me and as he came upon the scene I heard him scream, "Fuck."

The other two men spread out quickly and I heard more gunfire. I decided now would be a good time to take a seat on the floor before I fell.

After what seemed like an eternity, two older men walked into the bathroom. I remained in shock, probably slowly slipping toward a catatonic state. I was grateful I had my bathroom episode earlier.

"And you are?" the man in authority asked.

"Mary Collier," I said and felt myself start to quiver from the adrenaline rush.

"And why is Mary Collier here?" he asked stepping closer and then squatting to eye level with me.

"Sir, I'm afraid no matter what answer I give will not be to your liking. And I would prefer not to get gunned down if I can avoid it. What's the chances?" I asked, now fully pumped with the adrenaline coursing through me.

He studied me and as he was about to answer, Marcello Ghiaccio walked out with the men that had gone in to get him.

The men embraced. It was apparent they were closely related—probably father and son.

"Everyone accounted for?" the older man asked, and everyone responded in the affirmative. "*Andiamo*. Marcello, help Ms. Mary up please."

I was brought to my feet and with a thoughtful eye Marcello assessed me. "You were there, but you weren't with them."

"It's a long and complicated story," I said, fluffing my hair a bit. The older man was quite attractive, and I had nothing on my plate at this time. Obviously, my mind was still somewhere in Cleveland to be thinking such inappropriate thoughts.

"Come, let's go." He held the door open for me.

Outside were the bodies of Tyler, Lozar, and the two other men, laid out and oozing blood. Obviously dead. I stood for a moment taking in the scene and made the sign of the cross offering a silent prayer.

We walked to the cars. I was helped inside the car that Mr. Ghiaccio senior occupied, we all strapped in and took off.

About five minutes after we left, the car was clearing the entrance to the area when there was an explosion that I swear shook the ground. There was an accompanying fireball large enough that it sent orange flames as high as the trees.

"Crematorium furnace was old, and some kids must have been playing. Hope no one got hurt," Mr. Ghiaccio said.

"Italian?" I asked. He nodded.

"Mafioso?" I asked. He shrugged.

"What do you know about the Vatican Bank?" I asked, and he chuckled.

The drive back even in a state of shock could be termed pleasant, surreal more appropriate. We spoke about Italian food, Italian artists, and if Italy and the Vatican should have joined the eurozone in light of all the new regulations. If the man was not a criminal I might have enjoyed the conversation more. Or maybe I did because he was one?

My instructions were clear, we never met or the next time we met things might not end well. I could tell my story, but names were never mentioned, and my memory was fuzzy for descriptions. I thought that sounded reasonable.

The group was dropped at Richmond Airport. Once they boarded their private jet and it cleared the runway, a phone they'd given me automatically activated allowing me to call for someone to pick me up.

Strangely enough, my call went to Jackson.

TWENTY-SEVEN

Jackson

THIS WAS ABSOLUTELY MIND-BOGGLING THAT WE'D DRIVEN TO A place where Azar's phone was located, and it was deader than a door-nail. An old house in east bumblefuck that appeared to have been abandoned for years. No heat, no running water, no power, and no Azar. No tire tracks and no sign of life. Either someone was setting us up for an ambush or she had been here for a minute and left. We finally breached the doors. The dust that coated the counters looked undisturbed and the stains in the sink and toilets from well water were there a very long time. The floor was coated with a light sheet of dirt and no shoes or bare feet had been here in probably years.

My next worry was Mary and Tyler. Where were they and why had they gone radio silent? This was insane. I received three texts from Tyler saying they were chasing down another lead and then nothing. The chewing out I would get from Nathaniel was a given for wasting government resources and time and someone had to be the scapegoat. That person was likely me. The private sector was looking more attractive, and after I received a reprimand for this clusterfuck, life at the Bureau would be unbearable.

My phone reminded me the real world of the FBI was still a priority. I picked up a number I didn't recognize.

"Evans," I answered.

ONE

"I need a ride," Mary said as if I'd forgotten to pick her up from the mall.

"Where the hell are you? Why haven't you been in touch?" I drilled out. She was the cause of my pain and she was going to get an earful. "Where's that dipshit Tyler?"

"All in good time, Jackie boy. Right now, I need one of you to pick me up at Richmond Airport. I'm in the terminal having a Starbucks. How long do you think?" she asked in an annoyed voice. An actual annoyed voice.

"What the ever-loving hell are you talking about? Answer me. Where's that little prick Tyler. Put him on the phone," I demanded. Yeah, he was hiding from me, he didn't want to take any blame in this international shit show.

"Sorry, no can do," she said as I heard her name called for her coffee order.

"Mary, so help me, put him on the phone right now." I was quickly tipping over the edge where foul and abusive language would pour recklessly from my mouth.

"Give me a minute. I see a table that is actually empty and secluded," she said, and I waited. I heard her rustling around and then she began. "I can't talk on this line. But you need to get with Virginia. There was an explosion in the national forest area."

"You have lost your ever-loving mind. Why the hell should I care if some yahoos are blowing things up in the national forest. That's why they have forest rangers. Now put Tyler on. I'm not saying it again."

"I absolutely cannot share anything with you because I am the only one here and that's why I need you to have someone immediately investigate what I just told you. A member of my party was left behind. This is not a secure phone. Do I need to slow down for you or are you getting my message," she said as calm as could be. Too calm.

"You okay?" I asked.

"No, and don't ask any more questions."

I told her to hang on.

"All right, listen up. I have you on a flight leaving Richmond in twenty minutes. Stand outside the Starbucks and I will have the TSA grab you and get you to the gate. Now chop chop, get moving and I will meet you in a little over an hour at the gate here. Turn the phone off but bring it with you. And why didn't you call from yours?" I asked.

"My battery was removed and confiscated," she said. "Is my seat first class?"

"It's a commuter flight. Now get going," I said trying to piece everything together. "Which national forest?"

"Jackson, they have thermal imaging and they have eyes and ears. By now trees might be on fire. Just call. And tell them to be on the lookout for twelve bodies," she said.

"Jesus, what the hell? Were you in some type of counter revolution? And how did you make it out?"

"Brains and stealth," she said. This woman was over the top. "I see your man. Got to go."

After calling Eloise to tell her Mary was okay and to spread the word, I knew my next call should be Nathaniel, but I wanted more information before I reported back to him.

I arrived early at the gate and as I waited a call came in from the forest supervisor letting me know that multiple agencies were on the scene and he would keep me in the loop. They had come upon a scene that had a limited area engulfed in fire and had no information yet about the bodies. At first, they thought it had been kids that started a fire, but once I told them about the bodies all options were on the table and one was a bomb.

As I finished the call, Mary walked out the door on the arm of a young attractive man who found something she said amusing. I just didn't get it. If I had just left a place that might have been bombed and littered with bodies after some type of armed fight I would be home in bed with my friend Jameson and on leave for PTSD for at least two weeks. Yet here she was, rolling out like royalty, laughing.

There is something unhinged with that woman.

"Ah, there's my ride," I heard her say. "Thank you so much for taking such good care of me and sneaking me in the extra-large cups of coffee." A quick hand brush to his cheek and he was gone.

"Your ride?"

"You want to spar, or you want to get us to the car, so I can spill the beans? And the TSA confiscated most of my weapons so tomorrow I need to replenish," she said shoving her bag at me.

As we travelled a few steps toward the arrival area, a people carrier stopped and inquired if he could give Mary a ride to the front. Perfect, just perfect. I handed her the enormous bag back and after propping it on her lap went into surveillance mode.

Why me?

We made it to the car and I debriefed her.

"You have any idea who other people there were besides Tyler?"

"Not even a clue. I had my earbuds in and no one spoke anything other than English. I'm trying to give you everything I picked up, but even their accents could be Israeli or Middle Eastern. I have no idea and wouldn't be able to make an educated guess. The silver-hair guy had a twinge of a similar accent. However, he had clearly worked hard to lose it. Can't they do some Ancestry DNA test to find out the origin of everyone?" she asked.

That was a great idea.

"I would think if they were government issue like Tyler they would be in some government database. Now back to Azar and Adrien," I reminded her.

"I hate to admit it but once their brains were blown all over the room my mind went on a small vacation and I am having trouble recalling events—" She was clearly disappointed.

"What about the bio weapons?" I asked what was the most pressing.

"Oh, right. The other guy in the room had disposed of the samples that were in his possession. You know, the movie-star-looking guy? Azar said that unless she gave the go-ahead to launch the weapons no one had access to them. The important guys were going to reimburse the people who were out money from the plan as far as the agricultural sector. And they were going to take Adrien's money and compensate his victims," she said with a bit of hesitancy.

"What?" I said turning my head. "Somehow something doesn't feel right. I think that Tyler went rogue on this—"

"Ya think? You think many foreign governments are going to kidnap someone on US soil and then execute them on US soil? What was your first clue?" Her sarcasm in full force.

"We may never know all the players then, smarty pants. I have to ask. Why did you go with him? Why not call and say something didn't feel right?"

"I thought I might get lucky after the mission was concluded," she said with a shrug.

"Seriously. His story was off, why trust him?"

"I have no plausible answer so I'm not even going to try to come up with something. Will that suit you?" Her voice was quiet. She turned her head toward the window.

"The movie star guy, what happened to him?" I asked, trying to figure his angle.

"For all we know he could be wandering the forest dazed and buck naked. They talked about dosing him with ketamine."

"They sure picked an excellent place. No cameras anywhere and I suppose now NSA will get involved. And for the record, I don't know and don't want to know if they record everything every minute of the day everywhere to reverse engineer the movements right before the situation imploded. You sure you can't think of anything else?" I asked. Something felt off that she wasn't giving me a minute-by-minute replay.

"Jackie boy, I haven't had my nap and it's late. I almost got whacked today so I might have some of that PTSD. Once I'm better we can have another go at this."

"Fair enough." We were fifteen minutes outside the beltway. "We have to talk to Nathaniel so loath that I am to ask, you want to stop for lunch and coffee?"

"I'm not going to spend six hours being debriefed. I'm old and cranky, plus I need a nap. I have just been debriefed by an agent—"

"Nah, that's not going to fly, and you know it. Be prepared," I said as we rolled into the garage.

"Always am, Jackie boy," she said. "Good news is I have no weapons that they can confiscate."

"I want you to be careful what you say to Nathaniel. Think carefully and articulate your answers clearly. If you can't recall, then it's just that. Don't make anything up, don't dramatize anything," I said.

As I was ready to complete my directions I received a text: **Two outside dead, six dead in a room inside. Two inside ready to be burned, one female one male.**

All I could think was that Mary's story was inconsistent probably due to her age.

"Mary, when talking to the chief I would be a bit non-specific about your numbers because they found two outside dead not four, six inside plus two in the crematory to be burned. I can't coach you but I would say not to commit if you can't remember exactly. Maybe when you walked out you didn't have an unobstructed view. Or maybe when you were in the other room they walked as a group. Again, I never gave them your numbers. These are the numbers they gave me. You might even want to ask for a medical review first, so you can think clearly about this and possibly ask for a lawyer. I don't want to impede an investigation, but, Mary, you are Mary."

"Two outside, interesting," she said. "I have my theories."

"No. See, that's what I mean. No theories, no hypotheticals, no what-ifs. We good?" I asked.

"We are," she replied. "The place was a bit dark and my eyesight with the stress and dirt all around were not so great. I'm thinking I might need to rethink my account before I talk to Nathaniel," she said. I could see the wheels turning and ideas formulating.

"Mary, just so you are aware, Cillian and I are handing in our resignations. I love the Bureau, but the time has come to move in another direction. We are thinking of opening up our own firm—" I didn't even finish my sentence.

"I'm in."

THE END

ABOUT THE AUTHOR

K.J. McGillick is an author of psychological thrillers and draws from her background in the law, medicine and art history to engage her readers in her fast-paced thriller series, A Path of Deception and Betrayal. She draws upon her legal knowledge as a practicing attorney and experiences as an avid international traveler to produce page turning books filled with mystery and suspense.

CONNECT WITH
K. J. MCGILLICK

Official website: www.kjmcgillick.com

K.J.'s Facebook Page: www.facebook.com/KJMcGillickauthor

You can email her at kjmcgillick@gmail.com

Twitter: Kathleen McGillick@KJMcGillickAuth

OTHER BOOKS

A Path of Deception and Betrayal (Book1)

A Path of Deception and Betrayal (Book 2)

Made in the
USA
Columbia, SC